PENGUIN BOOKS
MAKER OF SAINTS

Thulani Davis teaches writing at Barnard College and is the author of the novel *1959*, which was nominated for the *Los Angeles Times* Book Award. She is a published poet, playwright, librettist, and a Grammy winner, now living in Brooklyn, New York.

Maker *of* Saints

a novel

Thulani Davis

PENGUIN BOOKS

PENGUIN BOOKS
Published by the Penguin Group
Penguin Putnam Inc., 375 Hudson Street,
New York, New York 10014, U.S.A.
Penguin Books Ltd, 27 Wrights Lane,
London W8 5TZ, England
Penguin Books Australia Ltd, Ringwood,
Victoria, Australia
Penguin Books Canada Ltd, 10 Alcorn Avenue,
Toronto, Ontario, Canada M4V 3B2
Penguin Books (N.Z.) Ltd, 182–190 Wairau Road,
Auckland 10, New Zealand

Penguin Books Ltd, Registered Offices:
Harmondsworth, Middlesex, England

First published in the United States of America by
Scribner, an imprint of Simon & Schuster, Inc. 1996
Published in Penguin Books 1997

1   3   5   7   9   10   8   6   4   2

PUBLISHER'S NOTE
This is a work of fiction. Names, characters, places, and incidents either are
the product of the author's imagination or are used fictitiously, and any resemblance
to actual persons, living or dead, events, or locales is entirely coincidental.

THE LIBRARY OF CONGRESS HAS CATALOGUED THE HARDCOVER AS FOLLOWS:
Davis, Thulani.
Maker of saints: a novel / Thulani Davis.
p.   cm.
ISBN 0-684-81225-8 (hc.)
ISBN 0 14 02.6735 2 (pbk.)
I. Title.
PS3554.A93779M34   1996
813´.54—dc20   96–25004

Printed in the United States of America
Set in Spectrum Monotype
Designed by Brooke Zimmer

With Namu
We are all named
We gon' let it shine
Namu Amida Butsu

You don't know what love is until someone lives with you while you write a book, so my first thanks must go to my husband Joseph Jarman, who is compassion.

Faith Hampton Childs, my agent, lived with me by phone, always gave enthusiastic support and sage advice, and wore my tired moccasins for that extra mile. The late Lee Goerner, my first editor, was a friend and a writer's champion, and he's missed. My editor Nan Graham earned my admiration for asking the right questions, and going toe to toe when the going got tough. My old school song will never be the same.

Much thanks to the MacDowell Colony, for great solitude, and Mark Ari, who sent great blues tapes. And to Rae C. Wright and Jessica Hagedorn for reading.

My teacher, Rev. Gyoko Saito, keeps me honest, and Salman Rushdie makes me want to keep working simply by staying alive and writing his pants off.

Their times were unsullied, and their joys were sweet, until they were visited by the terminator of delights and the separator of companions.
—*The Thousand and One Nights*

We are aging but still rampant.
—Christopher Walken, *Him*

Contents

Maker *of* Saints

I

STATIC

Way in the midnight when death comes slippin' in the room
You're gonna need somebody on your bond.
—BLIND WILLIE JOHNSON

1
Friday

B ird squirmed in her high-backed chair in the sound booth,
checked the needles quivering in their dials in front of her,
and twisted her neck several times to release the tension. The
needles were jumping too far to the left and right. The woman's
voice was rising and suddenly dropping, no good. She waved at the
director. She knew it would all go slower now. She was thinking
that listening to people was seldom startling, and even more
rarely, enlightening. Maybe it was because she spent her days listening to people talk that she thought she learned something
only when she wasn't trying to follow what they were saying.
She only heard when she wasn't listening.

She pulled the lever so the studio could hear her. Her wrists
were wrapped inside heavy black splints that gave a fearsome

gladiator look to hands and forearms that could no longer open jars or manage a pencil.

"Better take it again," Bird said into the mike, "you're getting tired."

Usually the people on the other side of the glass were trying to say something they'd said before, or simply something they thought appropriate. They were talking without being there. Sometimes they couldn't help it. The black woman on the other side of the double glass pane, who was laying down a narration track for a documentary, was fried. She'd only been at it for two hours. Bird felt a pang of compassion for her. While she was clearly an amateur, the woman seemed to fancy herself a professional and no doubt thought she still sounded good, but she was brain-dead.

"How about coffee, or juice?"

This was the only conversation Bird usually had with the people she studied while engineering radio shows or films like this one. For the most part, she sat speechless, as if there were a stone in her mouth in place of her tongue. She had been an artist until a few years ago when she gave it up. Bird had more or less stumbled into engineering while trying to produce radio plays with other artists in the early eighties. She was always so broke that she talked people at a community station into teaching her how to work the boards. After a while engineering paid the rent. Once she'd really given up painting, she retreated into the sound booth.

The glass barrier separating her booth from the studio made all the people on the other side more or less the same—great and small, famous and *petit* famous—the "petty famous," she called them. By the third visit in a day, she was as bored with the experts and the celebrated as they were with the questions. She had taped every man, woman, novelist, and disc jockey who ever ran for president or mayor, and had never met more than two she could even remember well. Politicians walked around with double glass panes in front of their eyes. She remembered one because he was the kind of man who didn't care what people thought about his wearing a Rolex encrusted with diamonds.

The other who left an impression was so absent from his body that it frightened her.

The most present person she'd ever taped was a serial killer in a Texas jail. She'd spent five days in a cell with earphones on listening to him run his mouth and watching him trying to be so present that he could leave inside her skin. He succeeded. When she got back to New York she locked herself in her apartment for three days. There was no glass wall in the jail cell, and unlike most people she taped, he didn't know how to put up one with his eyes. Didn't want to. The double glass window worked for Bird. If she didn't like the people, she only had to watch the needles. They couldn't tell what she was thinking, even if she said it out loud. It was her own sacred frontier. That's what they called the veil, the door to a harem, anything that kept the women safe from the eyes of the world. Sacred frontier. An ironic name. The glass booth was safe. No engagement. That hot early September morning Cynthia Kincaid, who was seldom called anything other than Bird, the chief sound engineer in a public radio station in New York, was bored and contented with her work.

The first job in the afternoon was simply listed in the log with the name of the culture reporter who'd booked the hour. Bird sat finishing a tuna sandwich, her wild curls straining against her earphones. When the reporter stuck his head in to say he was going into the studio for his interview, she simply nodded. She wrapped up the rest of the sandwich, spun her chair around, took a reel out of one of the dozens of thin boxes on the shelf, and slapped it on one of the big decks behind her board. When she spun back around she saw a tall, big-boned blond man adjusting himself in his seat, self-conscious, uncomfortable, preoccupied with wiping his hands on a handkerchief pulled from his jacket pocket. The habit was familiar. She saw a pile of crumpled, well-read newspapers on the table. Newsprint. An allergy to newsprint. Finishing with his hands, the man pulled notes from a briefcase. She knew the hands, the body, the crop of flax curving towards his right eye.

When he looked up he seemed to be caught by her face, and

stared at the window. Bird was aware that she too looked startled. She recognized the cutting, assessing blue eyes, the handsome high cheekbones and squared jaw, skin still smoothly sculpted over the bones. He looked down at the notes and told the reporter he'd need a second before putting on the earphones. When he looked up again at the booth Bird was gone.

She ran down the hall with the bathroom key jangling against the tape reel it was chained to, unlocked the door, and threw up before she could get into a stall. She turned on the faucet and threw cold water on her face. She scooped water into her mouth and spit it out.

When Bird reappeared in the studio and put on her earphones, the reporter looked annoyed and gestured to remind her that he didn't have much time. She spun her chair so her back was to the glass and hooked the end of the new reel through the heads and onto the pickup reel. Turning back around she looked at the dials. She turned on her mike into the studio, into their ears.

"Let's check the levels," she said. They nodded. "Could each of you say something into the mike?" She flipped the switch that brought the sound of their voices through the speakers in her booth. The anxious reporter told her that his guest was Frank Burton—

"Francis," the blond man interjected.

"—the art critic for the *New York*—"

"I know Mr. Burton," she said evenly. "How are you?" She watched the mike just below his lips. He said he was fine. "Say that again," she said, "I'm trying to get a level. Keep talking."

Since she wouldn't look at him, Frank, suddenly at ease, spoke to the reporter. "Bird Kincaid used to be a painter, did she ever tell you that?"

"No. Really?" The reporter looked baffled. "Bird, is that true? Wow. You should have told me. Bird, why'd you stop painting?"

Bird simply raised her armored wrists as if to say she'd lost her hands. She opened her speaker line. "Okay, you can start, I'm rolling tape."

They began the interview. Bird kept telling herself she could look at him, it was best to look at him, let him know she was not afraid of him. But how could she look at him, just calmly take in the face of the man she thought had killed her best friend? And got away with it. She kept wanting to look at the face of the only person in the world who really knew what had happened that night in the apartment next door. She wanted to look. She hadn't seen him since that night. This was the first face she saw after seeing Alex's broken body on the sidewalk. Now, he looked too healthy to suit Bird. She was a wreck and he was too smooth in the face, too untroubled, unscratched, unmarred in any way by the worst nightmare of Bird's life.

When she finally got the nerve and cooled her face enough to appear disinterested through the double glass, his eyes were waiting, fixed. He didn't look at the reporter the whole time they were talking. He ignored the fact of the taping, the protocol of an interview, spoke directly to Bird, perched somewhat above him in her booth.

"We should eat lunch sometime, Bird. It's long overdue. I'd like to talk to you. We've never talked since that night." It was as if he were not with the reporter at all but trying to make himself felt on the other side of the double window. The reporter groaned. Bird was speechless. She stopped the tape. She had been so sure, without even thinking it through, that she would never see him again, as if the gods would see to it, and she'd never have to find any words for what was between them.

"Shit," she said to herself. She flipped the switch so they could hear. She was talking in his ears. She knew the sound would be tinny, removed, not at all as intimate as the idea of speaking right into his ears might suggest, but like a scratchy long-distance call.

"It wouldn't make any sense," she said. "What's left in my head are the teeth of rabid dogs, not words." Burton watched her impassive face as the words came gritted with hate through the soft rubber muffs on his ears. The reporter instinctively pulled off his earphones, not knowing exactly what error he had made with this interview arrangement, but sure that he should not be party to it. "Unless you like having lunch with howling sick animals who retch at the sight of you, it's better to leave things as they are, to be through with it." She couldn't stop herself, things were all upside-down, her talking, the visitor listening, her words, coming from so close to her bones, passing through the glass wall that usually demanded her silence. She turned off her speaking switch and began to swivel her back towards the two men.

Regaining his charm, Frank Burton smiled at the reporter as if this kind of exchange were commonplace in his life. Maybe, but the reporter wasn't having any of it. "Look, whenever you're finished—"

"I'm sorry, just one second more," Frank said to him. "Bird, my life's been nearly ruined—"

She didn't like him speaking her name so casually, intimately. She turned around and flipped on her mike. "You're a free man."

"A court said I couldn't be tried, that's all. That doesn't end it—"

"End what? Your disgrace? Or your responsibility? What bothers you most, Frank? Some of us feel responsible."

"I'm the suspect."

"Well, there it is." She flicked off his mike.

"You're the guilty," she said to herself. "That's why you're not going to leave this alone." She flipped on her mike. "It's better if you don't say anything else." The reporter started to sputter and got up. She could only hear him faintly.

Realizing he was cut off, Burton stood up and shouted through the glass, "One can't just pick up and go on."

She lost track of herself. All she could think was, this is a man who beats people. The reporter's voice boomed from the door behind her, "Bird, you are losing it, what is this?"

She ignored him, and kept talking into the man's ears in the studio, her hand on the mike switch. "What do you think I'm trying to do? I'm packing up what's left of her life and shipping it out to the university, so people who care about her work can study it. And then I am moving on. I suggest you do the same." She flipped the switch again and turned on the reporter. "What did you think you were doing bringing that motherfucker in this studio on my shift?"

"I—I don't—"

"You don't read the fuckin' papers? You don't know who this man is or something?"

"No. What? I don't know all your fucking history, remember? I haven't been at this bureau but a couple of months." He was pleading.

"Shit." That was as close as she could come to "sorry." He left the studio. She could see Frank mouthing something into the mike.

The reporter returned to the studio, signaled Bird to turn his mike on, and said, "Let's just get it over with, folks. Maybe I can be of some help." The reporter's voice came calmly over the speakers, trying to sound nonchalant. "Bird, he's asking, just as a point of information, are you giving all of Alex Decatur's work to the university?"

Burton looked slightly rattled. She didn't want to say anything but felt caught by the etiquette of the situation, the need to regain a veneer of normalcy. "Everything I can. I can't keep that stuff." She couldn't tell what bothered Frank at the moment, but she was glad to see him off his high commanding horse.

"Okay, good, great," the reporter sputtered. "We're on our way." The reporter was relieved. Bird could hear Burton saying, "I thought her mother would take it all. Keep it, you know."

"Her mother doesn't want it," Bird said to no one and with a little superiority. "And I can't keep it. There's no room."

"What exactly—"

"Tell him, there'll be a press release."

"Right. Of course."

"I'll roll that back," she said, listening in the earphones as the tape whirred, watching the dials on her board. She looked up to let him know she had dismissed him. He was staring at her, trying to read her face for something. The reporter kept clearing his throat. "Okay, folks, we're rolling tape."

Once it was over she could hear Burton outside her door, trying to leave the station. She could hear the fool reporter making a remark about whatever it was between him and Bird being "so thick." Was she an ex-wife of his or something?

Burton said, "It's none of your business, but I've never been married."

Bird could feel Frank Burton's face one inch from her own.

2

Inscription on an Altarpiece

The once fall'n woman must for ever fall.
—Byron

On May 17, 1989, Alexandra Decatur, thirty-seven, an artist known for her atavistic clay works, died instantly when she fell eight floors from a window in her apartment. An investigation into whether she may have been the victim of foul play, including a grand jury probe into the possible involvement of her boyfriend, art critic Francis Burton, failed to produce an indictment. Her death was declared a probable suicide.

* * *

When exhibiting her work Decatur sometimes substituted "the primitive" for her proper name, a gesture regarded as an attempt to mock the art establishment. When she was in her twenties, Decatur was "discovered" by critics, one of whom labeled her a "primitive" artist after being told, erroneously, that the young woman was from the South Bronx and had never received formal training. The critic recanted his statement but said he felt he'd been made the victim of a prank.

Decatur often recalled the incident to interviewers, and complained that women artists like herself were not shown in the major museums. Critics frequently took issue with this charge, asserting that her work had not earned such recognition, that perhaps she had been ill-served by recognition already given. "If the art world has committed any wrong, it was to give too much too soon." Decatur was also reported to make unpleasant and intentionally cryptic remarks, most notably, that her work was a "ransom" for her life.

In the eighties the artist took up performance art and began to create scripted events that usually took place in storefront galleries. In her most famous piece, she took an ad out in the *Village Voice* asking "anyone who has something to bury" to bring it to a beach site on lower West Street. She and a band of others conducted a New Orleans–style funeral procession, or "second line," to the site and there handed out shovels. So many hundreds of people turned up carrying bundles that some waited over an hour for a shovel, while others used their hands. People who did not appear to be bona fide priests performed mysterious rites at the mass burial. Decatur told reporters at the event that they "should be grateful the people didn't try to bury the city itself. I'm surprised no one brought their landlords down here or their bosses."

Several days later the city health and sanitation departments issued citations and penalties to Decatur after having the ground turned over on a report that a stillborn baby had been interred at the site. No such remains were found. However, among the personal mementos and souvenirs uncovered, such as photographs, letters, bills, and records, were several recently deceased pets. The citations noted the inappropriate presence of organic material.

Decatur's death became the source of apocryphal rumor within the artistic community to which she belonged. Some of her immigrant neighbors, speaking through interpreters, called for prayer from all religious people. They likened the fall to visions appearing in dreams and attached spiritual significance to the mystery. Others spoke of neighbors who had allegedly seen Decatur fall and how, in that moment, she resembled a figure in a painting by Frida Kahlo. No such witnesses came forward to the police, and the painting *The Suicide of Dorothy Hale*, which depicts the headfirst plunge and landing of an elegantly coiffed woman in an evening gown with a corsage of white roses, cannot be said to be a realistic portrayal of what Decatur's neighbors might have seen.

In her death she resembled her own work. Clad only in her underwear, Decatur's body, which bore several glass cuts on the feet and back, fell onto an expanse of sidewalk under repair outside her apartment building. The area of half-dry poured concrete covered with a thin tarp gave under the impact of her falling weight. Two impressions were left by the impact: a bloodstained imprint in the translucent tarp, and a hollowed-out shape in the concrete resembling a grotesque sarcophagus fitted to a body in motion.

3
Friday Night

Something hit Bird's chest like a brick. Her head jerked up and her eyes opened, but all she could see was a grainy haze fading from a dream to become the piercing light of the television and the outline of her bedroom. "Alex?" she said. No, Alex was dead. Hit the sidewalk. The thud was in her chest. She thought the shadow man had come in there to kill her. She thought there was a specter that stood breathing in the doorway. She jerked herself up in the bed. The clock said 1:28. The shadow faded. No. Not there. She hadn't been hit, it was a door, she'd heard the door slam in her sleep. She got up and grabbed the *boken* she kept under the bed. It was a wooden sword she had learned to use when studying martial arts. She checked the connecting door to Alex's apartment. Then the front door. No, the locks were on. She walked back to the bedroom. She'd had some kind of fright. Her chest hurt as if she'd had a seizure. She sat on the edge of the bed. Only a sliver of light from the street eased through the curtain.

She heard the elevator out in the hallway shunt into gear and begin moving. A coincidence maybe. Bird was sweating. Her hair was wet. She sat on the bed staring across the room. The light showed eerie white pools on her thighs. She could not move—her arms and chest seemed frozen, tight. She sat back against the pillows, eyes watching the hall, feeling the sweat all over her. Bird remembered that night. Or her regular dream of that night.

Alex never backed down. He liked to provoke her. He liked to get loud about any curator, or gallery, any soul who wanted to show her work—as if he were angry that they were interested. He always said, "Right intention, wrong person." He usually said they were uninformed, misguided, made lousy presentations, or when he was impatient, simply, that they weren't shit, and always, that "it wouldn't be regarded as important" for her to show in their space. "You have to show in a significant venue."

"You don't understand."

"If you'd let me handle it . . ."

It was about some letters. A huge thud hit one of the bookcases on the other side of the wall. The wall shook. Books seemed to spill to the floor. She couldn't tell what the screaming was about. As long as she could hear Alex—

A body hit the door, the bookcase, the lamp by the door went down. Bird started screaming. She called Alex's name. Burton bellowed, "I will break down the fucking door, bitch, get away from there. Stay out of it. That your bitch, huh? That your bitch in there?" Bird slid down the door to the floor.

Bird untethered the dream, shaking it loose from her head. Maybe her own exhausted breathing had wakened her. She picked up the phone and called a man. It was an instinctive gesture, but the man she was calling was unlikely to be home. There was drumming in the street, surging up and fading. The machine answered and the man's voice quickly gave out the number she'd just dialed. She asked if he was there and held on. No response. She thought about it. Calling a man to help seemed a natural thing to do, but not with the men she knew. They weren't coming to any rescue. To call a man to the rescue, you'd have to know where to find one. In a movie he'd be out back fitting a shoe on a horse hoof, waiting for that excited yell. In a movie some kid would run down to the plant to get him, there hammering some molten metal into a powerfully useful tool. He'd run all the way.

The drumming was there in the street every night but Bird seldom paid it any attention. She was usually lost in thought, trying to separate life from what she'd been led to believe. She spent hours doing this. Her bedroom was at the front of the building and tonight the windows were open, no breeze coming through, only the rise and fall of Cuban congas. Friday night in September in New York and she couldn't tell if the drums were live or on somebody's box. Some nights they weren't Cuban, sometimes they were Puerto Rican, kin but distinct. Next door there was the fast stomping of someone running down the steps. A voice called from outside, "I got two dollars." The voice echoed. Bird hoped they'd be able to cop and be peaceful. She started to drift off, the television emitting blue-gray light across the sheets and a murmur that dulled the sound of Friday night.

"I'm still living in the Quarter," she said out loud.

She'd spent nearly all of the eighties indoors, working sequestered in her studio, or her apartment, living through the windows, as if hidden behind the ornately carved screens that obscured women on balconies in an Arab quarter somewhere. Hiding. Not by custom, but from some bleakness, some contagious despair in the street. Hiding because perhaps she'd already caught it. Too many people dying, for one thing. She knew lots of people who were now cloistered indoors as if there they could hide from an airborne virus. She'd spent a decade not being seen except in intimate moments, with people who were close. She knew her world of windows well, from sunup to the hours when the bright yellow crime lights came on automatically in the street.

New York's black bottom, despite the indoor plumbing and television in every home, still resembled a laborers' camp sitting at the fringe of rich plantation lands. Not much different from the small black side of town where she'd grown up in Carolina, just a lot more crowded. Surely someone must have succeeded with their schemes and plans and left the block. Usually, though, it seemed to Bird that the people who had lived on this block must have tried for decades, strived to make it in spite of grinding days, but then tired out and gave up. The weight of too much defeat caused the psychic structures—the efficient and delicate frames underneath the living flesh—simply to collapse.

It was a place that looked as if people had fallen there. The good life itself, if there really was one, had fallen elsewhere, maybe downtown. The Quarter sucked in people who couldn't pay more rent, every year a more complicated mix of temperaments and past fortunes, tastes and expectations. It sucked in carpetbaggers and passersby, music school graduates who had once had lofts with broad-beamed floors and now rented rooms as many musicians had done for decades before. A bass player lived for a while on the other side of her bedroom wall, playing old jams and strumming at odd hours of the day and night. The smell of reefer wafted from his window. The Quarter also took in untold children—grandchildren, cousins, nieces, all without parents, all temporary, only there till the goodwill ran out.

Even though Bird knew the drumming was probably the aging junkies near the corner who sometimes brought congas out on the sidewalk, the familiar rhythms had just then made her realize she'd always been inside that sound, the sound of a barracoon, the sound of dark bodies in a cramped Babel of passions and spirits. She drifted.

The yelling brought her back and without moving she listened to hear if she knew the voices. She looked at the bedroom door for the shadow man but he was gone. The sound was outside. Sneakers hitting the sidewalk hard, scuffling. "Give it to me, bitch." It was Naomi and Romeo, her man. "I ain't no punchin' bag, man!" The downstairs door slammed. She'd give it to him. They usually shared everything. It was other people they shorted. The door slammed a few more times. This time Naomi was yelling bloody murder. "Motherfucker, I ain't no fuckin' punchin' bag." She was trying to get out of the door.

Usually Naomi would threaten to call the police and go up to the corner to the phone. "Call 'em, bitch. What the fuck do I care?" His mother started yelling out of a window for them to shut up. She was telling Naomi to get the hell out of her place. "You don't pay no rent anyway. And I ain't never had the police in my house. Git out, git out, y' hear me?!" Bird thought about Ma calling the apartment a house. She did that too. Was that a Southern habit? Bird knew Ma was on the case, one way or the other. She was momentarily amazed at how she'd gotten used to the fighting, the sound of a body slamming against a wall.

Bird and Alex had different views. Even though their windows were side by side stretching along the front of the building, the two friends saw different sections of the street below. And they could not see each other unless they both leaned out dangerously far past the ledge. But Alex would never have done that. Bird could not have seen Alex going out the window, could not have seen if arms had held her or pushed her, only the arc of her fall. Only the fall announced with a common scream, then the arc of a scream, the arc of a falling body, gnarled hands and helpless arms flying first as if to break the fall. The arms going ahead as if to cushion the shattering of her skull and tiny bones. Her arms flew about the way babies' sometimes do as they emerge from the womb blind and confused.

The two women's different views seemed to Bird to be the evidence, the sign, that it was impossible for two people to know each other, even sharing a space. To Bird it seemed true now that any two people who lay in any proximity to each other night after night, convicts in a cell, sisters in a shared room, lovers in a bed, refugees packed in a cargo hold, soldiers on bivouac, would never know the dreaming inside the other. There was no shared reality. In her heart, in her body and mind, Bird knew Alex had not committed suicide or slipped watering the plants with the windows open, still, there had been a door between them. She didn't really know.

They had felt so lucky two years ago to find two empty apartments mirroring one another on the front side of the floor. They had rationalized about the cost, had told themselves and the folks who lent them money that they were getting "studio" space as well as living space and that was why they needed what amounted to eight rooms, if you thought in conventional terms. They were artists, though, and did not think in terms of conventional living rooms and so, as they looked at it, they were getting two one-bedroom apartments with large studio space built in. They told their families that they had roommates, and told their lovers that they had autonomy.

And in spite of what the landlord might charge them if he found out, they had had a friend come over and knock out an opening and put in a door between the two apartments, so they'd be connected.

The door, sometimes open, sometimes shut, and sometimes locked, defined two separate spheres that merely looked alike. If the door between 8A and 8B was open, one was in a huge double apartment of old oak tables and dressers, and rudely made pine bookshelves, crammed with books they could no longer neatly contain. Matching panels of faded blue and red "crocodile cloth" that a friend had brought from the Philippines adorned bedroom doors at opposite ends of the space. And folk carvings and figures, raided by both women from colored quarters all over, stood guardian duty from one end of the floor to another. All in all, their corresponding spaces were like a poor woman's museum of marketplace art. It was testimony to a shared taste for startling colors, jujus for spiritual protection, and small images of people with blank faces, knotty hairdos, and colonial powers somewhere in their past.

Alex's rooms were nearly overcome by Madonnas and weeping santos, bleeding santos in tin frames and wood boxes, dignified santos standing expressionless in pale robes, poor folk riding buses driven by smiling devils, and humorless *retablos* of souls caught in a disaster.

Bird's end, on the other hand, took a decidedly more African and Pacific view, peopled by hulking wood and stone creatures with implacable faces—Ibeji twins of all sizes, some nicked and bruised, some exquisitely smooth and well oiled; African market women bent over bowls of grain, Buddhas of brass and plastic, stone and clay; fat balsa baby angels from Bali, sitting, standing, and flying. One small wall outside Bird's kitchen was covered with dozens and dozens of postcards from all over the world.

When Alex died Bird noticed that her own place was a storehouse of the caprices of her friend: female-torso earrings, Chinese brocade jackets, Frida Kahlo postcards, clay monkey necklaces, ceramic plates glazed with whimsical obscene paintings and commentaries, gossipy letters, longing letters, angry letters, poems, and Aztec fertility pipes. The only piece in Bird's workspace, slowly converted into something like a greenhouse when Bird stopped painting, was a tiny Mexican figure squatting in the window. It was a clay woman giving birth to another fully developed being, maybe a god giving birth to a god. Bird remembered the story Alex told of finding it in a dusty bin in Guerrero somewhere, but forgot its supposed meaning. Alex said that it could represent the dual nature of the human spirit but Bird didn't think so. One of the reasons she liked it was that at different times it gave her different thoughts. It did not reveal itself, only possibilities.

Bird and Alex, floating in and out of their rooms, were like two planets revolving around one another, held in each other's sway by shared gravity. They had loved being connected yet having privacy, having somewhere to go when they fought. When no one else was there, they slept with the door open and had coffee in the morning in the same kitchen. Alex had come through the door sometimes to make announcements from the mail; Bird had yelled out to see what she needed from the grocery store.

If a lover was visiting, a note he would never see appeared on the inside of the other's apartment giving his name, description, and relative importance. "Let's see if this one can talk or if he just looks good." "Finally caught the fawn in the glen." "He's fine, he's Haitian, my niece thought I should meet him. Went dancing." Or just: "It's business, not fun," or, "Nick. He'll be leaving early."

Romeo's mother was on the case, bringing order from her window. Bird turned over. Naomi was Bird's private experience; Alex could never hear her. Naomi lived downstairs, on the other side of Bird. Now Bird had Naomi waking her on one side and the hollowness of Alex's untenanted space on the other. Compared to the silence there, Naomi's life was a relief, at least for being consistent, and for still going on.

The mother and son were now yelling for Naomi to get inside. Bird could hear her walking up and down the sidewalk. She could feel her standing there, watching the street. Bird could sleep once she knew Naomi had calmed down, whether she went in or not. Once she calmed down, Bird knew, she wouldn't get hit anymore. Naomi and Romeo were the most steady rhythm in Bird's head, the timekeepers who came in and out during the evening and roamed the sidewalks late at night. They were the last sound she heard on any night, and she depended on them to help her keep straight what was real.

Even that night, Naomi and Romeo had been the last sound she heard and the way she knew it was over, at least for that night. When all the squad cars had pulled off and the last EMS siren had whirred, when all the rest of them had gone and all the doors were sealed, Naomi and Romeo stood sentry as the streetlights blocked out the stars till the dawn came up the same orange-yellow and blotted out the lights. They murmured under the window till Bird slept.

The drumming took away all the reality, made everyone seem to be fragments crawling out of old stories in her mind, or turned them into hallucinations, except for Naomi, Romeo, and Mrs. Hayes—the woman they just called Ma. Romeo usually knew whoever was out there on the block: The manic walkers who belonged to the cracks and gangways between buildings. Even those who passed through, pausing at a door or window, yelling out to someone who lived there. Most of the time Romeo knew who they were, though of course he didn't always say. To him there were very few strangers, and no fragments of stories.

Bird knew Alex had never come to know the block this way even though she had lived right there. For one thing, Alex had put an air conditioner in her bedroom window, not for the heat, which didn't bother her, but because the noise of summer nights kept her awake. She was a country girl. At first she'd tried calling the police to report the noise. Then she discovered they wouldn't come for only one complaint. When Alex was home working she never heard anything, not even Bird's voice in her own doorway. Her mind was somewhere else. But Bird had never been satisfied with these, her own explanations for why Alex didn't experience the rhythms of the Quarter. She thought the real reason was because Alex came from someplace else, never grew up with runaway slaves in her head. She had no history of being black.

Alex had acquired her four hundred years of baggage all of a sudden, when she landed at Kennedy Airport twenty years ago. It was then that Alex had begun to look colored to everyone she encountered, and it was then that people had told her she was black, a lot of times saying "yella," "high yella," or "mariney," if they thought she was more red than tan. Sometimes with white folks at school it was just "nigger." These were new expressions to Alex but she had accepted them and all the black baggage that people gave her the same way she had accepted the stamp on her visa, as if it were a customs procedure. She had even accepted the rage that came to inhabit her body, just as it lived inside her friends'. Still, it was pretty humorous when she would sometimes confuse those people by displaying her odd lack of any memory of being black.

Alex had the details of black history as mixed up as her U.S. geography: she thought Michigan lay on the western edge of Delaware, Omaha outside St. Louis, and she was not quite able to imagine the country's vastness. For her, history was marked by the Conquistadors and the Civil War, of which she only knew Robert E. Lee, General Sherman, and the devastation of Vivien Leigh's beloved Tara. She had come to know Paul Robeson, Harriet Tubman, Jesse Jackson, and W.E.B. Du Bois simultaneously, and through conversation, so she often spoke of them in the present tense, as if Martin Luther King had been on the phone straightening her out on the location of Tubman's restaurant in Beaufort, South Carolina.

In Surinam, where Alex had grown up, she'd only known American Negroes who'd been either in the movies or the international news, a crew unlikely to eat dinner at the same table—Arthur Ashe, Eldridge Cleaver, Dorothy Dandridge, Harry Belafonte, Jackie Robinson, Angela Davis, and Diana Ross—no track runners or blues singers, no inventors of stoplights or blood plasma, no exotica like the Jewel Box Revue. When she did learn about the Jewel Box's spectacular drag queen revue, she was very excited and asked why they weren't on "The Ed Sullivan Show." American Negroes often laughed and said, "Girl, where you come from anyway?"

Alex Decatur was from a well-off corner of life in Latin America where she could think of herself as just Latin, and Catholic, even if she had Africans in the family tree. She mentioned sometimes, slipping back into a heavier accent, when she was a little girl at home riding the bus to school through the neighborhood of the blacks, or knowing a black guy who took the same bus. To Bird, it was as if Alex's childhood were white and her adulthood black. Of course, even looking at it that way, Bird realized, showed one of her own limitations, her Yankee mind, a race mind. All her life Bird had accepted the limitations she'd lived with—segregation, glass ceilings, even failure. She accepted the routine expectation in college, or on the job, or from haughty waiters, that she would not be suitable. Alex accepted a change of color, but no limitations. Bird lived in the Quarter, Alex didn't.

Romeo shouted, "Come on in here, now. I'm tellin' ya." He was calm. Ma added her two cents. "Girl, do like he says now." Downstairs, Naomi slammed the door shut. The street was quiet. Bird saw that the clock read 2:12 A.M., turned over, and went to sleep.

4

Saturday

Retablo: *m.* altarpiece; religious picture hung as a votive
offering; series of pictures that tell a story.
    —*University of Chicago English-Spanish Dictionary*

When Bird opened her eyes Saturday morning,
"Rhythm Revue" was coming through the window. It
was so loud she thought it was her clock radio. The
music was good. Then it dawned on her that the sound came
from her neighbor Cross outside. He had a new radio, with two
good speakers. He had discovered the same Saturday-morning
radio show that Bird liked. Naomi was yelling at someone, "Git
your ass across the street, git your *ass* out of the *street,* hear me?"
Bird looked out the window. Two kids were downstairs taking
apart what looked like an old bike.

Now that Alex was gone, Bird locked the inner door at night and kept it open in the day, taking care of Alex's plants and hoping all the little guardians would give some comfort. All the windows had been locked shut after the repairmen came. The apartment got stifling hot and very dusty. Sometimes she ran Alex's air conditioner rather than open her windows.

A note from Bird was still tacked on Alex's side of the door. "Documentary—long hours all weekend," it said. On the chipped and splintered side in Bird's apartment, Alex's hand had left the greeting "Anytime." The notes were very old, left up out of sentiment. One day after Frank Burton moved in with Alex he had had a new lock put on while they were out. After Alex died Bird had made the super replace it, even though the landlord had told her the door would soon become a wall again.

It had been two months since Alex died, and when she wasn't at work Bird was hiding out trying to "deal" with her feelings. At night sometimes she cooked, sometimes she didn't, and sooner or later crawled into bed to watch TV, dozing till 4:00 A.M. when the Bronx court bailiff who lived upstairs got up and ran his bath. She felt safer after he was up and running the water. She knew he had a gun. The stocky and stern middle-aged black man had come running down the steps that night, in his T-shirt, with a shoulder holster on. That night he became Bird's upstairs centurion. She waited to sleep when the bailiff was up.

Bird opened the door to Alex's and was delighted by the sunlight filling her view of the space. Hot air rushed towards her. Bird ran some water in a container, grabbed a cloth, and ventured into the domain of all small, seemingly exhausted guardians and whisked off the dust that had gathered on them during the week. Some of them were already cracking from the dry heat. She knew she probably should find the linseed oil and soak their thirsty wooden hides, but she wasn't sure if preserving them was her mission. To Bird they'd relinquished their protective roles in favor of observing. They had simply watched all that had passed. They had watched and begun to split, cracks running up the feet, around the limbs, along the smooth surface of a nose, sometimes across a skull. Her mind ran back to people who had given Alex one figure or another. Then she thought again about Alex's phonebook. She'd found it in the stuff the police had returned.

At first she'd just told herself, "Look, she *knew* my number and my address, that's why I'm not in there." Then Bird had looked up Alex's other close friends. They weren't in there either. That wasn't how phonebooks worked. Did people make phonebooks and leave out all the numbers they knew? It was a recent phonebook. An ancient, torn, wire-bound one was in the apartment, but the addresses in it were useless.

Bird had called several mutual friends and mentioned the new phonebook. When she told them that it gave her the creeps, usually they laughed and said that was pretty silly. Bird knew they hadn't really thought about it.

"It's ridiculous, doll," Alonso Essex said. He paced the floor when he talked, even on the phone. He was still upset that they'd blown it with the memorial. "The flowers should have been enormous, we were meant to be overwhelmed with scent. We wanted to weep."

"I know, Essex."

"And I tried to tell these fools we must play Marvin Gaye, 'Sexual Healing.' Sorry, doll, but I haven't gotten over it. We have to be real sometimes." Bird knew Essex had probably taken the funeral committee over the edge with his vision of how the last rites should be. People completely misread Essex on first sight, sometimes because there might be bracelets, sometimes because he could become florid over someone's physical beauty, sometimes because he gave extremely thoughtful, always un- solicited lectures on how every person living has some form of "drag." Alonso's "drag" was having once done all the right stuff the right way. He could put that on for family or business if needed, but usually didn't. "My former life was somewhat respectable," he'd say when he got drunk, finishing with a cheer- ful "oh, well."

"There is no music for what we're going through. 'Sexual

Healing' is as good as the next thing, *really.* It's dishonest, what we did, the whole bourgeois pretense to dignity. It's been years since we had any dignity to protect."

"It's true."

"It's beyond dignity what we've been through. I wanted to be taken somewhere, to be taken far."

"We probably didn't need to go where you might have taken it, babe."

"Doll, you're right, even you could not go where I could take it, and you are a jewel among us. I know. I know you, doll, I know you." Essex was just a tad drunk. "The women drummers were good, the libations were good, all wonderful, but playing only religious Aretha, no. It was a compromise and Bird, dear, the diva Alex was *never* about compromise. It's like what Lyndon Baines Johnson used to say about patriotism: It 'too often means concealing a world of error and wrong judgment beneath the flag.' Funerals are like that. Wrapping a world of error and wrong judgment in piety."

"You quoting LBJ now?"

"Yes, indeed. I'm reading about him. He's become my favorite doll of all the dolls. And much more quotable than that insipid Nixon, who never said anything witty. But even LBJ was probably buried like the rest. I have to look into who was at the funeral. You see, this is America and if you go, *high* you are likely to have a substantial and sympathetic black woman to put you away and ease the pain for the much bereaved, or not much bereaved, as the case may be. The highest of the most high among white folks nowadays have a cathedral and a black woman singing over their poor wracked, sinful, lying and thieving dead bodies. You're supposed to have a diva with a voice like a force of nature *hovering* over the casket, or *urn,* whatever you've got yourself in. It's the only succor there is in America, the black mother pietà moaning over our loss and wrapping us in the winding sheet. If we could only have gotten Jessye Norman. Not to have dignity, even though, of course, there is no greater dignity than that diva, but because it's the ritual, the rite. The rite of expiation, the catharsis. This is what I've been thinking about, because you know death is all the time, babe, and all of us."

"I know."

Basically Essex was right. The slides and videos of her work just didn't get it. If Essex had done the eulogy, he would have hailed her beauty, her arrogance, and her self-absorption, as if they were just as high on the moral scale as the selflessness and idealism her other friends had promoted. And they'd treated Alex like a Christian, a Catholic. She was more Hindu than Catholic. She didn't go to the hereafter, or a rest in peace, she went back for recycling. She went back as uncontainable energy to disturb the peace.

When the man Bird called the Prince of the Faithful appeared at the memorial it was disconcerting, because he had disappeared when Alex died, when Bird might have needed him. She called him the Prince of the Faithful, not because he was, but because she was. She'd been in love with him for years. He was prince to all who believed in him without question, but he was loyal to none. He was tall, handsome, and had been lanky for a long time, until even a daily two-mile run and weekend basketball failed to keep him skinny. His bone structure gave him the kind of good looks that would never abandon him, that could have put him in movies if he didn't know he was fabulous without being in the movies. That's what made him the Prince—he always acted as if he'd already been to the party and found it boring. But before anyone got close enough to find that out they couldn't help noticing that he dressed like a man who'd had a gentleman's gentleman hand him each article of clothing as he put it on. His clothes looked like they felt good but were not to be touched, mussed, or crushed. His clothes sent the right message for a man who was quiet, secretive, and content. Most people kept their distance.

He adored Bird, she knew that, but that was not enough for her. She felt like his favorite charm, a lucky penny. When the good luck came, he held her hand. She'd never divined to whom he gave his passion; it was not her, she knew that much. She'd never figured out to whom he'd once given his faithfulness. That, he did not even pretend to give Bird. She felt unforgiving that he hadn't been around before they put Alex away. She'd told him she couldn't sleep. He'd told her to see a shrink and get some pills. Some men disappear when a woman gets pregnant or gets sick; the Prince ran off because she wasn't listening. Maybe it was the same thing. When he called her that evening, she didn't pick up the phone. It was too late.

Everyone had to get drunk after the memorial. They should have made *pasteles* and plantains, some curried goat and rice and beans, and had a party.

"And this phonebook thing, doll, I think you are getting too crazy about the phonebook. It's probably some madness of the diva's that we cannot ever fathom."

Alex's family still had not come to get her things out of the apartment. They sent an agent to take the artwork, which was interesting to Bird because Alex had never been able to get represented while she was alive. Her mother did not want her cousins or anyone to take any of the Guatemalan shawls or street vendor jewelry, the size 5½ cowboy boots or the photos of her friends stuck on the refrigerator. She'd said very plainly she never wanted to see any of that stuff again.

Her mother had turned up unannounced at the apartment after the memorial to get some personal items and to look around. Bird heard her letting herself in through the hall door and then saw the stone-faced redhead standing paralyzed in the living room in a taupe silk suit. In her sixties, she still had the bearing of the woman who would have been a willing beauty queen had her family not punished her for any and all acts of vanity or public displays of flesh. She drew eyebrows in over the dark eyes that still refused to yield to the tiny folds wearying her face. Where her easy flirtatious smile had once created a shine across the skin, a wary look now sized up all strangers.

"Are you alright, Mrs. Decatur?"

"Reynolds, dear. Carlota, if you like."

Alex's mother regained her composure. An implacable mask borrowed from stern nuns at a convent school hid the wiles of a girl who had snuck off with her country cousins to local fairs where she strode the ramp in her sister's high heels and strapless swimsuit, chest poked out and ass in the air. Vain and trading public displays of flesh for enthusiastic catcalls. She still had the walk.

She paced through the apartment making a useless effort to look like she was planning to clean. She took pictures from the dresser and put them in a satchel she'd brought, ransacked a dresser drawer, pulled out lingerie and a diaphragm case, tossed them in the wastebasket, and closed the drawer. Next she fumbled with the socks and T-shirts, and losing interest, went back to the dresser top, pulling earrings and bracelets from little boxes and baskets. Some went into the satchel, some were left on the dresser top. It was amazing to Bird that she could distinguish between items, having feelings for some and not for others. Based on what? If she'd ever seen them? If she had given them to her daughter? What did she see so quickly, rummaging through Alex's favorite objects?

She trashed a nightgown hanging on a closet door, along with other worn personal items like slippers, a battered brush full of Alex's hair, small containers of makeup, tubes of lipstick. Carlota didn't look like she'd ever done too much cleaning, even though Bird suspected she probably had. In a sudden rush of passion the woman stripped the bed, rolled the sheets up into a pillowcase, walked out into the hall to the incinerator door, and threw the bundle in. She rolled up the throw rugs in the bedroom and shoved them in a corner. It was as if the first thing to do was to get rid of anything that might still have traces of Alex's skin cells, hair, or smell in it. Bird offered the woman some garbage bags from Alex's utility closet.

"Oh, God, I don't think I'll need those. I won't be doing much more of this."

Bird stood in horror as Carlota waved her hand at the overflow of novels and art books. "Perhaps you'd like them—consider them yours." All Bird could think at the moment was that maybe no one at her house read books, which she knew was unfair, but shit—a few hundred books that probably went out of print as soon as they were published, books you couldn't get anywhere. Well, no, Bird realized, her family wouldn't be looking for any art books. What was she thinking? She panicked. Bird had dubbed the woman *grandassa*—it suited her feelings. She wanted to tell this sultaness of Long Island that she'd have to *pay* her to clean up Alex's life and all the wreckage created by useless police investigations and visits from fingerprint dusters and relatives looking for a "decent" dress to put her in to be cremated. What was that about? The cremation was the only wish to which they'd acquiesced. Alex had always been very loud about the fact that should she drop dead she wanted to be cremated and have one of her spiritual teacher/guides chant over her. No one had bothered to find any of the gurus or *madrinas*. Everyone had dropped the ball. Bird got lost in the question as the mother jabbered on about all the junk that was Alex. "We won't be able to use this, what is it? I could have a cleaning crew come in to throw stuff out."

Bird looked at the woman who would have been a beauty queen, who smiled at the traveling cloth salesman standing at the side of the makeshift stage in a small beach town in Guyana. The girl who wanted to be caressed in her red swimsuit and commit some sin. The woman who still had her posture. Her experience was useless to help her turn a nightmare into a cleaning job. "That's a good idea, Mrs. Reynolds, a cleaning company."

"That bastard sent me money. Can you believe his nerve? Sending me money!" She turned away and turned back towards Bird. "And it was not much either, I might add." Carlota mentioning the bastard made Bird's hair stand on end. "Well, you know what it costs. I sent it back. He kills my daughter and he never says a word, not a word. I know he killed her, and he sends me money! It's disgusting. He's not a human being."

Bird homed in on Carlota's rage as if locking onto a radio frequency. "He sent money to the memorial too. I took it and shoved it back in the messenger's hand. It's unbelievable."

They were silent, tuned in, humming together on that frequency. Two women who did not understand each other at all, matched pound for pound in rage. Neither of them would ever get over it, and yet they were together only in their fury. Each woman was alone. Whenever the mother spat out the man's name Bird jumped back on Carlota's channel. Otherwise Bird received her intrusion as static.

"Where are her sketchbooks?"

Bird thought the question odd.

"The agent said to look for sketchbooks and things where she put down ideas for her work."

"I don't know exactly. She drew on scraps of paper and I think she was starting to tape things, using tape to document how she made the pieces and making notes on tape."

"Tape? No, I don't mean tape. You know, drawings, that sort of thing."

Bird led Carlota to the shelves that held the black oversized drawing books in the hallway near the large back room she used as a makeshift studio. "These are pretty old, I think, but you should start by looking here."

"I'll tell him to take them and then he can go through them."

Bird walked away from her, back towards the kitchen. She could toss some junk from the refrigerator while she waited.

"Didn't she have a video camera? I should take that."

Bird blinked and tried to think if she'd seen it. No. "I packed her electronic equipment in those boxes on the floor there but I didn't see a camera."

"Oh, God. You think someone stole it already? What's in there?"

"A VCR, some cables."

"Well, I don't need that. I'll pick it up when I come back. And these crude little whatever they are—trinkets—you may give to her friends. She's got all this terrible plastic Madonna stuff, my God—it's everywhere in the markets at home. She's got it all mixed up with the nice pottery. Did she ever buy herself any good dishes? I used to tell her all that handmade crap was no good." The woman whose family always ate on good dishes.

Bird began to feel panic again. She walked towards the door to her own place. She saw herself in Alex's tin-framed mirror near the door. She'd seen herself there a thousand times, as if her face were part of the room, but only in passing, only when she was visiting.

"She bought some very expensive crystal glasses, you might look in the kitchen for those. She liked nice wineglasses." She could hear Carlota in the kitchen, opening and closing cabinet doors.

"That's something. Oh. These *are* nice."

Bird didn't like Alex's mother. She reminded her of her own mother, who always resorted to being hard-ass rather than let her feelings show.

Bird noticed the *retablos* Alex had collected, miniature disasters sitting on ledges around the room. She could understand why Carlota didn't want them. The gruesome little paintings Alex had picked up were like snapshots from ancient *telenovelas*. Tiny children taken by illness and turned into angels by an artist paid to commemorate them. They were made for people who allowed themselves to cry. Maybe that was one of the reasons Bird had liked Alex—she spoke of weeping as a grace earned by suffering.

Bird could not cry, much less weep. Weeping was crying without embarrassment. Her own mother, Angie, had shamed Bird whenever she cried. Pride was her mother's acid milk. Angie ate, drank, and slept anger and insult and she repaid the whole world by refusing comfort to all. Angie wouldn't take Bird to the first day at a new school in a new city. She told her the bus routes and not to get lost. When Bird was thirteen Angie told her how to pack her bag, how to take the subway from Grand Central to her uncle's place in Harlem, and put her on a train to New York. Later, when Bird went to boarding school, Angie told her not to come home for any holiday except Christmas. Bird's father let her do it as a kind of payoff for going along with the scholarship to boarding school. Angie thought she didn't need to go. Bird's father came from a kinder, gentler clan, but Angie the Terrible was tsarina of all the Kincaids. "Stay up there," she'd said cheerfully, "you'll find somewhere interesting to visit." You survive, you don't weep. Angie's marching orders and rallying cries were always taken from the same bit of scripture: Nobody takes care of black women, might as well get used to it. With Angie, basic training was worse than the war.

The little *retablos* were the penance of survivors. Colorful permanent ceremonies to the survivor's pain, and one thought, there but for the grace of God go I, Lord, it was my disaster but it was not me. Bird passed around the room gathering them all from their little ledges and piling them in a chair. Carlota was talking.

"At least she had some of her upbringing left. Not a good suit in the closet, but she's got Austrian crystal champagne flutes with the label still stuck on the bottom." There was a pause. "Oh, Alex." She began sobbing.

Bird wanted to reach out to the woman, but she could not. Even though this was her friend Alex's mother, she could not reach across what seemed an enormous void. Bird's isolation, the rupture between herself and others, seemed unbridgeable.

The breach separated Bird and the other survivors in their circle from everyone else who did not live with the constant presence of death invisibly sheltered in their rooms, sucking up the life they had made. The life they had made by separating themselves from mothers and fathers, from home ground. It was precisely this separation that had made each of them possible. And now the distance was too great. And it was the distance that irked and prodded the family to blame and accuse. Even when they didn't really want to, they would still say, "It is that life you made that is killing you." Even if they named sin in their complaints, it was not sin they blamed, it was straying from their watchful eyes. Not retribution for acts, but for separation, for declaring liberty.

Bird hugged the stranger Carlota, briefly and without feeling, taking in her perfume, the texture of the suit, measuring the way the cut fit the body. They all had some family people who were like strangers. Bird said good-bye to the woman, knowing she probably didn't hear her. Bird stood still where she was and listened to all the sounds of Carlota's departure from the apartment, the floor, the building.

She was thinking that a family was a strange creature. She often felt as if she really belonged to a branch of an ancient shogunate, would-be dynasty and womb of warlords—she had alliances among her relations, rather than kin. Her mother's clan—the Judahs—were all marked by the same accident of birth, the taut, fragile skin of full balloons. This thin membrane of outer protection left them disposed to explosions of rage over perceived insults and unthinking offenses. The clan fought over things that could be uttered and forgotten by other families, especially folks who couldn't move away from each other. Bird's folks liked a little distance with their family love.

They banished one another as if they'd taken each other's husbands or wives, or had denounced them in Congress, or on "Oprah." This was done by immediate announcement to all listening relations. The stingy, thin, nearly invisible gods of Slights, Affronts, Aspersions, and Indignities sat steaming in the family baths and kitchens, listening and chafing at bits of human conversation, bristling over phrases repeated on telephones. When debts were left owing, the niggardly deities crowed. They fed when angry ladles banged against sinks, belched when doors slammed, and farted contentedly when the curses erupted and retribution was sworn. The fiercest of the warlords, by any measure, were the Judah women; once engaged they could not be talked down, they got blood first. Bird too bore the fractious mark of the clan, and as far as she knew, she was more ashamed of it than most, but that rarely stopped her from drawing her sword. The family campaigns had epic duration. Bird had a niece who hadn't spoken to her in eight years. "Not my aunt," she told people, "my mother's sister."

But Bird thought if they could all talk, it would still remain difficult. She and her brother practically ran away from home because their parents lived in preparation against every disaster they could imagine. So did Carlota. They were frightened of scarcity, isolation, and public shame. They were scared of hatred aimed at their children. And they were used to privation, hatred, war once-removed. Yet they knew nothing of the demons Bird and Alex came to know so well. And the parents' fear of shame prevented them from hearing. They had never been visited by the night demon, incubus and succubus of youthful death, laying its breathless flesh upon their lives and entering their sleep as a lover might, sweetly or with sudden violence.

Bird had all kinds of names for gods and spirits, but especially demons. She had an encyclopedia of them. It was a list only a Judah would keep. In her Indian guru days she called them Rakshasas, after the demons who served Ravana, the Demon King, in the Indian classic, the Ramayana. Rakshasas were considerable foes, dangerous and numerous like gangbangers. The tontons macoutes of the heavenly ancients. In those days, they liked "kicking" by night, ate the flesh of anyone stepping into their zone. But Bird thought this new nocturnal demon, the one who could snatch the young by the thousands, this succubus, was Ravana himself. Ravana, who could seize her friends with his twenty arms and poison them with the ten tongues in his ten monstrous heads adorned with golden earrings. Ten heads that grew back if a mortal slashed them with a sword. The Demon King coveted lovers and stole mates. Ravana always traveled unseen, leaving his fortress through the Gate of Illusion, his twenty eyes undetected. Bird knew it was Ravana, who took not virgins, but the passionate—beauties in their prime—that he might have them for himself at the moment of their splendor.

Bird knew the red-eyed demon preferred roses in their second season, fully grown in size, lush in color, dusted with pollen. Having known their frost, these flowers opened in overabundance and intemperance when the sun touched their richly tinted flesh. Ravana's claws could not resist them.

Bird realized she was staring into space. She caught herself in Alex's living room mirror. Her skin, usually a burnished copper, looked washed out and her shiny marble eyes, sunken. She was tired already. She saw her wild corkscrew hair, almost dreaded but going in too many directions, saw it as Alex's mother probably had seen it moments ago. One spends all this time trying to deal with one's self, she thought, all the fucked-up shit. But the universe was crumbling because nothing was really created in her lifetime, nothing was made except themselves. Nothing was of consequence compared to the love between them, mutually consumed, inhaled from one another. The air was collapsing. Tiny lungs were imploding like stars. Bird saw that she'd forgotten to put any earrings on. She remembered that Alex always slept in hers.

Bird had xeroxed the phonebook and sent a copy to Bernard, a lawyer. He called up freaked out when he got it. Bird gloated, knowing that he'd first thought Bird's reaction to the missing names was just some problem between the two women. Bernard was not in the book either: no home phone, no office phone, no fax, no car phone. A guy with that many numbers expected to be in a friend's phonebook.

There were a few numbers with male first names, no last names, and no area codes. They didn't discuss those, but Bird had noticed that some of the numbers were New York exchanges. Bird was too skittish to call them and try to inquire into their relationship with her dead friend. She did *want* to call them, wanted to call them all. She wanted them to tell her everything. It was as if Alex had left these first-name-no-area-code guys just to be provocative. It was like her. But the other scenario, that they were secrets, was like her, too, and Bird figured they were handsome, spoke syrupy crap in foreign languages, bit her neck waiting for taxis, and licked her ears on escalators.

Bernard wasn't interested in Alex's sometime men. He

wanted to know who Bird had talked to, who was in the book if he wasn't in the book. Bird told him she had been calling them, a few every night since before the memorial, and she was now somewhere in the J's. She had skipped the no-last-name guys.

Most people shared every recollection of Alex, no information being too odd or too detailed to repeat. There was a couple, Sheri and Mustafa Baker, who ran Alex's favorite health food store. Whenever she was taking a trip, Sheri said, she bought bottles of papaya enzyme; pints of coconut oil and small bottles of almond oil; capped goldenseal; homeopathic stress tablets. Alex loved fragrant Indonesian rice, bought only pure aloe creams, never let mineral oil touch her skin. Mustafa said she took large doses, took too much of everything. Sometimes Bird jotted down what they said in her notebook, sometimes she didn't.

There was Roland Jeffreys, knew Alexandra Decatur in graduate school. Saw it in the paper, wanted to know exactly what happened. She told him she'd known Alex fifteen years or so. Yeah, it was a long time. He'd introduced himself at the memorial. Did they let so-and-so know in Seattle? A name in the book.

Everyone Bird spoke to had some past revel to share from old apartments, solitary beaches, or emptied wine bottles. People who couldn't get to the memorial sent warm notes, poems, snapshots, and memoirs. A letter said Alex once came by a ticket to England and boarded the plane quite penniless, sat next to this apparently well-heeled relic of the monarchy who found her a lot of fun, and wound up riding horses at his country house for a week. Greatly entertained the whole family. Two weeks later, he said, he thought she was sharing a chilly apartment with some African students in London. He always got cards from her.

There were stories from people who'd never met anyone like her, tales of her dramatic performances at dinner, and cards of remembrance. Those others like Bird and Bernard to whom Alex was not remarkable did not get mealtime theater or thank-you notes. They accepted her silences and expected her to turn up at any time, pick up wherever she'd left off.

"It's ghastly, Bernard. Most of these people have to be told. Then, whatever memory pops in their head, they tell me. They repeat themselves. She was so intense, so unexpected, so angry, so whatever they can think of, so colored, so pretty."

"Yeah, people are awkward. They don't know what the hell to say. They don't know you."

"They just want to know if it was grisly."

"What do you say?"

"I tell them it was."

Nearly all the people missing from the phonebook, about ten of them, used to hang out a lot in a bar called the Crescent, before the place switched from jazz to country and western. Alex called Bird, Reenie, and Essex "the Three Ladies of Baghdad" even though Essex, technically speaking, was not a woman, much less a lady. Alex called them that because Bird and Reenie used to wear these long, heavy cotton Moroccan dresses, hand-woven shawls, and African cloth headties (all flung on with "attitude" and a total indifference to matching colors) and lots of jewelry—would-be-African earrings, silver cuffs from North Africa. Essex tied up his head in a cloth so tight that it eradicated wrinkles, and draped a thin desert-white cloth around his neck. Alex called it "Middle East bizarre."

Two others from their crew had recently died: Randall, a producer, and Paul, who did hair. "You know, Bernard, Randall would have been in there. He just died, not a year ago. Maybe Paul wouldn't but, God, we all had a couple of addresses for where Randall was the last two years—his apartment, then in the country. His sister's, the hospice. I mean, she would have had all those. She used to take him food, call him, visit the hospital, the sister's. I don't get it."

Michael, a painter and one of Alex's "sometimes" men, before Frank, wasn't there. None of the five addresses he'd had in the past three years. Nor was Charles Marshall.

"My man Charles. How is Charles? I had to stop hanging out with him because we seemed to like the same women."

"Yeah, well, he should have been letting you have them since he's married and you ain't."

"Yeah, but he didn't."

"I even looked for him under B for 'Baguette.' "

"Baguette?"

"That's what Alex and I used to call him. I probably never told you that."

"Charming, sounds like you."

She laughed.

"No, you never told me that. I guess you probably have a nickname for me too?"

Bird demurred on that one. He laughed. "Don't take this the wrong way, but except for me and Charles, who are two upstanding citizens, it sounds like she left all the weirdos out of the book."

"Thanks. Well, it does seem kind of like a phonebook just for business and Christmas cards."

"Maybe it was something like that. Business contacts, old school friends. Maybe she just kept it in her studio for work-related calls, fund-raising, trying to get shows abroad, that kind of thing. In a way, that's what the Rolodex at the office is about."

"You've got me in your Rolodex, don't you? And we aren't doing any business."

"Well, yes, I see what you mean. On the other hand, sometimes I call people from here to let the office pay for it."

"And how would you explain who these oddball people are in your Rolodex? 'They're these strange people I know who're part of my secret life when I'm not in this office'? Would you look at your secretary slyly and say, 'I'm probably the straightest person they know'?"

Bernard cracked up. "Hell, no. I'd probably say you're in the news business. If I went around here saying I had a secret life, that would be too juicy. The sister would definitely be trying to get in my business. And she wouldn't be thinking about it with any imagination. First of all, she would *assume* I was fucking alla y'all, and that in my secret life I'm trying to divest young girls of their maidenheads, you know. It would be nasty."

"I should call her sometime and tell her that we're a cult and you are our wizard."

"She'd be fascinated. And probably relieved. She would *love* to know that I had a wild side."

"You do. We just need to help you set it free."

"Free me, baby." Bernard was laughing again.

"How is your social life anyway?"

"I only meet two kinds of women: the ones who want to marry me and the ones I really like."

"You're too good for any of them."

"Really. You could tell me about that at greater length."

"I will sometime."

"About Alex, Bird, you know she had a way of just cracking open the door and letting me peek at where she was going. That was it. She would allude to having a life that she thought I wouldn't totally accept, sometimes saying that it was because she was an artist, or alternatively, that she was just a more daring person. 'You don't need to go there,' she'd say. She was careful to shut the door firmly behind her. I think she assumed that I wouldn't make it in that part of her life."

"Maybe so. But maybe it was the other way around. Maybe she liked the idea of coming into your world and leaving the door to hers shut so she could pretend she was like you."

"Oh, yes. We did that dance too."

Bernard and Bird talked every day. His secretary had indeed gotten used to her calling and treated her like a relative. Bird dropped her radio voice with the woman and started doing sister-to-sister. Bird figured Bernard was going to solve the mysteries of Alex's death with the raw materials Bird would provide; he was going to figure out the sensible thing to do with the creative remains of her life. Bird would just try to keep their decisions honest, in some kind of Alex mode.

Bird realized she was groping in a dimly lit room for a door. Her gut was telling her that Alex had prepared to leave them all.

That she had kept her distance, even though no one took it that way. No one had even noticed.

"Bernard, I still think she's telling this story, not us. She was telling us something and we missed it." Alex would know they wouldn't notice. They were, all of them, too busy. She would know how to evade without causing hurt feelings. She would know how to pretend she was being there, call when the machine would definitely be on and no one would pick up. Do holidays through the mail. And yet there was not a person who knew her who believed she would willingly give up her life.

"No, Bird, you're tripping again. Alex did not take herself out of here, or know something was going to happen to her."

"How do you know?"

"I know."

And not one of them believed if she was sick or in trouble that she would not tell them. Each one insinuated that even if she would not tell the *others,* she would confide in her or him. Alex was not just friends with any of them; she was *very close* to them all. Everyone said or intimated, "I would know."

The jealousy of Alex's friends—even her own jealousy—was obnoxious to Bird. She, of course, also felt that she had been especially close, more close, closer to Alex than all the others, even though she knew her friend shared confidences with people who sat next to her on the subway. Alex did not crave privacy, except when she was working. She liked to get naked with people emotionally, take off all their outer garments, the superficial stories of their lives, and find out why they never went home, or disliked their mothers, or couldn't stand for anyone to look at the burn marks left on a shoulder blade from a childhood accident. She liked to take off her own clothes, too. And because they'd been naked with her, they knew they knew her. They knew because there was one moment, some conversation when they were sprawled across the couch at a lake house on a summer night and they were closer than anyone.

As Bird wound her way through Alex's other grieving friends, they all told her something they had done once when no one else was there. Alex had set them all up. Set them all up with a moment that obscured everything else. As each friend remembered Alex, they were always alone together.

"Bird," Bernard said.

"Yeah."

"Just look at the tapes if you can. Let's just concentrate on getting her work archived. We both know what happened, but there's no trace of evidence. We'll have to let it go."

"I saw him."

"You said you *thought* you saw him before."

"He came into my office."

"Oh. That's different. What happened?"

"He said we should have lunch."

"He came in there to see you?"

"No. He was there for an interview."

"And he said you should have lunch? Maybe he was just saying that to seem polite."

"No."

"What did you say?"

"I told him. I don't know exactly what I told him. I told him to leave it alone. I was trying to get on with my life and he should too."

"Sounds benign enough to me. That was the best thing to do."

"It wasn't. We both got weird."

"I guess it was bound to happen. It won't happen again— Bird?"

"I don't think you understand. It's like I'm in the middle of some game they were playing. It's like he's trying to see if I'm still in the game. I don't know what I'm saying but I wouldn't want him to know—"

"Know what?"

"I wouldn't want him to know that I'm still wondering."

"Bird. Forget it. He's probably happy as hell he's out of it. He'll stay well away if he knows what's good for him. Besides, you handled it."

"Yeah."

"Let's just catalog her stuff and get it out of there. I'll come help."

"Yeah. I'd like to get rid of it."

Static. Black and white. Black on white slowly becoming more white on black. Bird turned down the white noise. Why is static black and white, she wondered. Bird realized Alex's videos were *retablos. Color bars.* Moving *retablos.* Now that Alex was dead, it was easy to see the videos she made as tragic histories. *Trees. Greens. Muddy ground. Feet stepping on leaves. Trees with barely perceptible movement in the leaves. Breathing near the camera. Movement backward, more clear ground in view. Alex steps into the frame in baggy overalls, peasant blouse, jean jacket. Her black hair is in tied-up braids, like a girl's. Alex is golden brown, her face very Mayan.*

Bird's mind was drifting. She was thinking that this videotape was made before she knew Alex, before style and habit had been shaped into social facade. Before she became a New York artist, before she became petty famous without even having a dealer, just by being the most outrageous person to show in any group show. It was the only kind of famous most people got, if they got any at all, when they came to New York looking for the real thing. It meant you could sell about four hundred campaign buttons with your name on them if you ran for mayor. It meant you had a mailing list for openings and people usually came. The people who came to Alex's openings were folks who thought they knew her story, usually people who'd met her sometime after she'd started telling it, after she'd begun to think of her public side, even dabbled with changing her name.

Bernard had said someone had to look at the tapes of her work. Get them organized to give to the university archive. Alex had managed to get that famous after all. The school she'd gone to wanted her papers. Bird had her notebook but she could not think of anything to write down. Rewind.

Alex steps in view in baggy overalls, peasant blouse, jean jacket, moves to the clearing and, on her knees, examines the ground, runs her hands across the area, lightly, without leaving palm- or fingerprints.

At some point soon after Bird first met her, Alex had grown newly fascinated by the fact that she was born in South America. She began to become more Latin. Maybe she'd tired of keeping her childhood tucked away for the sake of becoming American. Alex's father Willem DeKadt was from Surinam. She barely knew him, since he was usually traveling around in Latin America on import/export business. He had given Alex her European first name, the Dutch surname that was on her birth certificate, and her African genes.

And Willem DeKadt gave her a taste for marketplaces, with their heaps of ochre, brown, black, and orange ground spices, and dazzling fabrics, whimsical baskets, and teetering pyramids of plastics—piles of Vaseline jars and baby powder, bins of wallets and heaps of rubber sandals tied in pairs. She remembered the pleasant tongue-clattering uproar of it all from trips with him to the Hindu and West Indian merchants in their alleyways in downtown Paramaribo. He gave her a yen for the smells of turmeric and curry, jasmine and sandalwood. And sparkling cloth. The Indians displayed huge rolls of bright reds and greens embedded with tiny mirrors. The West Indians favored gold and silver lamés and even sequined laces, all the fixings of feasts and Carnival, fantasies woven of grand mythologies and poverty. Her good-looking father evidently liked to be dazzled too, and he would let only the most beguiling market women sell him only the most dainty or lacy baubles for his princess, and only after a lengthy exchange of the most exaggerated compliments. Alex, waiting in her crinolines, stemmed her impatience by touching and eyeing the alluring textiles.

Alex picks out thorny sprigs, sharp-edged pebbles, large twigs. Using the backs of her arms, she pushes the dirt up into a rise. She repeats this motion, moving slowly around the dirt space until an oval shape begins to appear, an oval big enough to fit the length of her body.

Alex's mother Carlota was from Guyana, but she had never returned there after she upset her family by marrying somebody who was going to take their young girl off to another country, even if it was just Surinam, the country next door. Carlota was not big on talking about bloodlines, so it was only Alex's guess that she had exchanged her Indian blood for a plane ticket to the U.S. and the made-up name Decatur. When Alex was twelve and Carlota was facing the fact that she would soon be thirty, her mother packed them up while her father was away, wrote him a note telling him not to look for them, and moved to Long Island. She changed their name to Decatur to sound more English and found herself a white Yankee. Alex actually became much more like the American than her mother, whose temperament was still that of the petulant sixteen-year-old who'd been swept off her feet and abandoned to housekeeping in a muggy seaport. Alex taught Carlota the ins and outs of the malls, and ate all the fast foods for which her mother never developed a taste. Alex wore dark black eye makeup in ninth grade and became a blond temporarily in high school, which her mother found trashy. Alex held it against Carlota that she'd torn her away from her glamorous wandering father and the sultry gaiety of her backwater home.

As Alex got older, she added to her list of losses the vast and dense jungles of home that she'd only glimpsed on a few trips upriver, the enticing mysteries of the people there with whom no one admitted any connection, much less ancestry. As she got into her twenties, she wanted to claim the images in her mind of the place and people, not for politics or memory, but solely for their beauty. And compared to the ghosts wandering the glass and tile hallways of the Long Island malls, her home seemed to carry untold stories and unspoken connections to human origins.

Alex thought since her name was already made up, it was of little consequence if she made up another one. She wanted a name that sounded more earthy, and she tried using the name of a Brazilian tribe—Xingu, so she could have more x's. If you said it all at once it came out Alexingu. It had an effect. Too theatrical an effect, Bird thought. Sounded like Mata Hari or a magic act, and it quickly faded.

Alex moves out of the space, out of the frame. Feet on leaves, mud. Well, she was Mata Hari or a magic act. Bird laughed out loud. Alex must have worn hiking boots. Bird hadn't noticed. She wore hiking boots a lot. Bird was thinking about the boots because she knew Alex was taking off her clothes which had to be hard to manage with the mud. Where was she putting them down? Why didn't she put the camera on pause? Bird felt chilly watching the ground, the quivers in the trees, light shifting in them by fractions. I would worry about where to put my clothes, Bird thought.

Alex reenters the frame, this time nude, taking large steps to leave as few prints as possible. She is slim, bronze, girlish in her body, except for her hard-muscled thighs. She lies down on her back inside the oval. She takes a deep breath, pushing her rib cage out. She exhales roughly, using the force to press her whole body downward into the soil.

Bird had changed her name too, from Cynthia to Dunyazad, which she took out of a book. Most people found it required too much precision from their mouths, a sound they'd have to think about first, like "Ouagadougou." They stuck with "Bird." *Alex rises up gingerly from the impression now left in the earth, first pulling herself up from the waist, then supporting her weight on one fist. Her right foot steps back instinctively. She catches herself, weight on the toes rather than the whole foot. Out of frame. Sound of a drizzle coming through the leaves. Tiny pellet sounds hit the ground. On her hands and knees, still naked, Alex restores the place where she stood, sculpting back into the ground the indentations of her heels.* In a weird way she looked like a scrubwoman cleaning a floor that would never clean, a naked scrubwoman, as if she were becoming part of the dirt instead of cleaning it. The mud on her back ran in tiny rivers where the rain landed. She looked like a Xingu too. Her back was as much a painting as the ground was a sculpture. The Xingu were into body painting. *Alex erases a set of knuckle-prints, toes.*

Bird thought Alex's guardian spirits had sent her to Bird's place. There really was no other explanation. Well, that's what she had once thought. Bird was convinced, though, that it was something out-of-body, out-of-mind, like that. Even though Bird had been unable to protect her, she still felt that the guardians had sent Alex like a message to a mailbox. Bird was the drop for the letter or package or whatever it was in Alex that they were trying to secure. Something inside Alex had driven her to Bird's door more than a decade ago. That's how Bird knew she was the designated recipient. Alex had just showed up one day. Well, she called first. Bird never mentioned this idea to Alex or to anyone else because it just sounded so ridiculous to say she was somebody's spiritual mailbox. The phone rang. Bird grabbed it and the caller hung up.

Bird wasn't a relative, not even an artist, not anymore. But she was the designated receptacle; she could prove that with the evidence, an entire apartment of unclaimed stuff. Evidence. An inadequate word to cover the slim pickings that might show up in a court. The DA's office had taken everything they wanted, including the tapes, copied some of the items, examined every-thing for some signs of suicide or homicide or accident. Or so the DA's office said. Since Frank Burton's life was on the line, Bird assumed that he must have looked too. Hadn't he stopped and looked at these tapes when he came to claim his belongings? Bird knew she would have. Of course, she and Burton had precious little in common.

Bird finally made a note about the tape. "Graduate school project. Part of a series. 1975." Bird fast-forwarded through the tape. The plot, she thought, is that it rains and fills the space in the ground, the impression of the human body. It rains and destroys the space, and the impression of the human body is eaten away and absorbed into earth. Fast-forwarding. *Rain. Swelling, fullness, leaves, draining, moistness, drying. Rain. Erosion.*

"No, the plot here is the weather in New England." Bird was talking to herself. She refused to be respectful just because the woman was dead. Alex's work may look like grave sites, Bird thought contentedly, but Alex ain't in one.

A feeling of pique came over her. She resented the hell out of Alex. She disliked the reminder that she herself was a failure as an artist and had given up. Watching the tapes brought back the feeling Bird had these days when she ventured to someone's art opening, a discomfort, sometimes a rancor that made her leave.

She didn't like standing around at an art party with only friendship to justify her presence. She wanted to have her own claim to a place at the table of creative folk, wanted to have a tantalizing answer to the question, "So what do you do?" Bird had made a good life for herself. She enjoyed the competence she brought to her work, and the occasional scent of glamour when she could say that she had sat through an interview with whoever wrote the book they were all talking about that night. But that .wasn't enough, not like saying, I made that piece on the wall. I make objects that sometimes are beautiful. I try to make sense of what doesn't make sense. I explore, make journeys, investigate, ask questions, construct, consecrate, make, create. Verbs an artist might use.

Bird knew she'd given up because she could not abide the anger she had felt when she was trying to be an artist. Rage that popped off in a second, took her by surprise in the middle of the day when somebody said there was no check or no work, no place, no need. She resented the fact that Alex could *live* off all the anger, like it was feeding her body precious fuel.

Alex used it. She could light fires with it, singe anyone who came near. She could suffer the fools. Smile at them, sit next to them, invite them to share their opinions, which, she knew, would enrage her more, and then she would draw out her long knives and calmly murder them, put mayhem into their brains. Then, smiling, she would give them advice. Calm them down. Leave hating them because they were cowards and refused to defend themselves.

"We only talk about ourselves." Bird talking to herself again. It didn't matter what other subject she and Alex chose—politics, art, the economy—the imagination rarely went beyond the self, rarely tried for anything else. The Hundred-Pound Mouth, as Alex called herself, always talked about Number One, especially in her most passionate diatribes against other people. Bird knew all about this, of course. Sometimes when she heard herself coaching a college intern, she knew in midsentence that she was just going over her own past mistakes. The only concepts that

66

came out of her mouth were stored observations of herself. The self was her only subject too. Bird figured that's why they were friends.

Alex's death required Bird to live with the other woman's life. She was ill-equipped, she knew, to stay honest for too long with Alex's life. She would get bored. Alex's life was in no way boring, but it was somebody else's.

When the phone rang again, Bird had no idea how long she'd been watching the tapes, how long it had been since she'd said good-bye to Bernard. The call was from one of the mystery phone numbers in Alex's book. Bird had called them all, even though she said she wouldn't. Some she just dialed in case they were local numbers. It was a sweet, puzzled voice, a black woman saying she'd received a message for one of the no-last-name guys—Riley—"in reference to Alexandra Decatur." Bird explained that she hadn't really known who she was calling, that she was just contacting people who were friends of Alex.

"Oh, well, the man you were asking for used to stay here sometimes, when he was on the road, you know." Bird woke up. She had never thought it would be Dr. Swoon, the only Riley she knew.

"Most people call him 'Stack.' "

"Yeah, of course."

"He's a singer. Or maybe I should say he used to be. And he doesn't stay here anymore." Bird couldn't believe Alex had been in touch with Dr. Swoon. That was old, real old.

"What happened to him?"

"Crack."

"Right."

"He left some of his tapes here for a while. Came in the middle of the night one night, packed them up, said he'd be back, and that was the last I ever heard. That was more than a year ago. And your friend, she used to like to call my house at the damnedest hours, too. I don't miss hearing from her either."

"I'm sure. I'm just surprised they were still in touch. It's been twelve or thirteen years since I've heard her mention his name." The sweet voice responded with a cynical laugh.

"You'd be surprised the women calling him over the years. Him and your friend, they really got on my nerves. They never saw each other, but what they were doing, I guess you'd call it phone sex."

Bird acted dumb. She remembered walking through the open door one day to find Alex sprawled out naked on the couch with the phone in one hand, cooing, "Okay, all I'm wearing now is buttons." Bird looked, and sure enough, Alex was wearing three strategically placed buttons. She had wanted to laugh because they looked so funny and Alex looked so serious. Alex shuddered and the buttons fell and rolled and she dug around in the couch for them, anxiously muttering, "Wait a minute," into the phone. She regained herself, put the buttons back, and then moaned into the phone, "If I do that, I'm not going to be able to keep 'em balanced."

Bird didn't know this woman she was talking to. It didn't make sense to have any more conversation. Should she tell her that when she'd left the room that day Alex was going, "Okay, okay, I'm taking off the first button"? That she had started groaning to the man not to hang up at the crucial moment? That Bird had once been crazy about the man herself for a month in 1976? She didn't think the woman would want to hear it.

5
1976

Bird's apartment in Boston was the most enormous place she'd ever lived in, and the only thing she liked about the city. The front door opened onto an L-shaped living and dining room, big enough to seat twenty at a table, and two bedrooms. When she moved in, she turned the second bedroom into a space to paint in because of its expanse of windows across one wall, but she could never pull herself out of the big wide L where the stereo was and all the plants, bare floors, and empty white walls.

A sudden bout of fear of starvation had compelled Bird to go to graduate school and she landed in Boston with too much work, too little money, and nobody with whom to talk. She'd been part of a free-floating crew that spent months at a time sleeping on each other's floors ever since college. For four or five years they'd gathered in different configurations, doing different kinds of poorly paid work, camping out in apartments without much furniture in Washington and San Francisco, L.A. or New York. One or two would move first, and then others would visit, and sooner or later, another would move in. One year she had lived near Reenie and Michael; another near Essex and Bernard; another, Michael and Bernard.

Bird thought she should have all that space because she would be indoors reading for the rest of her life, and it was cheap because the neighborhood was being adopted by refugees from Vietnam airlifts. She unrolled a tattered Oriental rug hauled across country and left her books stacked in boxes. Beneath the living room windowsills she set a discarded door on top of steel milk crates to make a table, and covered the table with African statues and candles and plants. The table became a dusty miniature jungle, useless for resting more than a drink, but hypnotic to look at if she stretched out on pillows and played some Stevie Wonder or Earth, Wind & Fire. Bird wanted to go to West Africa and find something "real," something nice, something you couldn't buy in the black nationalist stores where she got her nose pierced and bought Somali Rose incense, Kente cloth, and African novels.

Since Bird had no furniture, she kept everything low to the ground. Michael had come and hammered together some very short record cases on which she could put the stereo and she found some tiny rose-tinted Victorian lamps that didn't give off much light. She'd finally tossed the waterbed at the last place after her mother had had a Sealy Posturepedic shipped to her door to save her back. She put the dining table her mother had given her into the spare bedroom and began to work in the larger space. Bird's mother, Angie, was worried about decent furnishings. Worried that everything be right if, say, some sudden calamity forced her to move in with her daughter. Angie left a bottle of her brand of vodka in the kitchen. Bird prayed for her mother to stay in good health and happily married.

Most of the time Bird piled her books and homework on the

dining table and spent all weekend painting. By the time she'd been in the apartment for two months, the top end of the L-shaped room was covered in eerie self-portraits, about life-size, on small canvases. Bird, who built her solitary life around music, made the canvases during marathon three-day binges of her entire Coltrane collection, Cecil Taylor, or the Art Ensemble of Chicago. All day and all night gorging on coffee, cigarettes, and Trane or cognac, cigarettes, and CT. It wasn't exactly the three *c*'s of the high life: champagne, coke, and cognac? champagne, coke, and caviar? She couldn't remember what it was that Michael had told her in a club one night—champagne, coke, and something. Something Miles Davis would do. And it wasn't exactly nights in SoHo or a life of free jazz at Ornette's on Prince Street, those nights and lives she'd heard about, but it was definitely something a hell of a lot more interesting than the lectures on nineteenth-century landscapes and her professor's endless stream of anecdotes on the artistic journals of poets who liked painting. Her paintings were scary and intense, which she rather liked. They were private, though. Maybe she would never have made them if she had not found herself alone. And she would not have intentionally shown them to anyone.

Alex Decatur called from New York, which was strange because Bird didn't know her very well and they'd never phoned each other. The two women had mutual friends, but Bird hadn't seen much of her before she left New York. Alex wanted to come stay for "a while" and have some surgery.

"Surgery? What kind of surgery?"

"I have some kind of infection in my tubes. I seem to have had it a long time. But I'm trying to go to India and the doctor said I have to do this before I can go."

"You're going to India?"

"Well, yeah, to see Baba."

"Which Baba? Is that Satchidananda?"

"No, that's Swami Satchidananda. It's Baba, Baba Muktananda."

Oh, right, Bird thought, Satchidananda, Alice Coltrane, *early* seventies. Bird had a memory of Alex telling her she should come to see Baba. Bird flushed, remembering just then that she and Reenie used to laugh behind everybody's back during the swami days. Everybody had one. They invented some fake gurus and sent their wise sayings back and forth in the mails. Sri Justovayondah, who was very down-home; Sri Siesta, who slept during all audiences; Sri Vincent, who was very gay, hairdresser to the gurus.

"Oh. Yes, of course. Whatever happened to Swami Satchidananda?"

Alex laughed. "He's around, Bird." Alex laughed again. "I mean, I was going to go to India anyway. I have to go. But Baba talked to me and he told me I have to deal with my illness before I can come be with him in India."

"And you're having the surgery in Boston?"

"No, it's not that. Actually, Baba told me that you were the person to help me. I will need you to help me find a doctor."

"Baba told you to call me?"

"So to speak." Alex laughed. She knew Bird was going to have trouble with that one. Bird resisted asking how Baba knew about her.

"The main thing is, I need you to wait at the hospital while they do the surgery and then if they want to take anything out while I'm under, you should sign the paper giving permission."

"Oh God, Alex. Don't you want somebody in your family to do that?"

"Oh, no. Not at all." She was cheerful. "It'll be fine, believe me. Baba's with us."

"Right. What are they likely to take?"

"Well, maybe everything. I don't know, you know how the doctors at these clinics don't think anything about telling us they need to get rid of our reproductive stuff—I went to two, and they were hardly even civil. They both said the same thing. I don't really know what to do. I *have* to go to India, and if that's what it's going to take, well, that's how it is."

Bird was thinking maybe she didn't even like Alex Decatur. She'd heard a lot about her even before meeting her and this fit perfectly into what she'd heard. "I think you probably should get some other opinions. I know a really good doctor right there in New York."

"No, I have to come there. I'll be there Friday, okay?"

"Only if you promise to get—"

"Okay to whatever. Long as I'm in your hands. I'll let you know what train I'm going to take. Okay? Thanks so much. You're very sweet and I know Baba is right about you." She hung up.

"Right. Great. Why me, Baba?"

Baba did not answer. Bird was relieved at least that Alex wasn't into chanting anymore. She thought she remembered Alex being into "Nam Myoho Renge Kyo." Chanters had called her and hounded her for weeks on end to come to the temple, or ashram, or whatever. They were very aggressive.

It turned out that Alex had given up Buddhist chanting for Hindu chanting. It was all the same to Bird. Alex moved into Bird's walk-in linen closet, which was very deep and had shuttered doors. She set up a mat, a little altar with Baba's picture, an incense burner, and a tape player and played tapes of crowds of people chanting with Baba. Three times a day, smoke and a muttering drone wedged through every slat in the doors, wafted and hovered throughout the apartment. Bird's prickly household gods tried to get offended about the sheets and towels smelling like Hindu incense, but Bird decided it was harmless. She had set up a pallet in the spare room, but Alex, who was seemingly in mortal pain when she was not in the linen closet, said she had to sleep in Bird's bed. There she stayed curled up in a fetal position all day and all night.

Alex found three doctors through some women at the university. She picked the wealthiest-, healthiest-looking women she could find to ask for their personal doctors, people who'd never been to a clinic and didn't know the name of one. She got three horrible snooty doctors who said Alex needed to have any-where from half of her parts removed to all. Bird was desperate not to sign away Alex's reproductive organs even though she didn't know her very well.

"It's okay, I'm giving my life to Baba. I haven't had sex in a while and I'm not going to have any children if I go to live in India. I'm going to train to be a swami, you know."

"Oh. What about your art? Didn't you just get an MFA in painting or sculpture?"

"Sculpture, yeah. But you see what grad school's about, right? I will probably always do some art, but I have to practice non-attachment for a while before I'll understand anything, you know?"

"No. I don't really know. But I can imagine, sort of. I don't know why I'm sitting here. Well, all I know is, I was having fun in New York and now I'm up here without pot nor window, as Aunt Sugar would say."

"Potnawinda?"

"Pitiful—'Not a pot to piss in nor a window to throw it out.' " Alex's Latin origins and Long Island upbringing were bringing her up short. "It's a country expression—pre-plumbing."

"Oh." Alex nodded at the paintings on the walls. "Well, obviously school is not what you're about. Wanna tell me about those?"

"I was going to take them down, but I'm still looking at them. Can't decide if they're done. I couldn't really take them down before you came."

"Don't take them down!" Alex was alarmed. "They're beautiful. Tell me about them, what's going on with those faces of yours? All the colors, the markings or—what are they? I mean they're gorgeous."

Without ever meaning to at all, Bird let Alex in the door. As soon as Alex loved the paintings, said they were gorgeous, and as soon as Bird knew she was going to tell her what they were about, she had to allow Alex respect, make her some space. Alex gave birth to Bird the artist simply by being the first person to look at her paintings and see them as art. Alex couldn't see Bird any other way, except as another artist. Bird had never been that to herself. Bird felt a connection she knew she would never be able to sever.

> **Appaloosa:** *n.* [prob. fr. *Palouse*, an Indian people of Wash. and Idaho]: a rugged saddle horse of a breed developed in western No. America that has a mottled skin, vertically striped hooves, and a blotched or dotted patch of white hair over the rump and loins.
>
> —*Webster's New Collegiate Dictionary*

The heads in the paintings had twisted locks of brown-black hair, loose or pulled back, and elongated faces with small Negroid features in coppery coloring disfigured by islands of beige, or sometimes blank white canvas. One or two showed one hand, also in two pigments, held near the head or palm forward as if to stop the viewer. The faces were set against bleak land-scapes, black volcanic rock, or in rooms hung with mirrors in ornamental frames. The blotches of pigment were the shapes of continents or spilled water dried on paper, soft, rounded, irregu-lar. The most frightening of the paintings were two in which the light color traced the edges of the copper lips, and the rims of the eyes. Alex stared at these and declared them daring.

"You're taking on a whole iconography here. It's fascinating. She doesn't have the traditional African face, yet she wears the minstrel mask, the grotesque usually made with big lips, wide noses, and all of that. Is that where you're going? Is this about painting the face? Are you taking on what 'blackface' means, or meant, or whatever? Because none of these colors are real skin tones. Plus, it's a female face, it raises questions. It's so interesting, taking on those masks."

"Yeah, the mask thing is there but there's some accident involved in these images. Those last two with the white around the lips and eyes just came up in what I was doing. I can't decide if the discolorations are being imposed like that, like you say, or if they're coming from underneath. You know, I looked up 'pigment' in the dictionary—have you ever looked it up? I was making notes about skin pigment. The definition of pigment is very strange."

"What's that?"

"It says pigment is 'a substance that imparts black or white,' then it says, 'or a color to other materials.' " They both laughed. "You know, if you think of it as skin color, which it doesn't really mention, then it's like your skin color makes you black or white first, then a color. I mean they didn't mean it as a sequence, and I guess they were distinguishing black or white from a color, but there it is. Your pigment makes you black or white, and then you have a color too." Both women laughed.

"Yeah, that's for sure. For me, it was the other way, I used to have a color and then I found out that the tone of it, the shade, had also made me black or white and I just didn't know it."

"Was that lucky, you think?"

"I don't know. I feel good both ways, but then maybe I was in the dark." They laughed again. "You know I don't use color in my work—well, of course I use a hundred and three different colors of dirt brown, earth, you could even say they're all skin colors, but I'm never thinking about color like that. I like to put my body in the clay and be of the same color, but even if I'm not, I'm instantly just part of the clay, the dirt, the ground. I become the ground. You know what I'm saying?"

"Well, that kind of answers the question about whether the white coming through is imposed or underneath. That's funny. It has to be ground, clay, dirt, underneath. I'm really puzzling over whether to let this bare canvas come through or to paint that color. I'm thinking I should apply a color and then take it out. There are one or two here like that. But bleaching is not the right method. I need something more organic. It's funny, if you think about it. If I put enough ultraviolet light on paint it would lose color naturally. That's sort of what I'm after. Something organic. Sometimes when skin pigment does that on its own, loses color—"

"When does it do that?"

"In disease." Bird was looking at the paintings and not at Alex. "When the skin does that the books say that it's because there is a disorder in which the body recognizes its own pigment cells as foreign and attacks them."

"Attacks them with what?"

"I don't know, other cells—deformed cells, I guess. Whatever it attacks them with, it causes the color to go. I've seen people who have that."

"Albinos, you mean?"

"No, that's something else, I think. I call them Appaloosas. But that just describes the people I used to see, you know, like at a certain moment. They're not like Appaloosas, which basically have mottled markings. I mean these people, some of them, are turning white."

"I don't think I've ever seen that." Alex strained to imagine what people Bird was talking about. "Anyway, that's fascinating what you're doing, but it's not about that disease though, right—what you're painting?"

"It's about pigment. A distraction. It's about distraction."

Bird had gotten the Appaloosa first under her arms. When she got it years ago, she was told it might go away. It worked symmetrically, the doctor told her, and that was one aspect of the disease that struck her as absurd and intriguing. Like the rest of the body, the Appaloosa was sort of symmetrical and sort of not. One side would grow faster, but the other always caught up. If she painted someone like that, it would look hokey, too much like something man-made, like minstrel makeup, symmetrical. The disease did sometimes ring the lips and eyes. Genes that could deform you into a minstrel mask—it was too baffling to think about, too hurtful. Even trying to imagine her own genes being at war with her, what—her race?—was tough.

Her knowledge of her skin, her impressions of what color it was or wasn't, were a personal history, a long journey into what one brown skin meant to every pair of eyes that had ever looked at her. White people probably had that experience enough times to count on one or two hands, but a black person feels decisions made by anybody, black or white, who looks and takes them in.

Sometimes she got lost when a white person said to her something like, "You know, I really believe some people transcend color or race." Black people never said this. Maybe enlightened beings lost interest in color. She thought what white people meant by "transcended" was that the person was no longer racist. But when they said they or someone else did not notice a person's color, she clicked to another channel in her brain. She was relieved even to touch on the subject with Alex because she had run up against the block of language long ago and stopped trying to locate words with which to talk about color. At least with the paints there she could think about it. What was being erased? A mask, such as Alex saw? Or just the possibility of beauty? Or if the mind and body always had to struggle to be one, would the self be transmuted?

When the Appaloosa began to grow, she started doing self-portraits. Just heads. She was not comfortable doing a body with discolored loins and thighs. She was not comfortable with the idea of scars that did not merely rest here and there as history, markings of moments to be forgiven or prized, but scars that tried to take the whole body and blot out its history.

Bird could not believe the guy was calling her house. She let Alex stay there and one day she picked up the phone and a man who had crushed her the year before was asking for Alex as if he didn't know Bird.

"Hello, Alex?" His voice was unmistakable, that was for sure, like a radio voice, too deep, too rich, too clear for a normal person. It was Dr. Swoon.

"No. Bird." Without missing a beat he said hi and identified himself and said she sounded like Alex. Sounded like Alex. She couldn't think of anything to say to make him feel like an asshole for calling her house. And wasn't Alex a novice guru practicing celibacy? She hadn't mentioned having trouble going into novicehood because she'd met this devastatingly handsome, molasses-voiced, tall, slender jerk of a singer who had a lot of women strung around the countryside but was *really* in love with *her*. She hadn't mentioned any of that. Bird wanted to strangle the bitch.

She'd made Alex go to doctor number four, who had turned out to be a genius who put her in the hospital for three days, infused her entire body with some no doubt Baba-sent antibiotic cure, and nobody had to lose any parts or sign any papers. And Alex was still staying in her apartment, running around buying supplies to go to India. Bird thought evil thoughts about Alex's reproductive parts as this man coolly asked when she thought Alex would be returning, adding that he was in town for a few days.

Bird wanted to scream. She was embarrassed. She made her voice as sexless, raceless, nameless, as blank and dead as possible, and said she thought it would be two hours.

Bird had driven a hundred miles one night to talk to this man for five minutes before she had gotten the message. She was ashamed of having ever fallen for his suave bullshit, and dinner. It was like falling for song lyrics. And she was definitely ashamed of having been kidnapped and kept overnight in a bedroom in a houseful of men stoned on Twinkies, pot, and Sly and the Family Stone. Afterwards she had thought that if he didn't discard her it might be okay; it would mean it hadn't been reefer rape. But it was. And she didn't learn either. A couple of months later she'd gotten stone-cold knock-down-sober raped by an artist who was a houseguest and that's when she got real about being dumb.

Bird hung up and angrily tossed some dinner together before she realized that Alex wouldn't know anything about the fact that she used to see that man. And Alex took it rather blithely when she heard.

"Oh, God. An asshole, huh? But he's so fine, what a shame! He's been so nice. Well, I just met him. He's been calling me and asking me to meet him places, but you know, sick as I was, I wasn't meeting no man anywhere! He's pretty though, ain't he?" she bubbled.

"Yeah." Bird was still annoyed. "Dr. Swoon."

"Look, Bird, I know you're going to hate this, but I told him to come here to get me."

Bird's eyes got big.

"I'll make him wait outside. I don't know, I was just going to go out and have a drink or coffee, or something. I can't get into any trouble anyway right now."

"You're saving yourself for Baba, right?"

"We don't put it quite that way, Bird, but yes, I am saving it all for Baba." She laughed. "I guess we'll have to be friends. I knew I'd be in karmic debt to you, but I guess if I have to put down a pretty man, we'd better be friends."

"Well, don't put him down for me. You may need to stay someplace else if you're going to be hanging out with him, but who am I to say what? Hey, my name is Bennett and I already been in it."

Alex found out that the handsome man's real passion was not her but getting high. She was philosophical. The man was, she said, like Maricha, the demon who turned himself into a golden deer, an illusion never to be pierced by the arrow, who leads the hunter off into the forest.

"I'm supposed to keep my feet 'on the path.' " And she packed up for India as planned, reassured she must let go of earthly desires.

By the time the women talked again Bird had finished the year she needed for her master's and had taken the last of her grant money, which should have gone to rent, and bought a cheap ticket on a charter for folks in search of the motherland.

6
Saturday

Bird had lost interest in the rest of the phonebook; she started to call the no-area-code, no-last-name guys, one after another. Suspecting a whole network of Alex's secret sex life, she wanted to see who the next one might be. The number looked like a local New York exchange. Bird asked the woman, who sounded older, for Surabi.

"I'm his mother. He's not living here. He's at the ashram."

Bird was startled. She asked for the number of the monk's residence, and the mother told her she didn't think they would necessarily let her speak to him. Bird thanked the woman. She looked for the other no-area-codes to see if any of them were also the ashram number. One other name had the same number. These two at least were part of Alex's spiritual network. Bird's downstairs buzzer rang before she could dial the number.

She asked who it was on the intercom but there was no answer. This was not that strange on a busy Saturday, but at the same time Bird had a little gnawing paranoia that someone might simply be checking if she was there or not.

When she got the ashram, she was told that both men were busy doing chores. It was suggested that she come to the ashram, see the swami. She couldn't tell if the invitation was an explanation of how to visit Alex's friends or a total change of subject. Maybe they were just saying come on over. After years of joking about gurus, and so long after they had gone out of fashion, she couldn't believe she was going to see one.

When Bird finally got herself together she took the Broadway bus. She realized she must still be a little shaky from the night before when she thought she saw Burton through the bus window, waiting at a bus stop on the other side of Broadway. His bus would be going uptown towards her street.

She used to think Burton was obnoxious, but harmless. Not harmless, no, he liked to inflict sudden wounds, like letting Alex know if he was seeing someone else. Still, Bird had thought there was something pitiful about him. He had invited her out to lunch once, really to try to get rid of her, but he was extremely charming, courtly.

She knew he'd swept Alex off her feet by taking her to lunch and being so nervous that he could not eat. Bird had been a tiny bit annoyed that her friend had even eaten lunch with him. Bird considered Frank Burton a nemesis without having ever met him. He'd written hateful things about Bird's work. Alex wasn't thinking about any of that, of course. She had taken Frank Burton's lack of appetite as a tribute to her charisma. Right then he'd invited Alex to Europe and she'd declined. He next suggested the Yucatan. Alex had liked that better, but since she'd just met him, she said no. But Alex had loved the invitation and had returned blithering about her conquest, blithering about courtship being "the lie of beauty." Alex worshipped Frida Kahlo but pretended not to. She once slipped and said of Burton, "He's my Diego." That was rubbish, though, because she wasn't Frida the Mexican painter who freed herself from every shackle but her body and her passions   Alex was a brown-skinned woman in America, descendant of Africans, Dutchmen, Frenchmen, and anybody else who wanted some. She was angrier, hungrier, and the baggage she chose to carry was heavy. Tiny as she was, she was steely, and joyous, especially when things got harsh. And to Bird's eyes, Burton did not have one scintilla of the joy, the creativity, nor even the compassion. All he had was the craving. Bird had decided sight unseen that he was a weirdo when Alex described him sweating through the lunch.

When it came time for Bird's lunch with Frank Burton, she had found him better than expected, but artless. Artless was asking about her work, saying, "You have a lot of promise." He pretended he'd never said her paintings were confused, possibly didactic. He knew the only way into an artist's good graces was to praise her work. Food alone would not do it. And he had wanted to be in her good graces just enough to tell her to back off. Maybe she had been artless too. She'd pretended he'd never said her paintings were muddled, or muddling, possibly didactic, maybe political, still lacking the unique signature of a mature artist with universal appeal. She couldn't resist saying, however, that it's easy to be brilliant when you don't have to practice what you preach. Bird had pretended she was still painting. Alex had probably told him she wasn't.

"You remind me of a woman I was with for a while."

Bird had had no response.

"She was very beautiful. A Southerner too. You are a Southerner, aren't you? In fact, I must say, I used to be a real sap for any woman with a Carolinian or Virginian accent. But you don't really have one. What happened?"

"I'm not from that part of Carolina," Bird had cracked. She'd decided this was his way of being nice, though it felt pretty hostile.

"You like sparring, don't you? I like that too. You and I understand each other in a way. We both had it a little harder than Alex coming up."

Bird wondered where he had got that idea.

He became cheerful. "I grew up with just my mother, working-class family, you know, put myself through school. I went to high school in Brooklyn, and when the little rich kids started signing up to go to boarding school, I thought, 'They must be pretty dumb if their fathers have to send them away to school.' "

Bird inspected the bread basket and sipped her wine. She thought since she didn't know this man, she wouldn't start by telling him her father Arthur Kincaid, self-made lawyer and ardent devotee of a white folks' higher education, had, when the chance arose, sent her off as a scholarship shock troop to integrate a stuffy girls' school in Newton, Mass.

"You should have the seafood bisque," he had insisted. He'd recommended a wine. He looked at her with near disdain when she refused the wine.

She didn't want to say she couldn't man the board at work with a buzz.

"You must have one of these tiny bread loaves with black olives." He made mmm-ing noises. "I went off to Columbia and, believe me, Allen Ginsberg aside, they looked at me like they'd never seen my kind before. I'm sure you know what I mean. Not that I'm like Allen Ginsberg—"

"Do you mean you're not gay, not Jewish, or not bohemian?" Bird asked.

"None of the above."

Bird was a little confused. Burton was rather handsome, in a square-jawed sort of way. She couldn't imagine that anyone had looked at him like an outcast.

"Well, you know I can't say that they thought I was any of those things either," she said.

"I mean I didn't have money," he said. "And you're—"

"Black? Yes. They noticed I was that."

"Where did you go to school?" The waiter appeared with plates that looked like a set designer's miniatures. Frank made one or two more requests.

"So, you know, even in the sixties, they were all rich kids. Except for a few scholarship students like me and, I guess, some of the blacks."

"You didn't know them?"

"Well, no, you know, they were into the black thing."

Bird got lost in her own thoughts, debating as she chewed whether she would tell him she too went to Columbia, and trying to imagine in which corner of the campus surrounded by protest barricades he'd hidden himself. "Sure." And which kind of rich kid he'd pretended to be. Bird reflected as he talked and decided that she could really just hate Frank Burton.

"Have you been to the Yucatan yet?" he asked as if he knew she had not. "It has such an impact on an artist. I think there's a grant one can apply for to get down there. Maybe I could help you. I look at it as a pilgrimage one must make."

Bird thought she'd really like to go study the work there. If he was trying to appeal to the basic whore in her, he was beginning to make progress.

"Well, you know," he said. "Alex has told you, I'm sure. She told me how much it meant for her."

Alex knew no more about Mayan art or any other Mexican art than Bird. "Alex lied. She's never been to the Yucatan." Catching Alex's lie had made Bird cheerful.

"Really?"

"Really. I think she just told you as an excuse not to go when she first met you. Probably couldn't ever come clean." Bird chomped on her olive loaf.

"Really? I don't believe she'd lie about something like that."

"It was the 'lie of beauty.' You heard what was pleasing. It's like a postcard from Egypt."

"What's a postcard from Egypt?"

"Sometimes if someone we know is going to Egypt, one of us will have a card sent to a man we know. You know, 'See you in a month,' signed Alex, something like that. 'Sorry to stand you up Friday but had to make a trip. Love, Bird.' Postage art."

He laughed, though she could see his wheels turning. "They have the most wonderful desserts here." He signaled the waiter to come, ordered an espresso, and told the man to show Bird the pastries.

"I'm with Alex now," he said. "I know you're very close friends, and I don't want to get in the middle of that, but I have to have her to myself. You understand?"

Bird didn't say a word.

Feeling awkward in the silence, Frank Burton continued, ending with something like "we'll all be friends." She felt none of the giddiness Alex had about how worldly and quirky he was. She thought much of his worldliness was fake, too quickly acquired. But the worst thing Bird could have said about Burton that day was that he didn't interest her.

After Alex's death it bothered Bird that she thought there was not one friend to whom he might have told the real truth. She couldn't think of one person who would know what Frank knew. The idea made her nervous. If there was no one he'd tell, she was the somebody who came nearest to knowing something.

When Bird set eyes on Swami Viswamitra all she could think was that America was a weird place. To go in search of one life was to enter so many strange worlds that didn't seem American at all, and yet that was exactly what the place had become. Many thousands of tiny universes, an infinity of unaccountable encounters. Swami Viswamitra was a tiny brown man sitting on a mat on a wooden floor that shone like glass in an otherwise empty room. The space was filled with such a heavy scent, such a thick mixture of fresh flowers and slightly acrid incense, that Bird felt for a minute she could not breathe in the room. Once her two bare feet stepped into the interior, she felt unsteady and yet as if she could not back out. She was in there.

Romeo was at his post outside the apartment building watching the street when he saw the man coming down the hill. Romeo didn't forget a man's walk or attitude. He studied the man coming towards him on the sidewalk. Romeo stepped back and looked away until the man was right on him, then turned, checked him, and said, "What's up?" The man grunted something. Romeo wasn't looking for a response. He just wanted the man to know he'd checked him. Then he watched as the man took out a door key and went in.

Swami Viswamitra looked enormously happy to see Bird, and continued to look enormously happy after she sat down on the floor with him. It finally dawned on her that he looked this way all the time, eyes lit with an almost mischievous brightness, unfettered energy filling the room where he sat, even though every muscle was slack and relaxed; the skin of his face, placid. He seemed to listen to her and yet he did not seem to dwell on what she was saying. He narrowed his smile when she spoke of Alex's death, seemingly more out of politeness or convention than because it was distressing to him. She became aware that this was probably good because she would not want him to smile while she talked about the death. It would have struck her as inappropriate. She was suddenly aware of what she thought appropriate and inappropriate, even though she'd never seen this man before. She was aware that she was thinking of him as an immigrant, someone who didn't speak English, didn't know the customs, because he was sitting there looking like a guru out of a magazine. As if he wouldn't have a clue as to how he should act with her. She was suddenly aware that he knew her expectations. She was suddenly aware that he might, in other circumstances, smile throughout an entire discussion of someone being vaulted through a pane glass window. She was suddenly aware of demands she was silently putting forward.

"Do you know the Ramayana?"

"No," Bird said. Bird thought it only a slight lie, because she realized that knowing a little meant nothing. To say that she'd read it once wouldn't be much of a claim. How could she say she never took gurus seriously and read such books without having any useful thoughts, used the names of the story as she pleased?

"One day King Dasaratha receives an old sage who asks him to lend his son, Rama, to protect him because demons in the forest keep him from praying. The king asks him why this is so." Swami Viswamitra became an old sage in India: " 'Majesty,' he says, 'we are living in declining days. Dharma is forgotten. This is a time of shifting visions, fast-changing illusions, curtains rise and fall, a time of deceit and lies. The worlds have fallen prey to inhuman scavengers, wanderers and night hunters.' "

"I can understand that." Bird could hear Bessie Smith singing, *Back in Black Mountain, a child will smack your face | Babies cryin' for liquor and all the birds sing bass.*

Swami Viswamitra looked enormously happy once again and slipped into something like vernacular American speech. "Well, it turns out that Vishnu, Preserver of the Three Worlds, had agreed for the sake of the universe to become a mortal for a while. Unknown to King Dasaratha, he was born as the king's first son to do battle with Ravana, the Demon King, the Destroyer. And so , as Rama, he goes with the sage, and he battles Ravana.

"His life as a mortal is temporary and in becoming a mortal, he becomes forgetful. He forgets his own true nature as Creator and Preserver. He does not remember that the Destroyer is no more than all the illusions which chase and hound us continually. Only after his arrows have pierced the heart of the Destroyer, after his arrows have scorched away Ravana's thick outer skin, the hides of ego, anger, craving, and cruelty which have covered and choked his real self, does Rama see. After he defeats the Destroyer, after he rules in peace, he returns to heaven, and all creation goes with him. We are like this. Forgetting our true nature. Always forgetting we create the universe and it goes with us.

"But even as he kills the Demon King, Ravana tells him: 'Lord, you see what I am. You see what I learned, that every life is only one day full. And all creatures that are separate from you, Preserver of the Worlds, are forever reborn, over and over.' "

"Are you saying she will be reborn?"

"She? What she?"

"Are you saying my friend will be reborn?"

"Not to heaven, not to a blind contentment such as you Americans seem to mean when you say 'reborn.' Reborn to suffer. Unless——"

"Are you saying she is forever? For me, she will be forever falling."

"Why that moment? Not forever living?"

"No. I feel she was just trashed."

"And we are trash too. We are all trashed, are we not? Doomed to be trash. I am not condoning a horrible crime, only saying even a sweet death is the trashing of the flower, falling apart and wasted on the ground. But where does it go?"

Bird supposed he was right. It didn't help.

"You want to know if the man killed her or if she took her life?"

"Well, yes, I'd like to know that."

"But why? What will you do?"

"I don't know. Nothing, maybe."

"Will you kill the man to avenge your friend?"

"I don't think so."

"Oh? Why not?"

"I just want to know."

"See what the man has seen."

"I can't see that. I can never see that. That is why she is forever falling." Bird started to weep. "I saw her legs and arms flying forward and down. I saw her falling. I heard a whimpering, muffled sound that was her, I know. I heard something break, not big like her body going through glass, but smaller, like something breaking one pane—well, I mean, I know something broke one pane on a different window, it was something that happened but

I don't know how. Then a scream at the window, a little scream really. I heard my own screaming in my throat so loud . . . I heard her scream . . . Heard it choke off . . . Heard her . . . land— it was a horrible sound—somewhere below . . . the ledge. But I don't know—"

"If he is a killer, see what the killer has seen."

"You can't see what someone else has seen."

"That is what you must do."

"No."

Bird felt her mind shut off. *Black Mountain people are bad as they can be / They uses gunpowder just to sweeten their tea.* Bird felt a wall emerge between where he sat with his legs crossed and where she sat with her legs crossed. She was, with all of her being, hostile. And she was alone.

"The teaching does not condone taking one's own life. This condemns us to more repeating, reliving the cycle. It's rather like a heavy debt, suicide."

Bird listened again.

"The teaching does not condone taking one's own life. This is a teaching your friend Alex understood. It is not the way to free-dom." Swami Viswamitra looked enormously happy again. "Or, so we believe."

"I would have killed him. That night. It wouldn't have both-ered me." *I'm gon' shoot if he stand still and cut him if he run.*

Again he narrowed his smile for her. He resumed his telling of the Ramayana: "He stopped his breathing. He closed his eyes and watched all light die before him. He saw every experience of his life as a mortal and thought, it's like something I once created."

"He's been in my apartment. He's been in there at night."

"Call the police."

"They won't believe me. He's always gone before I can fully wake up and get down the hall. I see him in a flash and the door shuts. I don't know what he wants. I don't know how he got in."

"Change the locks."

"I did."

"Are you sure?"

Swami Viswamitra's eyes closed. Bird was straining to under-stand. Bird was straining to think. Assuming the interview must be over, she rose and made a feeble bow in the guru's direction. He did not move at all or lift an eyelid.

"Will you come back and join us for a class sometime?" He sounded bright.

"I don't know. I have no idea. I'm pretty obsessed with this, this problem, this death. I don't sleep very well, so I think I need to——"

" 'My friend, we have not seen you for a moment in heaven, return to yourself.' " Swami Viswamitra's eyes were still smiling while closed.

Bird stepped out onto Riverside Drive. She had the sensation of falling.

Romeo was waiting across the street when the man who used to live on eight with Alex emerged from the building. Without looking at him he spoke.

"How y' doin'?" The man looked around, confused. Romeo crossed the street.

"Uh, fine."

"Yeah, I thought that was you. Haven't seen you in a long time. Nobody's home up there, huh?"

"Uh, no, doesn't seem to be."

"Right. I woulda guessed nobody up there is too anxious to see you, so I was surprised."

"I'm looking for mail, that's all."

"Yeah. You were gone so long I decided you went to pick up something in the old place, you know. But I don't see you carry-ing anything, so I figure I guessed wrong."

"Oh. Well, I didn't see any loose mail downstairs there on the table, so I thought I'd see if it was under the door."

"Oh. You find it?"

"No. No, I didn't. Well, look, I'll be seeing you." The tall blond man turned away.

"Look, man, you couldn't spare a dollar, could you?"

Frank Burton fumbled in his pocket and found a couple of singles. "You don't need to mention that you saw me. I don't want anybody upset over a stupid piece of mail, you know." He handed him the bills.

"No problem."

Burton strode up the street and Romeo dashed off in the opposite direction.

The bright sunlight on the Hudson River nearly blinded Bird. She was falling through the sunlight. She sat on the stone stoop of the ashram to steady herself. She closed her eyes and she was falling and when she landed, it was in a luscious mound of peat moss and flowers, leaves and pine needles, deep red berries. She had no face or skin or markings of herself left showing, she was entirely covered by the lavish harvest of the forest floor. The stupor subsided, and the moss and flowers fell from her view, but she felt covered with softness still. The hot late-afternoon sunlight baked itself over her body where she had once had skin. Once she made it home she stretched herself across the bed, pulled a cotton blanket over her clothes, and slept.

7
Sunday

Bird rewound a tape and pulled it from the VCR. She was going to devote the day to getting rid of some of the tapes. She was on the floor of her living room in a T-shirt and overalls. She put the cassette back in its box, then noticed that Alex had already dated it. No need for a new label. Alex kept good records. She would just repack them and stash them somewhere. In a month or so the other apartment would finally be cleaned out, the wall would be plastered, and somebody else would move in. They would probably replace the sidewalk out front too and Bird could give up playing caretaker to an urban memorial. Maybe if she was smart, Bird thought, she'd move then. She'd been giving away what she could to friends who would make the trip, walk through the apartment, and take a few items from among the folded, stacked linens on the bed or the dishes and utensils washed and left in boxes in the kitchen, a chair here or table there. Bird was leaving the baskets of jewelry and the little sculptures for last. She thought she needed to devise some kind of ceremony for that, or at least a party, invite the whole Diaspora over for that one and let them fix a lot of food. The buzzer rang. She answered the intercom but no one was there.

She pulled out another tape and just as quickly abandoned the idea of watching it. She felt a little on edge. She wanted to sleep, take a nap. She was afraid she'd dream about the tapes. She went into the kitchen and made coffee. Bird's apartment was full of sun. The plants seemed to be preening before the windows and yearning for someone to wipe off any dust dulling their leaves. After starting the coffee she stood in the kitchen window and stared at all the backyards on the block. This September it was still hot summer. Sometimes the heat of summer in New York just cruised right past Labor Day and cooked like Carolina. Her neighbors in the Quarter never seemed to be bothered. People liked it. They put on old slow jams, the Chi-Lites and the Manhattans, Teddy Pendergrass and some Jeffrey Osborne, and smoked and talked on the stoops till 2:00 A.M.

Of course to live there, one had to like music. Then it was sweet to work or eat or even to sleep with such extravagant romance coming through the windows. New York was full of hard-ass, hard-core, don't-blink motherfuckers who cried tears down their collars on the stoop at night over tragic love songs. Ever since she'd realized she was going to be an embittered evil bitch if she lived in New York too long, she'd learned to love the mix of reggae, jazz, and crooners coming through her windows every day. She loved the gray-haired man across the street trying to teach the boys how to harmonize. Harmonizing was gone nowadays. Hearing him going over the sounds, telling them how to make it pretty, made her forget the moment. It reminded her of when she was waiting on someone, when she sat up late drinking wine and painting, trying to make meaning out of love affairs, race war, and personal disaster.

She could see a few fallen tree limbs in the back of the buildings where telephone crews had been hacking and then left the debris. She knew by winter when the leaves had fallen she'd see the wreckage among the standing. Or the standing among the wreckage. They'd let the thousands of creeping vines they clipped fall in funeral mounds over all the gardens. The birds were making kissing sounds.

The tape was out of sequence. Out of boredom Bird had blindly picked one out of the box. Color bars. Alex as a talking head.

[P.R.—KHA, 1987, Entry #1]

"When I went into my workroom today a cricket was in there. Where would a cricket come from? Another immigrant to New York. She had attached herself to a still life I had set up. This one is branches of pines in water, one wildflower which has lasted four full days now, and something that looks like it's from outer space, I don't know what it is. It's a sea green globe, a perfect sphere of spiny leaves. I found it out in the park. The cricket crawled down one of the pine branches till she reached the very end. I only noticed it because the branch jumped all of a sudden, nearly slipped out of the bottle. Scared me to death. The cricket had tipped the branch right out of the water. Her body was frozen in place, holding on for dear life. When I walked away she flew to the spiny globe and couldn't find a comfortable place to rest. It was too prickly for her. Soon she abandoned the whole piece and flew at the window, smacked into it, and then she crawled about looking for an opening. She was trying to get to the other side of the glass. I was wondering if she could tell the still life is dead. When I look at it, it looks alive, still has a vivid color, but I know it is dead. Can this creature who is confused by my pane glass window know the living from the dead? She looked trapped. I picked her up and threw her out the window. Wherever she came from, it wasn't my workroom." Alex clicks off with the remote.

Bird pressed fast-forward. The next segment showed Alex pacing around the studio, apparently working, stepping over pieces. Alex's workroom was flooded with sun from the windows. The camera was set at an angle perpendicular to the windows and pointed downward towards the floor. Alex evidently was trying to avoid shooting into any light source, yet the tape was still washed out in places. It was hard to make out the objects Bird knew were on Alex's giant worktable under the window. Blurred out were her drawing paper, buckets of clay, and the still lifes she usually made and remade. The buckets beneath the windows, lined up and filled with plants, dried and alive, had disappeared. For the most part the camera was getting Alex in silhouette.

Likely Bird would have merely found the tape annoying when Alex was alive. At the moment it was eerie to her, fading out a life that was so vivid, a room that was so rich in every shade of brown and green, life gathered from forests and the florists' district on Sixth Avenue. In spite of its spaciousness the room had then seemed to Bird to be teeming and steamy. On hot days if the air conditioner was off, the clay in buckets and in shapes on drop cloths on the floor would sweat before drying hard. Alex would have to keep wetting it. The tape made the studio look arid, lifeless, fading out of existence before her eyes. Bird decided to watch it later. She ejected the tape and turned down the loud static sound on the TV but left it on.

She rummaged through the box and found one marked *Private Reel* and lots more with the letters *PR*. She piled them on one side of her living room rug and the documentary tapes on another side in stacks of five. Even though she didn't know what use Alex had had for the private tapes, Bird wondered if Alex had meant for them to be destroyed. Judging from the little she'd seen, she couldn't imagine they were meant for any library.

She put another tape on and found Alex telling a story about "the dealer and the two sheiks." The art dealer was really the art critic—Burton—whose name Alex had changed for no apparent reason, and the story had to do with when she first met him. The two "sheiks" were obvious enough—two friends of theirs who shared the name Sheik, a Malian dancer and musician and a Senegalese commodities expert. Bird wondered again if Frank Burton had watched the tapes. She kept finding more of them. She was beginning to feel dismayed. Burton couldn't have wanted to watch all these tapes. And knowing Alex, Bird thought, anything could be on them. Alex was uninhibited in a way that could sometimes freak people out. She wasn't an exhibitionist exactly—well, she could be when she was drunk, Bird remembered her ripping her shirt off in some young guy's face after a performance—but she wasn't really an exhibitionist so much as she didn't draw the line where most people would. Still, Bird thought, the tapes were probably quite boring, the artist talking about herself.

There were more than fifty tapes of her work, finished pieces, repeat performances in different sites, installations, even rehearsals. She arranged the documentary tapes by year while she had them out, and then looked through the private reels. There were at least twenty-five of them. Each box had a different strange name or code: KHA; JIM; DHAL; THA; ZAY; GHAYN; ALIF; WAW; MIM; YA. It would be impossible to put them in real order without looking at them. And there were a couple of *years'* worth of tapes.

"If these are private I should just destroy them." Bird talked aloud. "If Burton let go of them, they couldn't be of any value or even that private." One other possibility came to mind: Maybe he thought there'd be something in them she wouldn't enjoy watching. Maybe he'd left a minefield for her to walk through. Frank Burton was that kind of a son of a bitch. He'd do that.

She thought again about the story Alex was telling on the tape and went to get the phonebook from the bedroom. She flipped through for African names. Most of the Adibayos, Khalils, and Adizikwes were African Americans. She'd already talked to a lot of them—musicians, designers, jewelers, professors, brothers Alex knew from obscure religious groups or artist alliances. They were the kind of people Alex collected almost incidentally, names for the mailing lists, people she might connect with for a month and then lose. The Mahmouds and Ibrahims, Muslim names less common with the bloods, were more likely the real thing. She found the two Sheiks: Sheik without an *h*, in Bamako, Mali, and the other, Sheikh with an *h*, in Paris. The number for Sheikh Doumbia in Paris was the same one Bird had in her book.

Bird didn't think she could face calling. What was she doing anyway? She wanted to know if the story was like Alex told it. Why? Was she going to go through every incident in Alex's life? What for? To see if she jumped? Even if she had, it wasn't going to turn out to be because of two guys named Sheik. She hadn't wanted to go through her best friend's phonebook in the first place. It was gruesome and it meant Alex no longer had any privacy. Well, that wasn't true. Bird didn't know what she was looking at when she'd first looked at it, just like these tapes. The whole dilemma simply pointed up the obvious fact that no one knew what was going on in somebody else's life. And so what? Did she need to know? It seemed absurd when Bird thought about all the moments in her own life that she'd just forgotten because they were inconsequential. Did she really need to know about a few thousand more moments from someone else's life? No. Not at all. Bird dragged the phone across the rug. The impulse to call got her anyway. It was about midnight in Paris, probably about the same in Mali, but in Mali that was the middle of the night. It was safer to call Sheikh in Paris because she'd spent enough nights with him to know he never went to bed no matter what city he was in.

"Lalla Bird, *ça va?*" Sheikh Abdoulaye Doumbia always added "Lalla" to her name to show she was special. His permanent good cheer smiled through the static on the wire. He didn't seem surprised to hear from her. "What's happening? I'm so glad you called. I've been thinking about you."

Sheikh was Barry White with a French accent. Sheikh used his voice to take people's clothes off, mostly for his own amusement, but if he lucked out, he knew just how to pat them, fold them, and lay them down. Without the least effort or thought, every intonation was a persistent hand tugging at the listener's zippers. Bird appreciated how well he practiced the art.

"No you weren't—don't even tell that lie."

He laughed quietly under his breath. "Aw, how could you say

that?" Even when he talked about the falling price of bauxite or soybeans, it sounded like *Aww, baby. Come on, take me. Show me.* Sheikh knew she never believed him if he sweet-talked her too quickly, even when he meant it. She preferred to assume the worst.

"That woman of yours would probably have me turned into something on four legs."

"No. She's done that to me, my dear. You don't know. I've been through hell this summer. She had an affair and it had the worst effect on me. The thing was very bad. It was as if I turned into a raving, lunatic dog. All I can say is, it was very fortunate I was able to recover myself."

"How did you do that?"

"Well, a friend helped me to come back to myself."

"Not a woman friend by any chance?"

"Well, yes. She happens to be a woman."

Bird laughed.

"You shouldn't laugh. You would not have helped me, I know that." *Baby, I want you to take your time because we have all night. I just want you to—*

"You're a real shit talker, you know that?"

"Well, yes, maybe, but it's *real* shit."

"So what happened with your woman?"

"Gone. It's finished. She started to act like a real ass, trying to embarrass me with this man in front of our friends, all of that, you know, making scenes."

Bird asked him when he had last seen Alex.

"It was the last time I was there in New York. More than a year ago. Well, I don't know. It was either I saw her on the street, you know, or at the bar, that bar, you know. I don't remember the name." He paused. "You will laugh when I tell you this, but the thing which I remember best is that I saw a film of Eddie Murphy. *Coming to America.*" He started laughing. "You know, as an African I wanted to see it. Some Europeans told me maybe I would take offense, so I was very excited."

"Did you?"

"Oh, nooo." He laughed. "I enjoyed it." Now that Sheikh had

gotten to be forty and had one or two gray hairs, he had decided jeans were not *distingué,* and wore traditional robes or smartly cut European suits. Bird could see this Senegalese dignitary strolling into the cineplex in his *grand buba* to see Eddie Murphy fake it. She couldn't think what year that was.

"Yeah, you probably liked it 'cause you live like that at home, right? Giraffe loping across the palace lawn, beauty queens to soap you down?"

"Absolutely. You should come home with me, my Lalla."

"Yes, I should. So did you have dinner with Alex or visit or anything?"

"No, no, it was very quick, my trip there. I saw her just on the street and then for a second at the bar."

"Oh. Was she with a guy?"

"Yes, she was with a man. The white one. He was her lover?"

"Not then."

"No? I certainly remember that I thought he was her lover because we were all going to see each other again at the bar. Some of us went and she wasn't there and then it got so crazy. The man was there, waiting I guess, and he became very disagreeable with me. He threw a drink at me."

"Damn. I didn't hear about that. Did you kick his ass?"

"Ah, no. I might have been glad to do it. I've given that shit up. I try to behave myself. Actually Alex came in there and dragged him out. Did she love this guy?"

"I don't know."

"No? She's gone now, so I mean we only care about the ones she loved, no?"

"What do you mean?"

"Let him go on—live with his suffering. He's a dead man inside. Let him go, Lalla, that's all."

"Oh yeah. Don't worry. It's not that."

"You chasing the ghost? I know you and Alex were close. Maybe you were too close. You don't need to be in her shadow. Sometimes I used to think you were standing back in her shadow, not seeing yourself for what you are."

Bird thought about that all the time. "I don't think so."

"Of course. Sorry."

"I was just wondering. Was the other Sheik around?"

"Bird! C'mon."

Bird was silent.

"You mean Diouf?" Sheikh didn't buy into *h*'s as distinguishing traits, and used last names to avoid confusion. Besides, he probably knew a few other Sheiks as well. "Yeah, matter of fact, Diouf might have been in New York. Yeah—" He was thinking back. "You could call him in Bamako."

"I'm not calling Mali."

"I can dig it, sister. Well, take my advice. In the end you will have to leave that man alone."

"I miss seeing you. It's nice to talk to you."

"Nice is all? You know I want to see you." *Aww, baby. Come on, take me.*

"Ciao. Don't go home without letting me know."

"You know it, babe. You'll meet my mother."

"Babe?" The last sound she heard was Sheikh's self-satisfied laugh.

Sheikh's Alex was more of the same old Alex. Nothing to go over and over across the Atlantic. Bird had known as soon as she heard his voice that nothing he had to say was going to clear up why Alex was sitting in front of the video telling these anecdotes about running into two Sheiks on the street while she was with an art dealer. It was the same self-absorbed Alex, interested in exotic people, feasts, dancing, and rum. Alex always liked to tease Sheikh as if she had a thing about him because he was a ladies' man. But he wasn't really Alex's type. She admired how he looked, but she was content to collect him as a visual.

Bird could see herself sitting where Alex might, on the floor around a pot of *thiebou dienn* or at one of the hidden apartment "restaurants" where the new African immigrants went for elaborate pots of fish, okra, onions, chicken, and plantains. She would be eating politely with her hands, hungrily consuming faces with her eyes, happy not to play angry Negro as she did at the dinners downtown, the ones she called "art business." Bird watched as Alex would, watched the Africans moving with grace, knowing they were the true art in any gallery. Pigments in the skin so saturated she could get lost in their richness. She'd luxuriate in the colors and textures of their clothes. Watch them being so much at ease, not bothered by race and America. They were not in rage. Sure, they talked politics, Bird thought, but they weren't bothered like *we* were bothered. They were into doing business, making money, and meeting lovers, going dancing, going home. They could go back.

When she thought of those nights she remembered how different the two of them were: Bird the lascivious and Alex the withholding. Bird would be drunk on flirtation and language, Alex drunk on elegance, afraid of taking home their bodies, of wanting more. Not virtuous, just scared. Lust was attachment. Possible loss. It was absurd for Alex to have taped a story about two African guys named Sheik, insinuating she was having affairs with one or the other or both, because it had never happened.

And Bird remembered how Burton slowly got rid of all of those people, all of Alex's friends. That, Bird supposed, was another reason she stopped seeing them herself. Embarrassment that they couldn't really come to the apartment and expect to see Alex and Bird anymore, at least not without this man becoming very rude.

The last time they were all there was when Alex had had a dinner party and tried to mix her friends with his over some bouillabaisse and wine. It was a miserable night. Burton's friends assumed that everyone there worked in some menial capacity to pull off Alex's performance pieces. Not an ego in the room was happy. Essex had howled in pain for days after about a puffed-up woman in faded denim and red high heels who'd become agitated as soon as she saw Essex heading her way in his head rag.

"She asked me didn't I think going around in semi-drag was a bit passé. I told her I was trying to stay close to my roots. I wanted to tell the bitch anybody who looked that poorly ought to be looking at her own roots—which were not good—but she was some friend of Frank's and I was trying to be nice. I asked her if she knew what Lyndon Baines Johnson had said about his generation. She said, no, she didn't care for Lyndon Johnson, and I said, 'Honey, you have one of those Neanderthal minds that can only comprehend people who agree with you.' I told her, 'Lyndon said: "No member of our generation who wasn't a Communist or a dropout in the thirties is worth a damn." And any forty-year-old now who wasn't some kind of freak twenty years ago probably has nothing to say. At least not to me. If even LBJ knew where the smart money was in his youth, who am I to turn my back on our flamboyant and, I might add, *fabulous* past? We're all passé, babe'—she didn't care for 'babe'—'I look in the mirror every day and say, girlfriend, honor your fuckin' protest, swish-activist, high-heel, Earth-shoe, dropout roots.'

"She just glared at me with total contempt and said, 'You must not have children.' She called me a cliché right to my face! Offensive homosexual cliché, I believe she said. I told the bitch she was living proof that Lenny Bruce was right, 'You can't get snot off a suede jacket.' "

Needless to say, Alex didn't care to expose her friends to his friends again, and he was more than relieved. Bird sat on her living room rug surrounded by tapes of Alex Decatur's artwork and Alex Decatur's private life or thoughts or secrets, and all she wanted was to get out. The Good Humor chimes were working their way up the block. Bird crossed her legs and held her face. The box of tapes was still half full. She turned it over and dumped the rest on the floor.

A car alarm went off. Bells, chimes, barking dogs, the gospel choir rehearsing at the church. The low drone of the late afternoon was settling in. A muggy evening with little breeze would slowly take over. Bird started, thinking she heard a mariachi band. That's crazy, she thought, listening again, but there were guitars and trumpets coming down the street. As she walked towards a front window, she knew it had to be the Indians. It was not the usual clave, salsa, or funk. It was country music like when the Andean people had their eerie Good Friday processionals. Nothing beats this place, Bird thought—life comes from any century, any remote corner of the planet, right to this block, with a band. It's still the Quarter, but jets have changed who's in a quarter now—some of *all* the children of slavery, not just the African ones. She laughed when people said, "Oh, that's one of those *changing* neighborhoods." They had no idea. They thought changing meant black and white yuppies buying brownstones. Bird lived in a quarter where people were moving from medieval times into the end of the world.

The newest people in the neighborhood were Indians from somewhere in the highlands of South America. They didn't look anything like the Puerto Ricans, Cubans, or Dominicans who'd been in New York for decades. They were tiny people with straight black bowl-cut hair, high cheekbones, and ruddy skin. At first there were only one or two walking their children on the street. Bird hired one of them, a carpenter, to build her some bookcases. He worked so hard and did such a beautiful job that she was worried about him being exploited in New York. Her neighbor Cross told her one of the buildings on the block was a drop-off for illegals coming in. Late at night one or two cars would come and unload six or seven new people. Now they had a small congregation at the Spanish-speaking church down the street.

The first time the Indians appeared on Good Friday it scared Bird to death. She heard a dirge of crying trumpets and a pounding drum after dusk. Then only flickers of light came towards her building. When the small band passed, heads covered, carrying candles, she could make out a glass coffin held aloft on men's shoulders, and inside it, a body—the body of Christ, wrapped in silver. The drum sounded slowly, mourning Jesus' suffering on the cross, his death from this life. Bird had looked out and she could see black Baptists, in the windows and on the stoops, cross themselves like Catholics when the coffin passed. Bird did too, not knowing whether it was right to left or left to right. Everybody came to the States with their gods in their luggage, and in New York, at least, people learned to cross themselves in front of other messiahs. The spirit was understood if not the particulars.

The mourners passed into the dark. If she could, she would have asked them to make one of those ancient moaning marches past the building when Alex died, past the horrifying sculpture in the cement, a grave Bird felt she was tending in some way. She would have asked them to play their trumpets past her shadow in the walkway, throw flower petals or dead leaves. It would have been the perfect tribute.

The Indians who'd been in the neighborhood the longest now had twelve-year-old boys on the corner who watched the crack business relocate from one block to another down the street, the dreadlock reefer shops give way to Chinese take-out, the old junkies dying of AIDS sitting on the stoops trying to stay warm in the sun.

Now as she looked down to the street, men were approaching in black and gold boleros and tight pants. The trumpets were bright and melodious. Cheerful. A beautiful teenage bride strolled past Bird's building arm in arm with her groom in his black tux. Brothers on either side. Her veil flowed for two yards behind her, riding a ten-foot train held above the sidewalk by six boys in tiny black suits. Bird could see the gold brocade designs in the tops of the musicians' wide-brimmed hats. Black children in Nikes and T-shirts followed along at a discreet distance in the street, not daring to disturb the formality of the sidewalk procession. Except for two older women, and the bride in her elaborate ritual dress of dazzling white satin and tulle, the strollers were males in black, men and boys escorting the delicate bride, extraordinary flower of a clan from somewhere else. A place open and dusty and bright perhaps, where the wedding feast might be held under trees, children embracing and jumping to the music. The bride's bouquet was a blur of white petals and flowing ribbon. She carried it with both hands at her waist, and looked straight ahead. She walked past Alex's sidewalk crypt without seeing it at all, looking straight as she had always planned to do, letting the boys catch the skirt swiping the walk.

Bird thought about having never been decked out in ribbons when she was eighteen and beautiful because she lived in a runaway's turmoil—penniless, idealistic, wandering, and afraid of ribbons and lace, afraid of having children with loves who were also escapees from the old rites and feasts. She felt like Essex did, like she'd been declared extinct somewhere along the line. They were all runaways. No, Bird thought, that was a lie, she was just afraid of that girl's life. Afraid of having three children before she was twenty-one, afraid of not having enough money to get them sturdy shoes and braces. Bird never wanted to be a bride of any age. It scared the hell out of her. She went back to the living room. She stretched out on the rug and stared at the ceiling. The tapes formed rows down her sides from head to toe. The mute television was blinking out weather maps.

"Bernard?"

He'd be tossing the pasta in olive oil by now. Ready to sit down and do the Sunday crossword. He'd spend a half hour ferreting out another word for indigo dye or the entrance to a mine.

"Yeah. Hey! What's up, Bird?"

"I don't think I can do this by myself."

"Forget it. What are you doin', tryin' to make yourself crazy?" He had on his at-home voice.

"Maybe."

"Give it a rest."

"What if I told you Alex left a whole pile of private tapes with all her private thoughts and stuff on them?"

"What do you mean, 'private thoughts'?"

"Well, I guess they're like journals. I'm not sure."

"That's wonderful. Maybe we'll learn something."

"Maybe *we'll* learn something! You act like you're going to get a sound bite of each tape. I can't watch all these tapes. She made two and a half years' worth of these things."

"Damn."

"I can't do it, Bernard. I just cannot do this. We gotta think of some other way."

"Yeah, no. You can't do that. But what do you think is on them?"

"I don't know. I can barely tell what order they should be in. They have the year marked on them and then some code or something."

"Code like what?"

"Letters. Some of them look like acronyms, some don't."

"Like what?"

"Hold on." Bird grabbed some of the boxes. "Okay, like Alif, A-L-I-F; Mim, M-I-M; Shin, S-H-I-N. The one I watched was K-H-A."

"And they have years on them?"

"Yeah."

"Well, you can start by putting them in order by year."

"Yeah, I know. Thanks."

"Alif, that's something I've heard before. I don't know where."

"It probably just sounds familiar. I mean, it sounds like a word."

"Right. So, go ahead."

"Okay. There's stuff where she just sits and talks into the camera and stuff with her rambling around the studio. Inconsequential stuff, it seems like. I just lost it and called Paris to ask somebody about an incident she describes on one tape that is really so stupid I can't believe I paid any attention to it, except that I remembered part of it, and she was insinuating something that wasn't true and then Burton was in there, and she had changed his name. Well, she had my name changed too, sort of, I mean she calls me Cynthia, which she never called me. And I don't know why she even changed his name, really, except maybe she was worried that somebody might find it."

"Like the dude himself, Burton?"

"Yeah, that's one possibility. God knows you or I wouldn't care. The only thing it does make me think is that if she was planning to jump out of a window, she might have destroyed these things, especially if they're like her journals."

"Unless she forgot or was overwrought in the moment. Whatever happened that night wasn't planned, you know?"

"Yeah. Well, I'll tell you this. If the DA's office did look at them, they didn't get much."

"So, I guess that means we really ought to go through them, but you shouldn't do all of it by yourself."

"What should I do?"

"I think you should stop. Pack the stuff up. Take a break. Maybe I can come over and check them out with you sometime."

"Yeah, that would be good."

"Look, Bird, just put them away. Can't you take off, go away for a day or two, chill out? You ever see that man in your life?"

"Who are you talking about?"

"You never told me his name. You just said there was a man."

"Oh. No. I don't see him much. He's more like a friend." That was a lie, she thought as soon as she said it.

"A friend is what you need."

"Yeah. I know what you mean. The men in my life, I guess you could say, haven't really worked out. It's like I gave up being an artist, and the men didn't really work out, and then my best friend landed on the sidewalk, and here I fucking am, you know?"

Bird could now hear the trumpets coming through her back windows. The procession must have gone all the way around the block, or over to the park. They sounded proudly, heralding some happiness, some point of completion. She got up and turned up the sound on the TV to catch the news. After a minute she realized she didn't want to watch the news, but left it on in case there was something she should hear. The doorbell rang and she got off the phone. She asked who it was. It was Romeo. His brow was all curled up like he was worried and he had an embarrassed smile, but she knew the picture was fake.

"Bird, you got seventy-five cents you could spare?"

She went and looked in her purse. Knowing that he was hoping she didn't have exact change and would give him a dollar, she dug around till she found three quarters.

It was late afternoon and she still wanted to call someone. There was no one else to call. She called the Prince, the man she told Bernard was her friend. His machine was on. The buzzer rang again. No one answered. Bird lit a cigarette. That doorbell ringing was beginning to get on her nerves. It had happened a lot, she thought. Tears rolled off her chin and dropped to the floor. She still wanted to call somebody. She wanted to call home. That wasn't a good idea. At home, they went by the computer-problem rule: Most mishaps are due to operator error. Whatever it was Sheikh had back in Senegal—she knew it was probably not a state-owned apartment or a circle of mud-walled huts with worn tires crowning their thatched roofs, but even if it was, he wouldn't care—it was there and he could go. She didn't even want to call home.

Any friend she might call was going to talk about Alex. It was hard to talk to them, not just because Alex was dead but because so many people were dead. At any time any one of them might go off the deep end because this was the last death he or she could stand. Alex's was the last one she could stand. Among their circle of friends some were burying parents, which was sudden and amputating. But it was not just parents. Not just aunts and uncles, and people who got older, and middle-aged people who got cancer. They were burying thirty-year-olds, thirty-five-year-olds, people just crossing forty. They were burying people who had lost a lover to AIDS and died a year later. They were burying people who bled to death after being shot for their purses, strangled in abandoned buildings over drugs. They buried one person who dropped dead from a two-day headache—a brain tumor he never knew he had—and then another was lost to lung cancer he never knew he had. They were burying people who hadn't seen their kids into the fifth grade. Unlike their parents, they'd fallen in love too many times. They were burying people they had fallen in love with for life, over and over. They were on a roulette wheel that turned red to black and black to red—knowing the meaning of death but not of survival. They couldn't talk about it. They just couldn't make the journey every time. They couldn't go back and they couldn't be in the moment.

Bird washed her face. She opened the shutters. She decided to go out, get some things to make dinner. Naomi was standing on the sidewalk, head turned left, watching the corner. The sunset was passing golden across her tawny face. The light caught her eyes and she looked serene. Bird sometimes admired her face but not often, because Naomi usually looked worried, pressed, even if she stood in the same spot for two hours and didn't move. She usually gave a rushed hello without moving a muscle. Naomi wasn't in a hurry to get something done, she was in a hurry for something to come.

When Bird rounded the corner on her way back and was once again on the block, the sun had set, the sky was inky blue, just light enough to show the chimneys, antennas, and water towers atop the buildings in silhouette. The roofs looked like a Lilliputian village on a far horizon as the buildings below them disappeared. The orange lights flickered on, bringing back the tenements and their stoops and open windows. Naomi was gone. Bird entered the lobby and waited as the elevator shunted noisily down towards her. She got in and then it stopped on the second floor. The door opened. A man in a black jacket and knit ski mask jumped in, arms going for her package. "That's right, bitch, I'm going to kill you." A hoarse voice. A cotton knit glove in her teeth. The hand covered her mouth. Bird's scream shook in her throat. The throat swelled as she tried to get sound out. "Shut up, bitch!" The door tried to shut, hit his back, and he moved in. He yanked her head to one side and back. She could feel her hair caught in his arm, the arm with the gun in her ribs. Somehow he had her arms locked behind her. He yanked her head back and down, her back arching towards the floor. Bird threw one of her feet into the elevator door before it closed. The rubber bumper banged into her ankle. He banged her head into the floor. Inside her head it sounded like wood cracking. She felt brittle, breakable. She reared up and tried screaming really hard and bit the glove. He loosed his hand for a second. He didn't shoot. Her throat filled with air, vocal cords trembling in her neck. His hand bored down again, this time into her mouth, a ring coming through her lips, ripping her gums. She could taste the huge metal ring and her blood. The door slammed on her ankle again. He yanked her head back and rammed it into the floor and the back wall. Her whole body was arched backward except for the one leg held straight out. She kept her eye on her ankle, trying to hold it steady so the door would not shut. All she could think was that the door could not shut, and then, as her head slammed again into the floor: It's going to shatter. My face is a shell. My face is going to shatter into tiny shards of clay shell. Each blow made her cheekbones crack. Pressure socked her eyes. The hollow sound of her skull meeting the rubber baseboard of the elevator pounded in her ears. She yanked her body up again and pulled him with her. She threw her knee into his balls. He grunted, one hand let go of her, and the other swung out to knock back the door. He looked back and she grabbed at his mask. He yanked it back. She never saw his face. He ran.

As soon as his blur rounded the corner of the landing, her neighbors appeared in front of her. She was standing with one leg still in the door of the elevator, now shutting dumbly against her foot and sliding back. Some ran down the steps, some stared in disbelief, some helped her out. They were in their underwear, housecoats, jeans, T-shirts, carrying kitchen knives and baseball bats. Mr. Sloan, the bailiff who lived upstairs, had his gun. Ready to fight.

"We could hear you, baby, but we couldn't tell what floor." Mrs. Hayes sounded like she was hurt. "We've been coming, we were running up and down the stairwell."

"I never heard a thing," Bird said.

"Yeah, but that's okay, we heard you."

"I'm sorry, I'm sorry, I couldn't find you," one kept saying. "I'm sorry I couldn't get to you sooner." It was Rae, the white woman from across the hall, with a new lover in his sleeveless undershirt. Bird took in that he was handsome and that Rae was holding a long knife. The woman hugged Bird. "Girl, what you been through." Bird noticed that she said it like somebody from down home.

Bird touched her face. It was rubber, not wood, not porcelain, rubber. Rubber and blood. They put her in the elevator to go up to eight. Bird realized her legs were completely soaked. She started pulling the straps of her overalls back up, embarrassed.

The bailiff said, "Guess he was trying to get that off of you."

Bird had what she felt was a thought for the first time. She was pulling her straps back up and trying to fasten them because they were off. He must have pulled them off. She didn't remember that. All she remembered was deciding to scream anyway because she was going to die. She didn't remember anything about her clothes. Her lips were slowly blowing up into light rubber balloons. She couldn't feel the blood there anymore, only where it ran down her chin. When she put her keys in the door, an old piece of wood trim inside snapped and creaked, as it always did, and her knees became rubber and she went down slowly till her neighbors caught her sagging deadweight. Every board in the floor creaked. Her body was piss-sopped, sweat-soaked rubber.

II

COLOR BARS

Hey, hey, baby, I got blood in my eyes for you.
—MISSISSIPPI SHEIKS

1
Monday Night

The cops came and told her she'd handled the situation well, as if she'd wanted to be graded on how she managed as a crime victim. They also told her it was attempted rape. Couldn't she see that her clothes were halfway off her body? Bird told them the man said he was going to kill her. She was getting hoarse. The detectives said that sometimes that's what these guys say, but they also had to read their actions. They gave her a number to call, told her when she felt better all she had to do was call and one of them would come get her, take her to the sex offenders unit to look at pictures.

When they left, Rae was still standing in Bird's hallway asking Bird to let her take her to the hospital. Bird's voice was really raw from screaming. She thought she should call someone. She called her mother, which she knew was a stupid idea, but it seemed a natural thing to do, to call one's mother, say a man just tried to kill her in an elevator. Her mother knew to be alarmed as soon as she heard her, but she said, "What did you do?" Bird didn't understand the question. Her mother asked if Bird had said something, or looked at the man funny. "What did you do?" Suddenly her father was yelling in the background. Bird screamed at her with the remnant of her voice.

"Do you mean how did I make the man try to kill me?" She couldn't feel her lips.

Her father came on the line. "Don't listen to anything she's saying. Are you okay?"

Bird said she didn't know.

"I'm coming up there. Can somebody take you to the hospital?"

Bird said yes. "But don't bring her."

"No," he said, "I'm coming by myself."

She called Bernard who said he'd meet her at the hospital. She had the thought to call the Prince and realized there was no reason. She couldn't believe he had come to mind. She made a decision just then not to ever call him again.

After eight hours in an emergency room, X-rays, and advice to see a dentist about her bottom teeth being moved around and the gums cut up, she was told to go home and get some sleep. Bernard sat in her living room while Bird slept through the rest of the night and all of the next day, stumbling out only once to go to the bathroom. She couldn't straighten up and could barely move most of her left side.

Sometime on Monday, Bernard let in Bird's father and they sat together until Bird woke up that evening. When Bird stepped into the living room, Arthur Kincaid gasped. Her eyes were rimmed by charcoal gray bruises—two sizable black eyes—and her mouth was swollen, purple and black. Bruises on her cheekbones made her face appear sunken, and her hair stood crazily in every direction. She smiled at her father.

"Chief!" Both men jumped to their feet. Her father hugged her gingerly. "Bernard, I guess you've met the chief."

"Wish you wouldn't call me that. This looks like a sensible young man who might want to use my real name."

"Me and my brother call him Chief, or Kalif." Bird's speech sounded halted and muffled. "He didn't want to change his name in the sixties, so we changed it for him."

"Don't try to talk."

"I think I need some ice on my head," she said to no one in particular. Bernard went to the kitchen.

"Girl, you look pretty bad, I'm not going to kid you. You look like you been in one of those street-fighter movies. You look like you fought off six dudes with your bare hands and tore up the bar."

She cried. He hugged her and went to pat her hair into place, out of her face.

"Don't— Be careful."

His hand recoiled. She took his hand in hers and showed him where to touch her scalp. "I have these huge knots on my head. Can you feel them?" She wanted to be assured they were as big as they seemed to her.

"They're pretty bad—we'll make you an ice pack. I haven't seen knots like that since I got my ass kicked in brawls in the army."

"I'm much worse than I was yesterday. I didn't know what happened to me, but now I feel every bloody bit of it. I can't turn my head. I have these welts that feel like eggs on my head. My skull hurts. My whole frame hurts. It's weird. I feel like I want to kill somebody for this. I am so mad. I woke up mad enough to kill somebody."

"You're just hurt, baby. Come on, sit down," he said. "Your body went into shock at first, to protect you. You couldn't feel what had happened. Sometimes it takes weeks to know exactly where you were hurt." Arthur Kincaid knew something about injuries from thirty-five years of martial arts and thirty years of practicing law. He'd seen more clients with the same injuries than he cared to think about, especially since most of them

117

came as a result of being in the hands of the authorities, not from assailants on the street.

And he'd thought his days of worrying about his kids getting the same treatment were over years ago, after having to go from one precinct to another looking for his son the student protest leader in the sixties, and finding him mauled and stuporous in a Harlem jail. After finding witnesses who saw them drag the boy into the middle of an intersection, and beat him into the street in plain view, cars wheeling by, and throw him into a car and drive off. After getting Bird off a campus where the plainclothes police came in by busloads, stormed student barricades, and took kids by the hundreds. After they'd made it into adulthood without becoming drug addicts—well, as far as he knew, and not through any effort on his part, but more likely through dumb luck, he now guessed.

He thought both his kids had had their seven years of hard luck early because they'd spent their entire youth in harm's way. Bird's trouble, though, was not the trouble of youth or volatile times. An ass-kicking like this was the grown kind of trouble a leadbelly finds all down the line. It was out of blues places where you could hear tell of a sudden death or of a madman who roamed the streets out to kill a bitch with gun or knife or bare hands. This was the kind of trouble folks like Arthur Kincaid had moved away from long ago after hearing it once too often out the back door.

Arthur Kincaid did the only thing he knew how to do for Bird's kind of trouble. He told Bernard to get hold of somebody who could press the police real hard to find the assailant. He told Bird she had to get another apartment and he would pay for it if she didn't have the money. He told her to get the best dentist in town, and if her medical insurance didn't cover it, he would pay for it. He checked the sprained muscles in her neck and back, the bruises on her ankle, and told her to get rid of the elastic bandage the doctors put on, soak in some minerals he would get for her, and see a Chinese doctor for some acupressure. He told her to try just taking aspirin for the pain and swelling and to do without the codeine they gave her—it would mess her up. He told her she needed some hot food, and wondered aloud if she could chew and swallow. He asked Bernard to get some food and gave him enough money for dinner for six. When Bernard left he also told her that if Bernard was her boyfriend that was the best she'd done in a long time and she had his blessing.

He didn't tell her they would get the motherfucker who did this to her, because he just couldn't bring himself to tell her that any more than he would tell it to a client. He said he would make the police do everything they could to get the mother-fucker. That he could promise.

Bird liked to see her father click into gear with his man-of-action routine. There was a good energy to it that helped to clean the house of all its goblins and haints. He swept through the situation with a big broom to rid her of the lingering fear that no one would do anything. That's where she felt she got her nerve from. She might never have landed in so many scrapes, righteous as she thought they were, if she hadn't known Arthur Kincaid would try to wipe the floor with anybody who did her wrong. It was just that she no longer felt he could. This trouble was hers, and it had fallen to her to wipe the floor with the cul-prit who did it. It was no longer even Alex's trouble. It was her life she had to get back. With her father asleep that night on the couch, Bird stared out the back window at the brick walls of all the buildings, including her own.

Watched as if the man could scale one of those walls and come into the apartment if she wasn't looking. When Mr. Sloan upstairs got up for his 4:00 A.M. bath, she slept.

2

Wednesday

Bird tried going to work in order to get her father to go home. Her friends at the office badgered her into tending to one of the items on her father's list. She cried her way through the whole grueling business in the dentist's chair. It was a great relief, a simple, utterly sensible reason to have a good cry.

The "best" dentist in town, at least according to Bird's contacts at the radio station, turned out to be a periodontist—a bright-eyed Frenchwoman who so terrorized her patients about gum disease that they had organized a Dr. Colette Rousse support group. When she found Bird in the chair, Dr. Rousse seemed so taken aback by the black eyes and purple cheekbones that she began by reassuring Bird that the mouth healed very, very quickly. She made matter-of-fact descriptions of the condition of her mouth. Bird could feel indignation rising in the doctor as she made a catalog of Bird's injuries.

"You have some deep lacerations in your gums—they'll heal, they'll be fine—but I'm afraid I'm going to have to ask you what kind of instrument made these cuts?"

"A man's ring."

Dr. Rousse was horrified by whatever she envisioned. "But it really dug *in*—so deep—"

"I was attacked by a maniac of some kind. He had his hand over my mouth to keep me from screaming."

Dr. Rousse exhaled deeply. "Yes, well, the two front ones have been jarred loose. I will clean it out down there and they should go back where they belong when the gum heals. You'll have to keep them very clean." Dr. Rousse donned goggles and slid a white mask over her nose and mouth. They reminded Bird of the mugger.

All Bird could think about was the lights, her helplessness, the hands pulling and tugging. She tried to think of it as Zen, as an experience that forced one to stay in the moment, prevented a person from thinking of anything more than breathing in and breathing out.

"Oh, jeez. There's so much blood. It's going to be a little slow."

Zen didn't work. A sensation sat on her as heavily as the leaded X-ray apron spread across her body. The sensation pressing her down was a continual falling. First her own body was falling, headfirst, never landing. Then the falling belonged to Dorothy Hale in Frida Kahlo's painting: Dorothy Hale in an evening gown, falling through unnatural ethers, clouds with heavy bodies like fattened doves. Clouds in rows like the crinkled layers of little girls' crinolines. Dorothy on the ground, in an evening gown, with a corsage of white roses. Then Bird falling, on the elevator of the Eiffel Tower, falling upward, the ground zooming away, stomach churning, the loudspeaker warning of pickpockets.

"Head up. How can I work on you if your head keeps falling

down?" Dr. Rousse sounded impatient. Maybe that's how Bird had got on the Eiffel Tower elevator, Dr. Rousse's voice. The periodontist looked at Bird's face, soaking wet from tears. "Why do that now? It's almost over."

Bird rolled her eyes at Dr. Colette. "I need a break."

The doctor looked amazed. When Bird returned to the chair, Dr. Colette was suddenly cheerful. "When I was a girl in Tahiti, when we went to the movies they had a break in the middle, you know, before the feature, and everyone would jump up and run out for a *glace chocolat,* ice cream. Put your head back." She put her goggles back on and they were in Tahiti. "You know they would have a newsreel, then the short, and then a cartoon." Dr. Colette, mind-travel dentist. "We sat on benches outside . . ."

Bird wanted to ask her how she happened to grow up in Tahiti but there were three hands in her mouth; the assistant was leaning an elbow on her chest as she held a suction tube in place. Bird put herself on a bench outside in Tahiti, and then recalled that she'd seen a movie sitting on a hard wooden bench somewhere in the interior of Ghana. It was *Murder on the Orient Express.* She couldn't remember anything else about it except all the Ghanaians howling with laughter as Ingrid Bergman reminisced about her time as a missionary in black Africa with the "little brown babies." It was in 1977, when she met Sheikh.

Bird had asked Alex if she wanted to go on the charter flight to West Africa. Alex had accused her of looking for an adventure, "like a boy." She said it was like something Bird's brother would do, "going off to get lost in the bush." In fact, Bird's brother had hooked her up with a group of middle-class African nationalist intellectuals who ran annual trips to the Homeland for three hundred dollars, which was about all the money Bird had. He also let her hold two hundred dollars for "trinkets." Alex said Baba had told her such adventures were only metaphors for the inward journey.

"I'd like to say that after I've been somewhere," Bird said.

Besides, she pointed out, Alex had taken her life savings of six hundred dollars to go to India.

"I'm not going to have an adventure, I'm going there to live, to meditate."

"You could meditate right here."

"I have to be with Baba."

"I bet he sends you back."

Alex still declined to go on Bird's adventure, finally saying she'd probably say the wrong thing and get arrested. Besides, Alex thought she'd be in India indefinitely, that Baba would let her stay till she was old.

Bird didn't really have an agenda for her trip, just a book she'd read and some maps. She'd told the handsome young African sitting next to her on the plane going to Accra that she might meet him in Lagos, where he was going on business, or later in Abidjan, where he was going to hang out. He was the most bohemian African she'd ever set eyes on, a guy who only wore jeans and T-shirts, and kept an apartment in New York. She wondered if all that bohemianism meant he was pretending not to be fabulously wealthy from newly unearthed Nigerian oil. She'd met several sisters on the plane who were going to Nigeria to marry these new millionaires. She'd never even heard they existed before finding this charter flight. After a while it dawned on her that she was really acting ignorant.

He wasn't Nigerian, he was French-speaking. Senegalese, it turned out. "My name is Sheikh Abdoulaye Doumbia." He was finishing graduate school in business, interested in commodities trading, "raw goods, such as we survive on in the third world." He told her at length how the people of West African countries had traditionally grown a variety of crops that provided all the food they needed. But then the colonial governments had forced the people to forsake this practice and to just grow or dig up or chop down one product for export—groundnuts or rubber, lumber, what have you. Food could be bought, they reasoned. Slowly the prices for all such goods went to hell. Sheikh Abdoulaye Doumbia had a passion for overthrowing colonial agrarian economies that she found positively erotic. Still, though, his itinerary of "business" in Lagos, and "hanging out" in Abidjan, meant that he was doing better in the world than she was as a graduate student. She began to wonder, again with appalling dumbness, what kind of millionaire would the Senegalese variety be?

Bird did trek into the bush, albeit by bus and jitney. It didn't much compete with her brother going and living in a village in the interior and boating down the Volta but it was a start. Being somewhat proud of her ease at adventure, and finding the dollar went pretty far, she headed for Nigeria. She did try to call Lagos, but the Ghanaian phones were very moody and prone to disconnect after taking her money. She bought bus fare to Nigeria, but there was a coup while she was on the road, and lots of borders shut down. She was stopped before getting into Dahomey. She took the bus back to Accra and waited, thinking to go instead to Abidjan, but this involved flying. Bird was pretty sure she was too poor for the "pearl of Africa" anyway, and forgot the whole thing. She found it hard to make plans, hard to write down her thoughts, and hard to sleep. Wherever she went, the terrain was so alive, she sat up listening to the sounds of it, hundreds upon hundred of frogs, birds that squawked and cawed. It was never truly quiet.

One morning, shortly before leaving Ghana, she sat in her hotel window. The sun was just up in savannas too far away to see. Crows called and the air was light. Men and women ran down the road in her view. Across lush fields, on narrow paths, trucks trundled, soldiers strolled in high boots. She watched the morning. Leaning out of a high window, she saw a man swimming in the pool below.

She had never learned that stroke. The heart had to work so hard, as the arms pumped and the legs reached wide and cut in. He was doing laps, and the stroke was so strenuous she thought he would tire. Soon she forgot the runners and walkers, the maids, teachers, and hardhats going by.

Imagining the lean body to be a man who might have kept

her up, a night visitor never there, her eyes did laps in his endless stream of plunges and glides. He didn't tire. He kept going and she watched his body, unaware of time or sunrise, until at last he quit and emerged, wet and quite perfect. She wanted to take the towel and dry his hair as he wiped his face and stretched the towel across his back. She watched the cloth slide around his waist, down his legs. Saw him slip into loose trousers, zip up his jacket. She wanted to be the towel close around his neck. Only when he walked away, dressed, did she think she recognized the body, the head, the walk, of the man on the plane. She dressed for a swim. Stretched herself across the water. She stroked in the reflection and let his laps take her in. Crows called and the air was light. A white butterfly skimmed the water's gleaming surface.

The young African bohemian's unavailable body, just departed but closer than the lover she carried in her heart, was, in the moment, the only body she'd ever wanted. She entered a lust for the place she was in, the dust, the dazzling cloths and sculptured heads, bare arms, and gleaming laughter. The almost silent streets at night when the turmoil of markets, beggars, cars, and offices stopped. Unseen priests patiently watching the advancing phases of the moon, measuring a slice of light in the night sky. Hundreds of miles away, beyond the bush where the trees died as desert overtook them, old men chanted with an imam who called from the speakers of portable radios. They watched for signs of the length and breadth of the moon, of Allah's desire for prayer and vigilance. In the desert, old men gave up the world with practice and looked towards the crescent moon. Nothing else within sight gave off light. Bird saw them without looking for them, knew their slim, dutiful daughters, and their daughters' sons, bundled in cloth, bearing the faces of prime ministers, sleeping on a pallet unaware of heat or flies. Sometimes she learned only through her body.

At the airport in Accra, she found herself in a crowd of hundreds, all shoving towards the ticket counter. A man accidentally hit her in the face with his elbow, and she pounded him with a right uppercut to the jaw. Bird had totally lost her grasp of language. Alex might have thought she'd get herself arrested, but Bird definitely would have if the police could have gotten to her through the mob.

"I thought that was you over here, acting American." The bohemian turned up, squeezing through the crowd, laughing. Bird was embarrassed, knowing that the only words she had been able to get out of her mouth moments before had been a sackful of streetisms that only American blacks delivered with the requisite authority. People gave the bohemian room as if he were responsible for her.

He showed her how to sneak the small "dash" in someone's hand that was required to get one's luggage and body onto the plane before the crush. They waited sweltering on the empty plane for two more hours. The plane would fill first with those who knew the system. The bohemian said she owed him for the airport favor.

"What would the price be?" She was amused that he couldn't know she had been the towel around his neck only days ago.

"Cappuccino in New York."

"Done."

Sheikh Abdoulaye Doumbia told her the coup had only seemed eventful for the first few hours and that she had missed a very wacky adventure in the Côte d'Ivoire that landed him with only a swimsuit and a pair of jeans at the home of President Felix Houphouët-Boigny. Bird said to herself, this guy is not poor. One ruling elite partying with another. He'd been through a coup in the last two weeks and left to go visit somebody at the palace of a man rumored to keep live crocodiles in the yard.

"Do you know the Boignys or the Houphouët-Boignys, or Houphouëts-Boigny?"

"I'll tell you about it." He smiled. "My friends call me Abdoulaye."

It took Bird several cappuccinos in New York to get the man's whole story. After Baba sent Alex back, Bird told her the inner journey left out the possibility of the strangers next to you on a plane. Alex said a fellow traveler is also a part of karma.

Dr. Rousse gave lengthy advice for how best to survive after a dental catastrophe:

One should not cry (causes bleeding). Or talk too much (bleeding again), smoke (are you crazy?), sneeze (try not to), eat anything with sugar in it (causes at least two full minutes of extreme pain with an exposed nerve), drink orange juice or other citrus juices (ditto), coffee (ditto), cold drinks (water, milk shakes, certainly not iced coffee), ice cream, meat (how would you chew it anyway?), bread crust (you get the idea), alcohol (it will be shockingly bad and not worth it), tomatoes, lettuce, garlic, fruit (except soft bananas), little leafy garnishes, kissing on both cheeks, vigorous hugs against tall bodies, heavy earrings hanging on the chin line. "Soups and purees are good, but not tomato puree—with this medicine I'm giving you, you'll throw up right away. You don't want to throw up."

"What's left?"

"Salt water is good. Go to the beach."

"What about sex? Not that I'm having any."

"Very gently, of course. You know, *some* things you might want to forgo."

Bird chuckled in her throat. Her mouth was too crowded to laugh.

Bird got lost trying to get home on the subway. Even though she could read the signs for each stop, she couldn't keep straight what line she was on, or where it went. She got out, went up on the street, and called Bernard. Bernard told her to get a cab. For the first time she could ever remember, she accepted being helpless. She didn't feel bad; she accepted it, hung up, and hailed a cab. Bernard was there on the stoop with two briefcases of papers when she got home. She told him the dentist had said she should go to the beach and she thought that was exactly what she would do.

"I'm gonna get a map out here and draw lines in three directions till I hit a beach and then I will call and make a reservation at an inn or hotel in each one of those places and tomorrow I'm going to one of them. You wanna go?"

Bernard begged off but said he'd stay in the apartment till she got ready to go. Once inside, she dashed around to find a map and went into the bedroom and got on the phone. Bernard studied Bird's neatly arranged rows of videotapes, examining the labels and putting them back in place.

Bird wondered for a second how Bernard could keep leaving his office on a minute's notice to help her and yet would never think of jumping in a car with her and going to the beach the next day. That's just how Bernard was, never quite knowing when a moment was his to enjoy. All the same, he knew he could assume a place in Bird's life, on her couch, in her kitchen. They were close like that.

Bernard Henderson was fit without doing anything about it, simply lucky to have kept what God gave him: lustrous skin the color of dark rum; clear, bright black marble eyes; a complex and agile mind; and a muscular body that did not discredit him when he showed his pride at younger days of odd sports like squash or crew. Bird didn't care much for youthful athletics stories, and he learned to preface his with an apology. He had lost most of his hair very early and shaved the rest. Bird, who'd never seen him with hair, thought that loss had made him prematurely serious. No matter what he did, he had the air of a responsible grown-up, dressing the part as well, dark suits, white shirts, bursting briefcase, and always insisting on paying the bill in a restaurant. Many people she knew were still secret adolescents. But even if he could have pulled off wearing hightops and baseball caps, Bernard was doomed to be the most serious guy in the room. It was his best quality, as he wore it loosely, with self-deprecating humor and a mischievous twinkle in his eye that made one question the whole effect.

While in her bedroom, Bird called Charles Marshall, who loved to drive, and talked him into her little trip. When he heard about the elevator assault, it wasn't hard. Bird emerged waving a bathing suit and beach towel. "I've got these and a bottle of some kind of horrible strychnine kill-anything rinse, a mouthful of packing that can come out in a day, and pills if anything hurts. Long as I don't cry, chew, talk, smoke, drink, eat tomatoes, or have rough sex, I'm okay."

Bernard wanted to know how she was going to get there.

"I did what Alex would have done. I called the Baguette and told him he had to take me."

Bernard said, "Oh."

"You know why we called him the Baguette? 'Cause he's like the kind of sweet-smelling bread you take home for the night while it's fresh, but you don't try to hold onto for other days. And with Charles I don't have to worry about talking, smoking, drinking, fucking, or eating tomatoes. He hates anything with tomato sauce." Bird was astounded that her sense of humor had returned.

It seemed as if Bernard's had not. "You sure? You're talking about him like a hot loaf."

"You know the story of the distracted slave of love?"

"No."

"Without getting into it, 'cause you know I'm not supposed to talk too much, and it is a *very* long story, let me just say, he never gets any."

"Oh. Maybe that's me."

She was a little startled and winked. "I don't know about that. Anyway I've been a distracted slave of love, I know."

"If you've been one, I must have been one twice."

Bird laughed and headed for the kitchen. "Have some coffee for me, Bernard, I just want to smell it."

"Okay. Listen, Bird, I was looking at these tapes."

The room went silent for a second.

"Please don't. I'm feeling good for the first time in I don't know when. I even called Essex and gave him the rest of the phonebook stuff to do. I am going to bail out for a while. Don't start with the tapes, Bernard."

"No, listen. It's just that I saw something. We'll deal with it when you come back, okay? When you asked me about those nonsense words, I thought only one sounded familiar—Alif. I saw it a minute ago and I was thinking Hebrew. I know it from the crossword. It's a letter, the first letter of the Hebrew alphabet. But when I saw it, I realized the Hebrew is not spelled that way. It's Aleph. I think these are Arabic letters."

"Yeah," said Bird, "it would more likely be Arabic. Yeah, actually during one of those times when she was doing crazy patterns in everything, she was buying books of art of the Ottoman Empire, Suleyman the Magnificent, and all that. Yeah. Arabic fits. I'll get a dictionary."

The tapes fell into order by the year, from A to Z. Year One, 1987: ALIF to RA (or RE); Year Two, 1988: ZAY (ZE) to FA (FE); Year Three, 1989: QAF to YA (YE). They sat on the floor and rearranged the tape cassettes. Bird got the giggles again.

"At least she wasn't in her Hindu period. Shit, we would have been looking for some kind of Urdu or Sanskrit or Pali alphabet. Lord."

Bernard smiled. "Yeah, I'm afraid Urdu doesn't come up in the *New York Times* crossword."

They agreed to watch the tapes in order when she came back. Bernard heated up some food and Bird made soup. Bird still couldn't get over her good humor. With everything she'd been through, it was amazing that it was still so scary to go sit in the dentist's chair. She'd been through so much that she'd gotten stupid again. It felt good not to care anymore. She told Bernard, "First, I nearly get killed and then I have to go to the dentist. What else is there?"

Bernard settled in at her dining table with his pile of legal briefs. Bird took a pill and stretched out on the bed. She got up every now and again to fetch suntan oil or hair cream from the bathroom. She tossed each item in an open satchel. Every time, she went and stood at the back window and stared at the brick walls. When Mr. Sloan got up at 4:00 A.M. for his bath, she slept.

3
Thursday

In the morning when Bird walked out of the apartment to find Charles Marshall waiting in his car, she felt relieved just to be outside in the sun, reassured that the rest of the whole mundane world she knew was still there, still going on. In the months spent just going to work and back to her apartment, it was as if all the world she'd known, all that could not be framed by her front windows, had fallen away from her and could no longer be touched. Naomi was already in her spot, just where she'd been the night before, and right where she'd probably be when Bird returned. They exchanged smiles—Bird's was a little puffed and crooked—and Naomi studied her face for a second, then looked away. Charles looked a little shocked too when he saw Bird. Bird had on her good-luck leopard-print jacket and giant sunglasses to hide her bruises. She pulled off her sunglasses and flashed him a peek at her sunken, bruised eyes.

"Darkly mysterious, no?"

"I think you could lose the look," he said, turning the key in the ignition. "We'll work on it. I've decided on the Vineyard."

He wanted to go the longest distance. He had the black Porsche that he kept stashed in a garage. The fact that he had such a car in New York City showed a certain determination on his part to live a magazine-pretty life even when good sense advised otherwise. Bird figured the garage alone was $350 a month. The Baguette was tall, and handsome with an earnest, boyish look. The brown of his skin was warm, like his open, uncomplicated expressions. Even though he was a lot younger, Charles was straight like Bernard was straight—hardworking, taxpaying, co-op–buying, suit-wearing straight. But he was different from Bernard in two ways: he knew he was good-looking and he had at some point realized he was just as crazy as the people he admired for being crazy. He opened up in their presence like a plant starved for water stretching out in a rain.

For Bird, Charles's most endearing quality was that he loved it when someone asked him to do something he'd never done before, especially things he'd never thought of doing. Some people, like Bird's family, would want to know if a thing was hazardous before doing it. Some had already drawn the exact perimeters of the world in which they wanted to live, and saw no reason to waste time experimenting, they would say, merely for the sake of "sensation."

Until the eighties, Bird had thought life was like one of the ornate mazelike gaming palaces of Shanghai she'd heard about, where thousands of fascinating creatures from anywhere in the world, stranded by rumors of war, floated glittering in and out of chambers that defied one's sense of what was possible within four walls. Her Shanghai palace was a house of chance made from frames of thirties movies: chandeliered dog-racing tracks and ballrooms for big bands; mirrored galleries; imperial dining halls; smoky saloons thick with the smell of cognac. It was a stopover where one might simply sit and wait, or else be dragged away exhausted and impoverished, holding only specious tales of one's experiences. But in the eighties, troops had definitely occupied Bird's glittering pleasure mall and turned it into the setting for "The Masque of the Red Death."

Charles put on a Prince tape, opened the roof, and stepped on it. He was doing his favorite version of himself, behind the wheel, music up, talking about his woman troubles, the version that made it worthwhile to go to his job and worry about money sixty hours a week. He wore a hundred-dollar T-shirt, similarly pricey jeans, and Nikes. Charles went to the gym, worked out with weights. He was into his manliness. He would have been very annoyed to know Bird and Alex called him the Baguette. They had died with laughter every time one of them almost slipped and said it right in his face, right at one of those moments when he would take off the jacket to one of his Armani suits, signal the waiter, and buy all the drinks. He told them how he'd given up making tons of money to make merely a lot of money but he could not give up the suits, as if someone had asked him to lower his standard of dress.

"Yeah, going to the beach is just what I needed to do. You want to take the ferry from New Bedford or Woods Hole?"

He'd been going up to the Vineyard pretty often the past couple of years. "I've been getting invited to these quasi-social events. In fact, that's what I told my wife I was doing today, going up for two days to see clients who are still up there. It's turned into a scene these days. You know the new niggerati has moved in now."

"Oh yeah? Who is that anyway?"

"People who write books, TV types, filmmakers, some artists like yourself, I guess, except obviously they're making more money than you." He laughed.

"I'm a former artist. You sure they're artists?"

"I've met a couple of semi-best-selling authors, you know, like what's-his-name—I'll think of it."

"Semi-best-sellers? I can't wait."

"He wrote that book, you know the one, something about his life in the discos in the seventies."

Bird hated the book. "Oh God! Who else?"

"A couple of TV producers, and I met a guy who wrote an opera, a TV anchor from D.C.—"

"Not the same person?"

"No. C'mon, girl. Several black Harvard types."

"What are you, chopped liver?"

"Leave me alone. Anyway, one of them, I thought he said his name was Wallace D. Fard and my mouth fell open, but I think he was saying Ford."

"Oh yeah, Ford, sociology. I hope you didn't tell him you thought he was the original prophet of the Nation of Islam. I don't think he has a sense of humor."

"Doesn't. He looked at me like I was an illiterate idiot."

"Lord. I'm not ready for any scene. Plus, look at me." She laughed.

He turned his shining black eyes on her and smiled. "We don't have to do any scene. It's after Labor Day, maybe they've all gone home. We're just gonna hang out, get wet."

"Yeah." She looked away from his smile. When he smiled he got the Baguette look. She realized that within hours of leaving town, Bird the Lascivious was on the way back. He had crinkling jet black hair that gave a delicate look to an athletic body. His eyes danced and he was pretty enough to turn heads. His nickname was a tribute to his boyishness. He was ten years younger than any of the men Bird and Alex knew, which made him about ten years younger than Bird and Alex too. Even though Essex judged him beautiful, Charles's looks were like a clean slate. Not much living on his face. Bird secretly thought men were more appreciative of an innocent look on other men. Women liked a little experience and "edge." Charles's only edge was that he kept leaving his wife and home unannounced. He went alone to any place he really enjoyed. Memphis Minnie started singing with a laugh in Bird's head: *Wants to see my chauffeur / I wants him to drive me / I wants him to drive me downtown . . .*

He was the only male point of agreement between Alex and Bird. They didn't usually go for the same men. Alex liked pretty boys and Bird didn't. Usually. Alex liked them slight and troubled. Or young and foreign. She liked long hair. Bird liked them skinny but a little rugged. She liked men who'd been through something. But the Baguette could talk about almost anything that interested them—painting, music, plays, clothes, books. He was also good on a number of subjects they didn't care about, such as brokerage scams and vintage wines. Even though they weren't interested, it was nice when they ordered dinner to let him go on with the waiter about the esoteric wine blahblah. Alex would whisper, "He's cute and the waiter thinks so too. He doesn't even notice." *See, he drives so easy / I can't turn him down.* But Bird didn't know if he had the romance in him.

In the beginning they didn't hit on him simply because he was married. Then Alex started saying someone needed to hit on him to liberate the boy, but she only got forward with him when she was drunk and the Baguette couldn't take drunks. Bird never hit on him because bad timing was her middle name.

The reason they wondered about him was that he was very polite. They weren't used to men who were that polite. Men who were hard-core "lovers" were caring, solicitous, and gentlemanly and put their hands on you. They always wore one article of clothing that didn't fit in a magazine-perfect ensemble, white bucks, argyle socks, or no belt, something that said they weren't really that polite. The Baguette was always perfect.

He played Aretha and Bird fell quiet. Bird knew he wouldn't find it rude that she was staring out the window, and trying to smoke with gauze in her mouth. He was used to his older friends doing that. They always got quiet when someone put on music they remembered. She was listening to the old music and thinking she was no longer tiny enough to sensibly be called Bird. She was more like a big cat or a horse. A racehorse, she'd like to think, but a creature of strong bones and muscle nevertheless. For a long time she had been accustomed to people being attracted to her, took it for granted. It was a quality people often disliked about Bird. She had a casual assumption about desire, as if it was always there between two humans and could just as well be ignored. Charles, she knew, thought desire a sudden gift, a gift that demanded acknowledgment. He would think you could get up from your chair and lose it.

"What if I run you a hot bath when we get there and give you a massage?"

She looked at him as if he were ten. "You hitting on me after all this time, Charles?" As if desire was always there.

"Yeah."

"Maybe I'll just take the hot bath."

"Did you get us one room or two?"

"Oh, God, I forgot about that. I made one reservation last night. They were pretty packed. Shit." She panicked at the thought of sleeping with him.

"You don't have to sound that annoyed. It's cool." He was being cheerful again.

"Maybe they have another room."

Bird could be cold. He smiled. She wanted to put her hand in his hair. Bird stared out the window and laughed out loud.

She was thinking the word "shit." She reached in her bag for another cigarette. She felt truly ridiculous. It was funny. It was not a lack of lust, her fear of sleeping with Charles. She felt stupid because it was about taking off her clothes. It was that silly. She didn't think she was beautiful enough anymore to take off her clothes with a man who didn't know what happened to women's bodies. And what had happened to hers. Would she now, like a teenager, prefer the dark? She'd sooner fuck Charles in the back of his Porsche than share a hotel room. She didn't care about sharing a bed; she'd shared beds with her gay friends, men who thought she was beautiful no matter what and didn't want her body anyway. But Charles was the Baguette—poor thing, he should have perfect women, and if not perfect, swell at least.

Bird closed her eyes. She saw the stiffness of her sprained

muscles. Saw the even older ashen patches on her limbs, like watery translucent blots of a watercolor spilled along her skin. There were also the small things a man might not notice, tiny silver keloids on her hips and breasts where she'd once been pregnant too long and yet not long enough. The stitches from a small tumor, just dots really, and a quarter-moon scar. A man probably wouldn't see them if he wasn't looking for them. But not only were there dots and incisions, the memories had settled in there too, all the tubes, and blinding lights, the Hungarian doctor, the black surgeon assisting, the pain of the body stitching itself back together. Her body was like a map of incidents, of events whose witnesses were strangers long gone. And it was like a map with islands of lost color indicating buried fear, and pain. She was sorry that all the great joys, all the fun and love, had not left some markers too. The only scar of happiness she bore was a burn from swiping her right forearm against a hot oven, remnant of a delicious meal cooked for her first lover. Wouldn't it be better if God gave out extra eyelashes for every good love affair or single strands of red hair for every orgasm. How delicious to see a woman on the street, hair full of incongruent, unmatching fabulous red strands of hair.

The air was almost wet at Woods Hole. They got coffee and waited for the ferry, then rode it bundled up in sweatshirts, standing in the wind. Charles put his arm around Bird and kissed her forehead. She looked at him and raised her eyebrows and looked away but she didn't move. An arm was a good thing.

At the inn, the manager looked a little alarmed at Bird's bruised face and said rather coolly that the best he could do was a two-room suite. Bird and Charles said yes. Bird thought, in the abundance of water, why should the fool still thirst? Alex always said someone should throw this man down and make him happy but she had never done it. Bird thought she ought to screw up the courage and do it for the girl. She wouldn't be able to tell her about it—that would take some of the pleasure out of it. Telling Alex she'd taken care of that would have been a real enjoyment.

They drove to Edgartown to eat at a restaurant on the dock. When Bird got a good look at herself in the restroom mirror, she reached in her mouth and pulled out the packing. She decided that feeling loved was going to have to heal it, and in the meantime, she could look at least a little less gruesome. She tried powder on the cheeks, flinching as she brushed it on. She still looked like a police station Polaroid.

They weren't used to the ocean chill and the dampness and sat side by side at a table. He put a sweater around her shoulders and rubbed her arms. They'd given up the other subjects and had gotten into their "relationships," except for the most recent. He kept asking questions about men she'd been with. She asked for his stories. Every time he warmed her arms and hands, Bird silently toasted Alex and thanked her for leaving her the pleasure of Charles. She liked the awkward way he tried to tell her he was surprised to like her, how he was trying to talk without handing a line even though there was no line to hand. He told her how she had acted so bored when she first met him. She was embarrassed. She didn't tell him she had not been in the least bit bored. He was saying he was surprised to keep coming back. She thought he was really trying to say he was surprised to be lusting after her.

Charles muttered a quiet "Oh, no" as two young filmmakers from the city came in with their dates. Bird knew them too, but only because she'd seen them at work. "Phat and Buttah," she said. He started laughing, then she laughed, and by the time the four stood at their table, Charles and Bird could hardly get it together.

"Charles! Investment king to the black elite! My favorite broker!" one of them raved.

"Not yet. You have to give me some money first." Everyone laughed. Charles introduced the two men to Bird as the most undecided investors he knew. They introduced their dates and Bird instantly lost their names. One was either Tiffany or Brittany, and the other's rhymed with Keesha. Charles introduced Bird, saying, "You must know Cynthia Kincaid, from Public

Radio." This made them say yes, of course, whether they knew her or not. The possibility of having both a broker's brain and media person's to pick was too hard for the men to resist and they immediately invited themselves to join them for dinner. They pulled chairs from another table and sat down. All four of them looked puzzled once they took in Bird's laughing, bruised face with two black eyes.

"Car accident?" asked Phat.

"Yup," Charles answered quickly, "a doozy."

"Not in that Porsche?"

"Not me, not the Porsche." Bird was thinking snidely how nicely they'd handled the important stuff, without her saying a word.

"Can you talk?" Phat inquired, leaning in as if she might be deaf.

"Yeah, she can talk," Charles said. "Wanna order a drink?" Bird cracked up. After getting over Bird's face, Phat and Buttah seemed to notice very little, nothing but their careers. Throughout dinner Buttah went on about who said what to him and Phat dropped what star he was talking to last week; Buttah told which famous director called to ask for videos of his work; Phat announced how much bread was involved in their next projects. They both agreed that the Baguette should help them put together the money they needed. They were into budgets. Bird couldn't imagine being interested in budgets unless she had one. Charles talked easily to them, affably, seemingly interested in their shoptalk.

She knew Phat from the studio but she knew he didn't remember engineers, only people on the mike or in front of the camera. Only politicians spoke to the peons in an office, and only because peons vote. Movie people saved their energy. Phat was a terrible interview, memorable to anybody in the business for trying to answer every question with yes or no. When he'd started out, he was always "good copy" because he liked shooting off his mouth. But he'd learned, and now, in spite of the fact that he was hard to get because he was famous and fussy, he was considered a loathsome assignment, especially in radio. She didn't look at him much because she had long ago studied his tight, withholding face through the glass of her studio. She thought he'd be hard to paint. She kept lighting cigarettes, which made him squirm, and she started cracking jokes, which made all of them laugh nervously.

"Have you ever auditioned for me?" he said.

Bird said no.

"I know I've seen you in something."

"Bird's not——" She pinched Charles's thigh under the table.

"I know it's something I've seen, 'cause I know I don't know you. I don't know anyone who smokes. I make a point of it."

"You're right," she said. "And I'm too old to be in your movies. That's why I haven't auditioned for you."

"That's not true."

Bird tried to think if she really liked one of his movies.

"Yeah, I think I'd have to be somebody's mother who's out of it and doesn't know her son's on the corner, or an aging crackhead, or both." She got devilish. "I'm waiting for you to do a black Barbara Stanwyck movie. You know, one where the smart woman in the suit and fox stole gets the man, makes him take the fall, and walks off with the money." Bird started chuckling softly as she pulled the ego off his sleeve.

"I don't do the 'black version' of anything. I make *my* movies."

"Oh. Of course. It's just that I thought your second film, *in addition* to being your *own*, was also a 'tribute,' shall we say a hood tribute, to *Rocco and His Brothers*, or was that *Open City*?" Charles pinched her to stop.

"I'm not into Visconti."

"But you are into Rossellini. Yes, it was *Open City*." She laughed. The Phat man was wounded, and bristled as if she'd said women were more fit to lead the race. Bird noticed the two dates were perfect and quiet and smiled without being amused. Miss Phat and Miss All That. They drank wine and did not smoke, had never smoked in their young lives. She knew they didn't know what Etta James meant when she said, "I'd rather go blind than to see you walk away from me, Chile"—Etta always finished that with "Chile." They'd never had the shit kicked out of them in an elevator either, Bird thought. They were the right age and the right look for a man like Charles. They were perfect. They annoyed Bird, even though she knew she, too, had once been quiet. *I don't want him | To be riding these girls around | I'm gwine steal me a pistol | Shoot my chauffeur down.*

"That's not what I was doing. I'm not making *tributes* to Europeans." The Phat man was still tense.

"It's okay with *me.* Hell, I've seen at least one black film that was a tribute to Loretta Young." Everyone knew what that was and had to laugh. There were lots of people whose movies were worse than theirs.

She'd left Buttah alone because she considered him somewhat vulnerable. His films were notable to Bird only for showing that black men looked better than anybody in good suits and that black women pushed the limits of everything sold by Victoria's Secret. The Buttah man had on a suit straight from his last release. In his movies, black women understood foreplay to involve a well-rehearsed Vegas strip routine in chicken feathers and peach satin, punctuated with a few outtakes from African dance class, where they threw their heads and extensions back as they gyrated, hands on hips, hopping pelvis-forward towards the camera. Then they licked a loud cologne—she knew it was loud—off every inch of the hero's epidermis, and wiped themselves down with ice cubes before being left for some biddy in a better class of clothes. Buttah man still had on all his cologne. The whole bottle.

Bird knew she could never make it as a New Black Woman—all those dance classes, all that practicing of licking motions in the mirror, all that lingerie. She wondered if the filmmakers' dates tried to live up to the celluloid creations. Did they rub themselves with ice cubes in their hotels on Martha's Vineyard? Bird had thrown out all her little lace triangles when she switched to all-cotton underclothes. Cotton underwear is the sure sign of a has-been. She had been feeling very attractive before they sat down. And now she knew the two men were wondering what Charles was doing on the Vineyard having dinner with some has-been, cigarette-smoking, smart-ass bitch from an Italian film course.

By now Charles was sitting so close to Bird at the table that a thigh and an arm swept into her every time he breathed, as if asking her to pay attention. The hairs on his arm brushed against the hairs on her arm every time he turned the stem of his wineglass. She could tell his mind was thinking about the conversation while his body was thinking about sex.

"So, what was it I saw you in?" the Phat man asked. Charles grabbed her leg again while looking around as if to call the waitress.

"I know what it is," Buttah said with finality. "It was that suicide. The woman artist who jumped out the window. Aren't you her sister or something?"

"Something."

The women gasped, the first sounds they'd made all evening. The Phat man contributed, "Oh, shit, yeeaah." They all studied Bird's black eyes and sunken cheeks with renewed interest.

"And then you were in a car wreck—man!"

The two men began to sense that they were at the end of all their possible responses to an awkward impasse and fought over who should pay the check. Then Tiffany and Lateesha got up to go to the ladies' room. Bird laughed to herself because she knew that she and the Baguette were the only subject in the room. Guided unconsciously by the intimacy between Charles and Bird, their touching arms and occasional whispers, by the way her hair kept clinging to the invisible electricity in his shirt, the two men did everything they could to find out what Bird and the Baguette were doing up on the island together. Charles tried to make it sound boring, like they'd bumped into each other at a Laundromat and decided to fold towels together. Phat and Buttah weren't buying it. When the women returned, all four headed out to Buttah's Mercedes. Charles and Bird laughed with relief. They walked out onto the pier.

"I'm definitely not ready for the scene here," she said.

"Yeah, I'm hip. You know, in the middle of that whole conversation, I realized I was bored out of my mind. I talk to guys like that week in and week out." She didn't respond and he went on, "I noticed during dinner that I was drinking and nodding attentively, uh-huh, yeah, the whole bit, and all the while my brain was buried in the thighs sitting next to me. I'm not just saying that because I'm hitting on you, even though obviously—well—but I was shocked because I just don't get my shit mixed up like that."

Charles didn't make her feel ten years younger, he made her feel glad life had made her old enough to dismiss young girls, and to know a man like Charles should be appreciated. If she had to be a leadbelly, at least she'd know what was worth a fight and a blade in the dark, that's what the blues was about—knowing when it was that good to you. She felt bad for his wife. One day he'd be talkin' 'bout "no use to askin' me, babe, 'cause I'll never be back." It was hard for a wife to liberate a man. And to be of lasting interest, men had to be freed from their habits and prejudices, their business and collections, their own creations, and their suits.

Bird took hold of the hair at the back of his neck and he gasped with surprise. She had never touched him like that. She felt a shiver run down his body. Instantly he turned towards her, kissing her very gently. The air blowing round them on the pier was cold. He pulled at her, kissed her face, lips, breathing deeply in her mouth. Breathing hard with his whole body. She had meant to startle him and now he startled her. She pulled his hands down her body.

Then it seemed as though his mind clicked on and he decided he might blow it by being too eager. She could tell he was thinking. When they got back to the inn, he was very polite. He told her he'd let her get some rest, and left the room and closed the door.

4
Friday

When the door closed she was so stunned she thought she'd stop breathing for a second. She just sat there on the edge of her bed with her clothes twisted all around. He blocked out everything else in her dreams all night. In the morning she wondered if she'd been talking or groaning in her sleep. She felt like she'd slept in a sauna.

They had coffee and Bird acted like she'd read a novel in bed all night, almost bored, like he'd done exactly what she meant for him to do by leaving her in a heat. She was downright sunny about trying to forget she'd ever had a carnal thought about the man. In reality, it was as if the lust for Charles had brought Bird's mind from a deep sleep, back into her body. Even the frustration was delicious. She realized she was completely taken in, totally distracted just by being away with this man. Worrying about

Charles's willingness to commit adultery was perfectly, completely entertaining, not a problem. It was none of the terrors she was running from. She knew problems, and this was not a problem—not life or death, entertainment. Being distracted was good. Being the distracted slave of love was not.

They drove to Gay Head, wound their way down the sandy cliff to the beach. When she took out a novel to read, he asked her about the last time she was in love. She said it had been a while. Sometimes she loved to talk about the old days because no one knew anymore what they had been like. On the other hand, it often turned into a performance.

"I used to see a couple of men sort of at the same time."

His eyes widened slightly.

She smiled, and started sounding apologetic. "Well, you could do that then. At least we didn't know any reason we *couldn't* do that. I feel *fortunate* for that time. It was less complicated, believe me."

"I don't see why."

"It's simpler. You know that most of the relationships you're going to get into, ninety percent of them, are not going to work out, right?"

"That's pretty cynical."

"No, no. Most of them are *not* going to work out. That's a fact. It ain't tragic either. Why try to turn every encounter into something it's just never going to be? If one of them is going to work, you'll know to let the others go, but in the meantime—"

"I thought that's how men are supposed to think."

"People have it wrong about men. They like being with one person, they like settling down, they just like sex with different people. They like what they think they can't have."

"Oh, I see." He started laughing. "And women don't like settling down?"

"My theory is that since women like the part of the relationship that comes at the beginning, they should have a couple of partners so they can do more courtship and less housework. Ask your wife sometime if she wouldn't be happier with a couple of

148

guys calling your house asking her out." Bird laughed out loud. She saw him walking into his kitchen at home and asking her that. "Seriously, women like the chase. They love the moment when they know a person is interested. That's their moment, the moment when everything they know how to do gets to be played out."

"And what is that?"

"A power field. That is the moment when they have to make just the right analysis and just the right move."

"Like what?"

"Dropping an embroidered handkerchief, feasting on him with one eye." Bird turned her head and gave a coy, sideways look. "When the guy retrieves it and hands it back to her, she looks bored, thanks him very sweetly, and turns away. Makes him question whether he saw what he saw. Hot then cold. The oldest game in courtship."

"Hmm. I sure know that one."

Bird opened the book again.

"But the one you loved, what was he like?"

"The one I loved? They were *all* like heavy weather." She laughed.

Bird always dubbed them with princely titles because she'd hardly ever met a brother who did not deal with power first and affection second. And they all had the one trait seemingly brought by every African captive forced into slavery and passed on to every Negro in America—a propensity to get royal if the occasion allowed. From the long green Cadillacs to the self-declaring mouth of Muhammad Ali, from James Brown's robe and crown to Marvin Gaye's smoking jackets and white silk bathrobe. All those poems of sphinx builders and Dahomey kings. The Five Royales, the Royaltones, the Marvelettes, the Supremes, and the Imperials; the Queen of Soul, the Duke, the Count, the Duke of Earl, Lady Day, the Prez, Nat "King" Cole, and the King of Soul. The men she knew were no different, every one a chief, and a freak for elegant raiment. She knew more chiefs than Indians.

But their coolness was not just clothes, not just jazz, it was total shutdown, a code of deadly impassivity. They used the same stare-down tactic for white men, black women, and the wild-eyed boys who looked like them and might turn and kill them. It was noble when they gave the stare-down in the face of Mississippi fire-hoses, but it was really scary when they used it to face their families.

"Stay cool, uh, stay calm, and stay collected." Bird remembered chanting it at football games. "Stay cool, uh, stay calm, and stay collected." Coasters, Drifters, Moonglows, Midnighters, Blue Notes. They were, each and every one, extremely unlikely to shower one with presents or to kiss in public. Breaking a crack in the cool meant standing up to a rage that flayed skin from muscle and bone. A man who walked with open palms was rare in Bird's experience. Hands closed around the thumbs. The men she knew didn't regard themselves as difficult, just manly. No more scary than their own fathers, no more remote. Less so, they would say. Their fathers were the most remote beings on the planet, absent without a note or excuse, a lie or a phone message. Arthur "the Chief" Kincaid had been her first instructor: Don't you *ever,* I don't care what went wrong, cry in front of a teacher or a boss. Her brother was next: If they invite you to a fight after school, you better show up, I better *not ever* hear you ran away, and you need to try to kick their ass, but if they kick yours, don't show it. Just get up and walk away. And, don't you ever give a boy a note. Tell him you *like* him? Are you kidding? Years later, a ladies' man gave Bird two tips: God, whatever you do, never send a man a poem, and never tell him you love him—he'll be gone. Bird felt like a walking encyclopedia on cool and the black man's science.

The men who taught her had personal rules and bylaws: "I never give money—to women." And rules for the pack, rules laid down like high school that lived on long after: Once you get a female on the line, don't call for a couple of weeks, make her wonder, make her want you more. Let her hear you were out with somebody else. Tell her she looks good but her ankles are too thin, or too thick. If she shaves tell her your women don't. If she doesn't, tell her your women do. Maybe she ought to do something with her hair. You really cannot be seen with her on a beach unless she loses a few pounds. Or quits smoking. Let her think she's got to be up to the standard of your "other females," the ones who supposedly went before, even if she's the finest thing you ever came near. Call women "females," it keeps them from thinking they're special. Tell her she's not who you thought she was. Make her paranoid. Get rid of her girlfriends 'cause all they do is cause you trouble. Never let a woman embarrass you in a public place. If one of your boys takes your girl, act like you don't care. She was a ho' anyway. If she gives it up, tell her that was nice, real nice, but you want to show her a few things. If she doesn't, say she did. It wasn't that good either. I mean, you know, man, all pussy is good but you know what I mean, no big thing. The boys come first. Black high school in the South was a rough training ground but everybody left there prepared. That's why Bird thought most of the men she'd known never sent cards—because Hallmark didn't print any that said "control" instead of "love." Bird learned to play too.

"They were all difficult," said Bird.

"What does 'difficult' mean?" Charles asked.

"I don't know. One of them, I can definitely tell you, would wait two years to tell you that something you did had gotten on his nerves. He stayed away when I was into him, and called me when I was busy. I don't know what he was like. He was hard to get."

"You mean hard to understand?"

"No, I mean he was hard to get. That's what he was like." She laughed.

He had come into the Crescent one night in a sparkling white shirt that made her realize she had it bad. He took his hat off to her three times before she noticed him. That's what he said. She had tried locking him in her rooms all winter. He always left at sunup. She liked a lot of things about him, the way he looked, the way he talked. But it was the way he kissed her with his head to the side that made her feel she was the sweetheart of rock and roll. That night he came in with another woman. *Let her hear you were out with somebody else.* She was sitting at a table with Alex and Michael, who were tense and trying to drink it away. Bird was fighting with Alex, too. Alex had been trying to bring Bird back from the brink a devastating review had sent her to. She'd been trying to bully Bird into doing a piece for a women's group show. Bird got up and strolled to the bar. That night the man who was hard to get came in with another woman and tipped his black Borsalino at her and smiled so broadly from across the room that everyone looked up. *Never let a man embarrass you in a public place.* She turned away so she could be cool. *If one of your men takes out another woman, act like you don't care.*

Blades was tall and wiry with a headful of dreadlocks that could not be contained or even obscured by an Italian fedora. He almost always wore a big sweater and dark jeans under his forties overcoats and tuxedo scarves. She sank as she cruised his beautiful handmade white shirt. Did he dress for this biddy too? He came over and asked her how she was. She said fine, blankly, as she checked the woman seated at a table. *Never let a man embarrass you in public.* Blades went back to his seat.

Lanka, a piano player, was standing nearby studying the band, particularly the pianist. Lanka was always the most splendidly dressed man in the room. He talked out of the side of his mouth so no one would hear, which made anyone he talked to feel like a confidante. Lanka was rough to hang with because he was easily bored. And rough to hang with because hardly anyone over twenty-nine could hang out as long as Lanka. Those who'd tried were usually humbled by seven or eight A.M., as Bird was when this man nearly twenty years older dropped her at her door and blithely strolled off for a morning swim. He did the clubs till they closed, then the after-hours bars, then breakfast and the baths. He never went to bed till noon the next day. Then he got up, cleaned the house, practiced for five hours, got dressed, and did it all over again. If it was music, he danced to it. If it wasn't, he talked about it bad. The only thing that truly kept Lanka's attention and affection was masterful improvisation. If your number lacked variations, it was soon up.

"People repeat on you," he'd say. He said that once he turned forty he could see the wrong ones coming his way before they rounded the corner.

Lanka turned to her. "La Serena, how are you?"

She made a "so-so" face.

Lanka muttered, "And who, my dear, is *that?*"

"Lanka," she muttered back at him, "there is no one but you."

"I know. I just wondered who the man was, making you look grim."

"The Sultan of Evasion."

Lanka laughed loudly. Lanka studied him with an approving raised eyebrow. "But he came in with another woman, my dear."

"Thanks for reminding me."

"I'm sure you'll handle it." Lanka turned back to the music.

Blades sauntered down the aisle by the bar and sat with his shirt leaning so close that his cologne opened her nose and singed her eyes. Without taking a breath, Bird broke a rule and said right into his ear, "I'm thinking maybe you didn't know I gave you my heart too." Said it with a bored sound, like baby, you're fine but your ankles are kinda thin.

He ignored what she said. *Act like you don't care.* He brought his lips near her eyes. *Hot.* "There's a lot about me you don't know." *Then cold.*

"Too much," she said, lowering her voice. *Hot.* "As Chaka Khan says, 'What you hold against me is what I miss.' "

Blades laughed, too heartily for Bird.

"Here, my dear." Lanka handed over a Rémy straight up with a soda back and disappeared.

"You ignored me when I came in. I tipped my hat to you three times and you left me standing there looking stupid."

Then cold. "All I could see was your woman. Do it again."

He obliged.

She got ready to do something really dumb. "Look, I wish we could—"

Alex burst in on them with a drunken stage whisper in Bird's ear. "I've decided I love you, even though I'm not sure you love me." The words spit.

Never let a woman embarrass you in a public place. Bird knew it was over. *Girlfriends cause trouble.* The white shirt moved out of Bird's line of vision.

Alex's eyes watered. Bird was afraid she'd get louder. Alex didn't know Blades had been coming to Bird's apartment all winter, singing in her ear, kissing with his head to one side. But she could spot the intimacy blindfolded. Bird could see her thinking.

Bird watched Blades put a coat over his white shirt and gather up his date. When the idea of what was going on was fully formed in Alex's mind and she'd realized that at the moment she was irrelevant to Bird, she too decided to leave. Bird's eyes watched Alex walk away while the rest of her was already in a cab headed uptown. The Sultan of Evasion had his rules. Bird didn't hear from him for a year.

"Why didn't it work?"

"Can't say that anybody ever told me. I mean sometimes you can be deeply in love with someone and nothing comes of it, you never even do a thing about it, you know?"

The Sultan of Evasion was a winter. The Prince of the Faithful was the most difficult of all, six years' worth of difficult. Bird was a little like Lanka about getting bored, and the most unboring thing in Bird's world was frustration, being strung out on the line, and the man of six years was prince of frustraters. She had never had an affair with him at all in the normal sense. Their separation was not of the body, nor was their togetherness. His body got her in her sleep. His mind had her the rest of the time. She suffered enormously whenever he abandoned her, mourned every day of separation from him, and in return, since she was no longer a girl and knew how to do it, she punished him. She dogged him and let him suffer. And he was faithful to her and mourned and was not bored. He had always left her free—no reason not to love the one you're with. Bird laughed to herself and looked Charles straight in the eyes.

"You know it's like Mike Tyson says, everybody has a plan till they get hit," she said. He smiled sadly. She liked the Baguette's eyes. "Don't you want to get wet?" He didn't answer.

It was Charles's eyes and collarbone or maybe the crinkles of his hair that interested her. She thought of slowly moving up his body, pondering each of his seven chakras. Of course he wasn't weird enough to know he had any chakras. However, if she told him his body had seven little temples running straight up from his groin, he'd be all ears. If she told him she had to lick every one of those seven little temples, he wouldn't know she was pulling his leg, but he'd be all ears, all legs, all temples. And still he'd want to know that she was interested in his mind. He was vain about his mind. But she took for granted that she could always touch that. He gave a tender look that asked what she was doing with him. He looked like the adoring man who expected to be refused. What was she doing? She got up and took off her shorts, briefly noticing on her legs the long islands and inlets of whitened flesh that would quickly freckle, then burn. She put some heavy-duty cream on her upper legs and arms where the disease made her vulnerable to the sun, and didn't bother with the rest. She'd always been free to run all summer without a thing on her skin, until she got the turning-white thing—that is, until the whole neighborhood started to go. She didn't look at Charles again, acknowledging that deep inside she felt foolish.

The cold water shot the blood to her head, and tightened the skin on her scalp so suddenly and completely it gave her a headache. She felt like she'd jumped headfirst out of a dusty attic window into an icy waterfall. She popped up gasping, chest heaving. The waves kept coming and she stumbled this way and that. It was as if her eyes and skin had never before burned from harsh salt water. As if waves had never pounded against the small of her back, never touched her before, as if it were the first time she'd known an ocean to be alive. She totally immersed herself—it was the only way.

Bird knew Charles was innocently trying to help and maybe figure her out. She and her friends had always thought they were so bad because they'd been through so much shit, "the struggle" and all—they could tell you about it. But now it seemed as if they were just flamboyant, damaged creatures with hungry spirits. She thought about all the battles she routinely had on her job with younger reporters who called her an "embittered passé relic of the sixties." She thought they were spineless little revisionists who had no convictions of their own. Everyone in her crew was always in one battle or another. They probably needed someone to take care of them at this point. Of course, no one could. They were always in too deep.

Bird had acted as if she would tell Charles anything he wanted to know, but she had left out the most important parts. By answering him each time very specifically what he'd asked, she had told him about the white man who'd tried to rape her in college, about watching some of her friends get beaten by New York City detectives during protests in '68. She'd mentioned people now dead who had taught her how to talk, how to dance; people now dead who'd taught her how to dress; people she'd put on planes for home or in the hospital when they were splintering into jabbering or silent pieces. When he brought up the marches she said she didn't like huge crowds because horses had once stamped through her right arm and leg at a rally. She had only given up snatches of whole years that made her quixotic, emphatic, extreme, a hundred percent there when she was there and a hundred percent gone when she was gone.

Bird emerged from the water shivering, and set off at a trot hoping the air would dry her quickly. She didn't want to look back at the Baguette sitting on the beach waiting for her to return. She wanted to enjoy the sensation of being away from everyone: the man who had smashed her head into the elevator floor, the X-ray machines, the medical labs that couldn't find her blood tests, her bills, the cops waiting for her to come look at sex offenders. She wanted to run from the cluttered, scrambled dustbin of all the old shit she lived with buried in that apartment. She wanted to get away from the soundtrack: Tammy Bakker and Gary Hart, the earthquake in L.A., Imelda

Marcos, Tawana Brawley, the uncounted maimed of Chernobyl, the Crips and the Bloods, and the men running for mayor, all mouths spraying barren language into her earphones. She wondered if there couldn't be an electronic harmattan, a dust storm that could blow a clean silence through the airwaves now and again.

She wanted to stay running cold on a beach away from the years cluttered into one long continuous day-to-night, night-to-day opening and closing of windows, curtains, blinds, turning on fans for air, putting on the news reports, entombing herself under covers, in layers of sweatshirts on top of T-shirts, socks, jeans, sometimes wearing the same clothes all weekend and never combing her hair, sometimes crawling in the bed with all the clothes and books and Alex's dolls and bathrobe and God knows, anything to hold on to. And Charles was very nicely trying to root around in the past, where she'd stopped going years ago. She didn't like it because when he asked about it and she answered, it sounded tragic to her and yet she didn't ever remember feeling tragic about any of it really, not then, not till she'd disappeared behind the walls of her place after giving up trying to be even a part-time painter.

She knew one vicious review of a small show downtown by a critic trying to make a name for himself—Francis Burton—was one reason she was a full-time top-of-the-line radio engineer, a woman who could sit with murderers but who'd lost her nerve to be an artist. Once she couldn't paint anymore, she'd "lost access to the world," as she called it. She couldn't live in the light. She couldn't see where she had the right to taste fully anymore because she couldn't savor those tastes, or thoughts even, couldn't love tastes and thoughts again and again as she remade them in her work. A person has to know she has a right. Frank Burton made her question her right to make something of the world in her head. And in a weird way, it was as if it had happened to everyone, not just her.

People seemed to hide out inside disasters. They were taken by surprise like Bird when an explosion blew up a couple hundred.Marines in Beirut. Or they were ambushed by the secret untelevised invasion of a little island named Grenada. When the TV anchors couldn't get in there, nobody could leave their sets. In Bird's mind, that's how it started. Some went inside and stayed through the Iran-Contra hearings, studying Poindexter, North, McFarlane, and Secord. And the stock market crash didn't help. Bird's little pension, which had amazed her with its seventeen percent fattening every month, dried up. They were desperate for news to go with the pictures from Tienanmen Square, thirteen hours ahead of New York time, and she'd worked day and night making tape from news that came over a fax machine they'd just installed at the job. Regular programming was now seemingly permanently interrupted. It made some people stop getting the paper. It made some people crazy. Lack of sleep nearly took Bird over the brink.

Bird was up all night when the ayatollah called for the death of Salman Rushdie. She was going through her life but she lived inside the disaster. By then there were so many people like Bird sitting up all night worrying about what was going on in the world, even though they had to go to work, that Ted Koppel had a new job. She sat up to hear if Rushdie would tell Ted how many artists were in danger all over the world. He tried to explain his book, which Ted probably hadn't read and simply let someone brief him on, and which Bird wasn't reading for watching Ted. It was during the spring, not long before Alex died, that Bird took to calling late-night news shows and correcting facts they had wrong, racist views they were passing along, and information left out. She called Ted to tell him lots of governments were hunting, maiming, killing writers. She gave some kindly voice on the phone the names of famous South American and African novelists she'd been reading who were all in exile. She knew she'd lost it when she called a local station to say it almost made her throw up to hear one of the newscasters say someone caught in a fire had been "burnt to a crisp." She worked at a news station; she knew they weren't going to pass it on. But she knew she wasn't alone.

When the Exxon *Valdez* ran aground in Alaska, a woman in Bird's office came around begging for dollars to help her go there to clean up animals. Bird gave her ten dollars and asked if she'd be back. She went to wipe the muck off animals whose skin couldn't breathe, because that particular event had crushed her idea of the world. Bird could dig it, sort of. Bird wished the woman had lost it like that when crack hit the streets of New York. Wished she had wanted to run out and wipe the muck off children. Bird was self-righteous but she didn't do that either. When the National Guard swooped down on black college kids in Virginia Beach, her nephew was there and she freaked out and started calling the city council to find out why folks in the Quarter couldn't get cable TV. She had already started waiting to see how Noriega would go down, was ready to sit up for the late news after the polls closed to find out if David Dinkins could beat Ed Koch.

She never even saw the gang anymore. The Crescent closed and everybody went home. Alonso Jackson Essex, bless his heart, had found a school that would let him influence young minds. Reenie stayed out there doing performance work but she wasn't like Reenie anymore. One night during intermission in a performance with Bird and Alex, Reenie had a miscarriage in the trash can in the dressing room. She couldn't get to the bathroom. And Bird was frozen in place, and the stage manager got sick, and Alex had to shake Bird, and shake her again, to make her go on. She couldn't be like the old Reenie anymore because she was going to keep the next baby.

Not like Reenie at the eclipse in 1970, stoned out of her mind, wandering around Central Park with a camera, snapping the children and balloons, witch covens dancing in circles on the Great Lawn, hippies staring at the blackening skyline of New York City. Reenie drinking champagne at the fountain with Michael and Bird and Lanka, making plans to run away, see California by car. Reenie, who could party in any language. Reenie, who passed up going to Woodstock because she already had a party to go to. Reenie, who slinked through the dank crowds at the Fillmore East in a haze of smoke to stand up under the four-teen-foot walls of speakers that blew out your ears on the first chord, slinking down front to give Jimi Hendrix a serious appraisal. Reenie, who said she didn't see how he could be so hung up on white girls when he could have her, well, once at least. Reenie, who knew talent when she saw it. Reenie, who'd been hauled half-dead to the hospital twice for homemade abor-tions and lived to laugh about her fear of getting arrested in an emergency room somewhere in New Jersey. Reenie, who carried a tambourine in her purse.

Frank Burton had made Bird too scared to go on painting but something else had gotten to Michael. Whatever happened to Michael? They never talked again about what a lady's man he thought he was until he moved in with Paul the hairdresser extraordinaire, who did do's for the stars and hurt Michael's ego by making women more frequently than meals. Was Michael still to be found backstage at all the jazz sets in an aqua silk jacket sampling the dope? Maybe he was still there and just never men-tioned it. Michael, an expert on cognacs, champagnes, and beer, sipping and sampling, doing the galleries on Saturdays.

She saw herself for a second, caught herself dancing at the Corso in the seventies with a slim Latin man in a tuxedo shirt, his hair combed back and glistening. She could see his left hand holding her right hand. Their palms were damp from the sud-den intimacy of wanting each other. She could see a cuff link made out of a shiny dime. A dime from the forties. She had her left hand on his right shoulder. She could see a diamond stud in his right ear. His arm was around her waist, his eyes lowered, and his mouth was parted slightly, about to whisper something, a sweet warm breath brushed her right eye, her right cheek, her right ear. She didn't recall his name.

"What about Randall, Alex?" Bird screamed out at the ocean. "What am I going to do about Randall?" She meant it to sound angry but an impulse pulled her back to the water and not thinking, not even feeling her own aches anymore, she ventured back in. The water was heavy, holding back her calves as she pushed against it. Finally she fell backwards laughing. A wave crashed on top of her and plunged her headfirst towards the bottom. Bird's heart raced and she forced her feet down, finding the velvety bottom, and yanked her body upward. But the next wave socked her and she tumbled onto an unseen rock. Her arm scraped along the sharp edges and her shin scraped the rock's side. She forced herself up, frightened, and flashing on Dr. Rousse's warning about rough waves or rough hugs, or whatever it was she was not supposed to do to her mouth. This fit the list. She coughed and spat as she recovered, then caught her breath and laughed. Randall had driven her into the brine, she thought. He was too devilish a character to yell about. She felt really good. She tried to float and yelled out at Alex.

"Who's going to keep Randall alive, Alex?" She lowered her voice and became confidential, as if the ether held ears that should not hear. "Who am I going to laugh with about Randall telling us all those lies and outrageous stories? We believed him, didn't we? Every time. Well, the stories were so good. God. You thought you were extraordinary, I thought I was extraordinary, shit, everybody we knew thought they were extraordinary, but Randall really was."

Randall was the high-water mark to Bird and Alex against which they measured anybody who tried to say they'd "been there" or "done that." Randall had. Randall, the producer extraordinaire, had been everyone's something—stage manager, mentor, best friend, organizer, club member, fund-raiser, or good-time guide. He could be found backstage at the Met with LaBelle in silver, or backstage at the Met with Jessye Norman in black and white. Randall asking the next one he had his eye on, "Do you want fame, power, or money? Choose one. It's hard to get all three." Randall had picked fame and then, in the end, he kept saying maybe he should have gone for money. "Money helps," he said. Randall last year receiving a compliment on his outfit of all-black Yamamoto: "Yes, isn't it flawless?"

Randall, backstage with Stevie Wonder: "Yes, I'll give him your lyrics. You need to have them printed in braille, go to the

Lighthouse, they'll do it for you. Babe, I just have to tell you, though, Stevie don't need a thing." Randall, backstage on Broadway: "He's stunning but he needs to come live with me for a year. I'll make him a real star." And: "He needs to get rid of that wife. She's holding him back." Randall, backstage at the Rainbow Room, telling Bird: "Honey, marrying for money is not all you may think it is." As if he had. As if she could. Always as if Bird could. Always as if he already had. Randall, backstage in Harlem, 4:00 A.M., eating grits and chicken black and orange with pepper and hot sauce. Randall with four biscuits slathered in butter.

Everyone at the Ritz, young, chic, sexy, and on the prowl, chanting with Dr. Buzzard and the Savannah Band: "They're all the same, the sluts and the saints." Randall, backstage: "He needs to get rid of that wife. She's holding him back." He said it a lot. Randall, backstage at the party for Sly and the Family Stone, asking if she wanted to come in. Backstage with Aretha: "I've always wanted to see her wig collection." Backstage with friends at Buckingham Palace in 1960 for Princess Margaret's wedding, saying it was a very nice service, saying the Earl of Snowden used to hang out with "us" on the Lower East Side. In the eighties Randall laughed as he said he'd had affairs with the Princess, the Dalai Lama, and Lyndon Baines Johnson. Adding the Dalai was Randall's way of staying current. Always Negroes doing fabulous, unheard-of things and always with style, even if the minks and gloves were borrowed.

Bird lifted her legs slowly, trying to walk out, standing up against the ocean that shoved her heavily forward and dragged the sand out from under her feet. She started feeling cold again. Her ankle and chin were bleeding slightly, her hand gushing. She sat at the edge of the water, washing the cuts.

Randall was backstage at *The Blacks,* backstage with Marvin Gaye, at Ali-Liston, Ali-Frazier, Ali-Foreman, all of them. Randall, backstage talking about love, and how he wasn't sure he'd ever been in love. Backstage at the Black Power convention in Gary, in dashiki and sandals. Backstage at the Democratic convention, knowing all the deals, knowing who flew on the private planes. Randall, who didn't want a piece of any deal. Randall, backstage at the mayor's office, shoes off, sitting lotus on the couch: "I can pull it together for you. We'll do a nice gala. It will be flawless." Bird learned by watching Randall backstage at Carnegie Hall, holding women at bay for a matinee idol he swore was really gay. Randall whispered that everyone she'd ever heard of in her life was really gay, didn't she know? "Come see me, dear, I'm interested in your career. Next opening I ought to give you a party. I want to give the party."

He left Bird in a greenroom at Lincoln Center, sitting speechless in iridescent cowboy boots, sparkling eyes, sparkling shirt, and sparkling scarf next to Melvin Van Peebles, while Al Green took off his all-white clothes soaked through with sweat and tears. Randall whispered to her about what to wear, what to ask for from a man desperate with love, where to eat if she was having an affair with a married man, a celebrity or politician, or anyone else she didn't want people to see. That's how Bird knew to make a man sit on his hands for months at a time. That was why she had the patience. That was why she told a man who was hard to get that she loved him only when he wouldn't believe it anyway—in a public place with a lot of noise and a lot of alcohol. With most of them, she wasn't going to need half of what Randall had taught her.

Before life in the orbit of Randall, the glam guru, she'd met Miles Davis and he'd scared her to death and introduced her to his hairdresser as a whore he'd picked up on the streets of San Francisco. But she'd learned what stupid, obscene things men said at gigs and a year later when Miles leaned over to her at a bar and asked if they had ever fucked. She stared into his giant black shades and told him she didn't recall. She never sang "Lean on Me" to men like him who said bitches were never there when you needed them. He said he wanted to fuck her brain. Definitely not your usual line. When he pushed her against a wall, she pushed him away. His music had been in her body for years. She told him he'd done that years ago, and she'd been meaning to thank him for it, and walked away. And she didn't lie one bit.

A girl who has practiced on Miles Davis would be waiting for someone supremely difficult to call. She was just a kid when she got her own copy of "Someday My Prince Will Come," and Miles played the shit out of it.

Bird was feeling good in her muscles, good in her skin, her hair, possibly even beautiful, which only salt water and sex made her feel. But her arm was still bleeding like crazy—she'd have to go back, rinsing the blood from her hand as she went.

She remembered the rest. Randall, backstage in his own life, listening to Aretha, bundled up in blankets, weighing ninety-eight pounds, on liquid morphine, incontinent, in pain down to his bones, smiling, watching the sunrise, dreaming about Aretha's voice carrying him to Paris or Barbados for one last fling. Thinking too about Donny Hathaway singing, *Yes, thank you, yes, thank you, Master, for my soul*. They played it at the funeral. Randall, asking in a whisper, with elegance and dignity still intact in his hospital bed, what was the telephone, and how did it work.

If Randall missed an event in the sixties, seventies, or eighties, it was because it wasn't sold out. Randall only went when it was hard to get in. Randall backstage at Newport: "They had a better night about twenty years ago." Bird smiled back at the ocean blowing spray towards her face. She started back, noticing her footprints behind her, sometimes heavy, sometimes light, some-times leaving blood in the sand. She'd once told Randall how Frank Burton had stopped her from painting, and he'd laughed. "He ain't never had a better night twenty years ago."

"We did have fun, didn't we?" Bird said to Alex, to Randall, to no one. "I'd forgotten that." Bird knew Randall would tell her that if Frank Burton was going to do her any more harm, she should go ahead and fuck him up. She dipped her hand in the water and watched the blood run thin across her skin. She knew she was going to do what Randall would've said. She would fuck him up.

Frank Burton was the reason she'd gotten her head busted, she was sure. She couldn't prove it, but she also couldn't go home and lose herself in the television news. This was her own disaster. She would fix it so he had to show himself. Bird walked back to the blanket. She looked pretty cold. She was laughing. "That was ridiculous. You should go in there. You won't remember your own name when that water hits you."

"You want that massage I promised you?"

"Sure. I cut my hand, though. I need to get some kind of bandage."

"Let's see it. I probably have something in the car. Hot bath before the massage?"

"Sounds good."

She fell asleep stretched across the bed, bandages on her ankle, knee, and hand, like a kid in from a day at the park. Her body was warm and damp in a kimono, and her hair was wrapped up wet in a towel. He put his arm around her, cradled her head in his arm, and let her sleep. He wanted to wake her. He wanted to talk to her. He kissed her face. Her voice said "uh-huh" in agreement somewhere down in her throat. She curled up. He let her sleep.

In her dream he was talking and talking in her ear, his voice deep and soothing. He was telling her how he would pay attention to every move she made. In the dream she no longer lived in the Quarter and there was no screaming. It was very quiet. Just his voice in her ear. The shadow man in the hallway backed off.

5

Saturday

Bird told Charles about the tapes. She told him she was supposed to watch them with Bernard, and Charles said he wanted to help. She didn't think it was a bad idea. When they entered the apartment, Bird put on a light and headed for the kitchen to check the answering machine. No blinking red light. She was pleased. John Coltrane music was rolling in even with the window closed. Cross was on his fire escape playing his box so loud that it was as if he hoped to provide the neighborhood with some ecstasy by giving them "My Favorite Things." He seemed to be hauling in clothes off the line. She could hear the squeal of the pulley when Trane took a breath. Clothes were inching their way towards the building.

Charles wondered what she was looking at out the back window. Trane didn't send him and he wasn't used to neighbors like Cross who shared their passions with several hundred people at a time. Charles hadn't been cut up in the Korean War, didn't fight in the street like Cross had till he got hit so bad he lost part of his skull and had to have a plate put in. Charles didn't wait for the end of the month to drink his gin and he wouldn't drink it straight. Bird hadn't done any of those things either but she loved Cross's music and she liked her liquor straight. And she knew Cross, knew he was cool.

Bird immediately started rattling pots and pans in the kitchen. She made Charles some chicken and dumplings, something she thought he might never have had in his life, in spite of being black. To Bird, the new black people were like that. She never had any way of knowing if they'd chomped their way through a chitling or not. Not that she would miss chitlings if they became extinct. For Bird, it was a cultural issue. Pronto, Essex was on the phone.

"Darling, that is perfect. You ran *off* with the Baguette. Hmmm. He's so beautiful. And were you very naughty with him? I hope so."

"Not very. I really can't talk about it right now, babe."

"Oh! What was wrong? Didn't you like him after all? Of course, it's none of my business. But he adores you, you know."

"When'd you get that idea? Just now?"

"Oh, no. I could see by how he's lookin' at you. It's there."

"Yeah? When?"

"All the time. That's why I don't flirt with him." Essex flirted with everyone.

"Well, thank God for small favors."

Essex laughed a husky laugh. He was forty and handsome and did almost nothing but work, so he no longer studied flirting as hard as when he was young and cute and wild. People fell for the mature Essex more often than the former cute one, men and women, although mostly younger men and older women. "We have to expect this kind of thing now that we're forty, my dear. We're going to have a lot of younger lovers, you know. They look around at the people they know and they look at us, and they know that we're fabulous."

"I'm not forty yet, babe."

"*So* sorry, Miss Thing. Well, I am and I am in my *prime.*"

"And I bet you let them all get close enough to taste too."

"I do the best I can. The dolls don't look at me at the dance halls anymore. I look at them."

"Alonso, you're too modest."

"Well, a little." He laughed heartily.

When she hung up, Bird stepped into the living room to offer Charles a drink. She noticed the tapes were strewn all over the floor. Charles was sitting in the middle of them all, looking at the boxes. Bird lost her cool.

"Why'd you do that? Oh, God. I don't believe this!"

"Do what?"

"This! Bernard and I methodically organized those fucking tapes! Man!"

"Whoa. Hold it, Bird. They were like this. I was getting ready to try to sort them for you. They were all over the floor like this. I haven't moved one."

Bird was flabbergasted. "That's not possible. I walked right through here."

"The shades were drawn."

Bird studied the room.

"Some of them are out of the boxes, like somebody's been looking at them," Charles said.

"Yes. Probably so."

"What does that mean?"

"It means that's probably what happened. Somebody was looking at them."

"Well, we should call the cops."

"What for? Does this place look like there was a break-in? They'll just make a note and leave."

"We want them to make a note."

Bird walked over to the door to Alex's apartment and studied the lock as if it could give a clue.

"Change the locks," Swami Viswamitra said.

"I did."

"What if nothing's missing? We tell the cops a burglar came in, we don't know how, and he didn't take anything. They'll say I forgot to clean up. No." She thought for a second, and looked around for the dictionary. "What needs to happen is I need to see the super." A calm came over her. The same calm she had felt on the beach. She handed him the dictionary. "The tapes are in a sequence matching the Arabic alphabet. If you put them in order, we can see if anything is missing. I'll be right back."

"You're saying someone was in here leisurely watching video-cassettes, like they knew you wouldn't be here, and watched tapes and maybe took some particular tapes?"

"I didn't say any of that, but yeah."

"And who would that be?"

"At this point, there's only two people with anything at stake. Me and him. I knew he wouldn't leave it alone. He's guilty and he can't leave it alone."

"Burton, I take it?"

"How he's looking to get rid of his guilt in this apartment, I don't know."

"What does that mean?"

"I don't know. But I am going to think of something before he does whatever he does next." Bird walked out the door and pushed the button for the elevator. She did not know what she was going to do, but she was sure she wasn't going to tell Charles. And she would not ask for his help. The only thing she could figure out about the situation was that if Burton knew somehow that she was away for the weekend, he might come back that night—it was Saturday and she was back early. Unless he was permanently camped outside her door somewhere and knew all her comings and goings. If he was camped nearby she knew one person who would know. When Bird got down to the first floor she detoured to the front door.

"How y' doin', Bird? You feelin' better? Healing up?" Romeo asked.

"Yeah, I'm doing great, great. How 'bout you? I was wondering, did you see the UPS come yesterday? I was kind of expecting a package. I was away overnight."

"Yeah. Seem like you left Thursday, wadn't it? Nope. I mean the guy came on the block, but he didn't stop here."

"The guy?"

"Yeah. The UPS guy."

"Right. Maybe you know the guy who used to live upstairs?" Romeo nodded. "Sure, I know him."

"He wasn't by here, was he?"

"Not that I saw. But he has been here. Was here like last week, said he was just looking for his mail."

"Mail?"

"Said he didn't find it."

Bird rang the super's bell. Joey was watching a game. The TV was loud.

"C'mon in! How are you feeling?"

"Cool, I'm okay."

"Sit down. It's the play-offs, you know."

"Oh yeah. I forgot it's play-off time. Look, I won't keep you, I just wanted to ask you about the lock."

"Lock's not workin'?"

"Yeah, no. It's working. But you know the one you changed? Between the apartments?"

"Yeah."

"You changed it right, you know, when I asked you to, after the——"

"Yeah, of course. Just like you asked. The holes where the screws go were just about worn out, 'cause you know I changed it before, for the man. If it's loose I could move it."

"Yeah, good. You know, I looked at it," Bird said, "and it

doesn't really look like a new lock. Did you put a new lock on there?"

Joey's face flushed. "Well, miss, I got so many locks round here. I hate to spend the money if it's no need."

"Where did you get the lock you put on there?"

Joey smelled trouble for himself but he didn't know why. "I put the old one back that you had before. You know I knew it would be the perfect fit. And it was like new. I found it with one key in it right in under the sink in the apartment, right where I had told Miss Alex it was when I took it off. You know, I figured it was her lock. So I left it with her. And when I put it back on, I gave you the one key."

Bird sighed. "Joey, you have any idea where the other key might be?"

"Probably still on Miss Alex's key ring. Somethin' wrong?"

"No, Joey, it's okay. You know I just get nervous."

"If it bothers you, I'll go get another lock and put it on for you. I can buy one."

Bird thought for a second; Joey turned back towards the TV.

"That might be a plan. Tell you what, Joey, I'll see if I can find that other key first. I'll come back tomorrow."

"Okay, miss. But tomorrow's Sunday, I won't be able to buy the lock till Monday morning. But I'll do it then, no problem."

Bird agreed. Monday was good. That gave her a day, she thought. She'd get everything done by then. She headed back upstairs.

It was late afternoon and as far as she knew, Charles had not yet called home to say he was back in town. She wondered about that. Bird hoped none of the tapes was missing. It occurred to her that until Bernard came and explained the Arabic alphabet, the tapes had been scattered all over the floor. If someone had been there and looked over them before, she wouldn't have noticed. She would have to watch them all to figure out what he could be looking for. It would have to be in the private reels, the ones with the changed names. But what? If Alex had had the video recorder on the night of her death, he would have known to take the tape then. It had to be something less obvious than that.

When she put her key in the front door and opened it, two cops were standing there, smirking, listening to Charles. Bird was shocked. They must have driven up right after she left the front stoop. She tried not to look surprised. Charles was explaining that yes, both of them had cleaned up the tapes, put them in boxes, and on and on. Obviously the cops had asked if maybe he'd forgotten to clean up.

"Is this your apartment?" one asked her.

"Yes."

"Any idea how this supposed burglar got in?"

"Yes. That door." She pointed to the door to Alex's place.

"Doesn't look forced."

"The lock is loose." She didn't mention that someone had a key. But she didn't lie either. "You could just unscrew it at this point."

"Well, better get it fixed. This doesn't look serious. Your friend says nothing's missing."

"That's a relief." She sounded cheerful. "I just saw the super. He's going to change the lock."

The cops were bored and nodded approvingly. "Good then. Well, we've made a note of it. But next time, try not to call 911 except for an emergency." He handed Charles a card with the precinct number. "We'll be going now." They walked past Bird and left without waiting for her to open the door. She stood there surveying her apartment and Charles, waiting for the elevator door to fetch the cops. When she heard the elevator door close she said, "Why was that necessary?"

"Your safety. You don't have all the answers, you know. This is serious business."

"You don't know those guys. They think that in this quarter of town we cause all our own problems. We jump out of our own windows, beat each other regularly—you name it, we're supposed to be doing it. Clearly you live in a better part of town."

"Maybe you should think about doing the same if you're so upset with the public servants up here."

"You're right. Clearly, I should move."

"It would take care of a lot of your problems. I don't really care if you didn't want to call the cops, you know. *I* feel better. I feel safer, okay? Shit, it looks like I'm the guard dog at this point."

"Nobody asked you to be the guard dog."

"Okay. I'm sorry. I didn't mean that. Seriously, though, all I'm saying is that your biggest problem is really just a real estate problem."

Bird didn't answer. She was too furious.

She went into Alex's apartment and looked for the keys on the dead woman's dresser and in the top drawer. She had never seen them anywhere but on the dining table or on the dresser. She looked on the shelves. Carlota had taken Alex's purse. Maybe they were in there. She turned the lights off and went back to her apartment without saying what she'd been looking for.

Charles wanted to know what was in the dumplings. He liked them—he just wanted to know what they were. Bird smiled to herself, thinking there was still hope. Charles had gone through the list using the alphabet and all the tapes were still there. Charles said he couldn't figure out if Burton was watching them systematically at all, but he had made a list of every tape that was out of its box or pulled from a stack. He said they might as well skip those, since the mere fact that Burton had left them meant they probably weren't important. He further suggested that they start with later tapes, the ones closer to the time of her death, and then go back.

[P.R.—NUN, 1989, Entry #1]

Alex is in her apartment. It's night and only a kitchen light is on at the back. The lights of apartment buildings across the street are coming through the windows behind her. Dishes, wine bottles, and glasses are on the table at the rear. She sits in a chair in a T-shirt. She looks wasted.

"Frank went out with some friends, drinking I guess." Alex sounds loaded,

depressed. *"I looked at my work recently and felt alienated from it. That was interesting in itself. It was like I had nothing to do with it and it was just there. Well, it's all tied to the natural world too much, not to the natural world but representation, it's too tied to representation, the density of objects in space. Who cares? Frank's friends were saying just keep going the way I'm going. He agrees with them when they're around, but when he's drunk, he doesn't mind telling me my work is shit. He doesn't say it's shit. He says, 'Not new.' Sometimes I say, man, what is this,* Gaslight? *So anyway, tonight his friends are going on about 'lots of these jerks who're so much in demand now are getting back into representation.' But those guys are not doing anything like what I'm doing. What are they talking about anyway? And what do I care what the other artists are doing?*

"They never say it, but they are only talking about white people, what white people are doing. None of these art guys ever just happen to mention what some artist of color might be doing. If we're working in a new area, the area doesn't exist, or it's not real terrain. If one of us does something new, we die in obscurity. If we don't die in obscurity, we were doing something somebody else did first. Did you ever hear a white artist admit they got something from a black artist? Who am I asking? Yeah, I know the Beatles were turned on by Chuck Berry.

"They go on about how Schnabel and the neo-Expressionists are dead. Everybody's passé, except the primitives—those kids from the South Bronx, that's what they call them. They seem to forget that at first they called me one of those kids from the Bronx. They talk down to me. I guess they figure Frank's the big shot, I'm just some little whore he's taken up with who does art. They like to make remarks that I'm so different from the other women he's been with. Other women he's been with, hah. What do they know? They're thinking about the women coming on to him in art bars and if I wasn't different from them, I'd kill myself. Sad. If you lined them all up against a wall you couldn't find one you'd want to look at twice. We used to call them 'star-fuckers.' But Frank really isn't an art star, and he ain't young no more, so he doesn't get the first-rate art-star-fuckers. He gets the real dumb ones and the ones who buy the drinks.

"They tell me just to take whatever advice he gives me. 'Frank knows what's happening, Frank knows who's moving what.' Not to worry. If I want to stay alive, I should probably take their advice and do what the white guys do." She pauses, looks blank. *"Fuck them anyway."*

Bird paused the tape. " 'If I want to stay alive'?"

"Pretty creepy, but, you know, we're reading into it. I mean, it does sound like she means staying alive as an artist, you know, making a living at it."

"Yeah. I guess. She never used expressions like that—'if I want to stay alive,' I mean."

"Well, if you take it literally, it's like saying she thought some-body would kill her for doing it her way."

"You're right. He is an ass but that's not the kind of ass he is. He's a jealous ass." Bird pushed play.

"I find myself looking at pattern again. Am I just doing the patterns turning up from nature? But pattern feels like a phase. I don't know what I'm doing with it. Rep-etition is stable, symmetry is stable. I used to think I was just using the symmetry that is there, but of course I'm imposing it." Alex reaches for something, a glass, gets up and walks back to the table and pours from a wine bottle. She is wearing only under-wear with the T-shirt. She looks incredibly small crossing the room, her bare feet tiny. Returns to her seat, takes a sip, returns her eyes to the camera.

"The work doesn't breathe anymore. If you reduce nature to pattern you lose the breath. I know I used to be real concerned with breath, and the coming and going, breathing in and breathing out. I've lost that." She pauses. Looks at the camera as if to say "Remember this face." Pause. "Frank's an asshole, along with his asshole friends. That's for the record." Alex presses the remote. Static.

Charles raised his eyebrows. "Feel like we missed something?"

Tears streamed down Bird's face. She pressed the stop button and looked at him. "Yeah, that looks like she was depressed, could've been suicidal. That's what the cops saw."

"That's what I saw," Charles said.

"Yeah, but you'd have to take her a lot farther down that road to get her to want to give up. She's not like me." As soon as she said that, she stopped. *Shit, he did get me to stop. It was easy. Maybe he was trying to discourage her. And yes, she was a lot tougher. It would take years.* All Bird said out loud was, "Obvi-ously she had a lousy time at her own dinner party or whatever it was." She started crying.

Charles moved close and put his arm around her. "It's okay, Bird."

"Yup."

He kissed the side of her face. She got up to get a Kleenex.

"I take it you weren't around for that occasion."

"Nope. I never got invited when those art guys came around."

Bird was still puzzled. She put on the first "private reel" tape.

[P.R.—ALIF, 1987, Entry #1]

Alex is in her bedroom, adjusting the camera, her fuzzy image looming too close to the lens. The room is white and bare except for a bed covered with a hand-woven Navajo blanket, two night tables piled with books, and a huge painting hanging over the bed. She adjusts the focus by setting a piece of sculpture on the bed, tightens the tripod. Picks up the sculpture, a large wooden man from the Congo, and sits down holding it.

"*September twenty-seventh. I don't know exactly what I'm going to do with this yet, but I'm going to try talking on the tape. I'm really happy being with Frank, living with him, but I can't work when he's around. It bothers me. I don't know why. Even if I can't actually see him, I can't work. I may have to find another space to work in. I don't really have enough time to myself. Not just for working.*" *Then Alex shouts:* "*Yeah, just a minute. I'm coming. Don't come in.*" *She gets up, goes to the door. A male voice, Burton's:* "*What do you mean, don't come in?*" *Alex:* "*It'll ruin the picture.*" *Static.*

Alex sitting again. "*Ruin the picture. That's a good one. Now he wants to know what I'm doing but I told him I'm working on an idea. I must have looked stupid grabbing the door with this carving in my arms. This is so intense, it's like I can't get away from it.*" *Static.*

Alex sitting again. "*And he's always telling me about myself which I am totally bored with. I'm bored with telling him about himself. It's just not that interesting, how he is, how I am. He thinks I'm a diva asshole. The way he says it is like, who do I think I am. I can't really discuss it with my friends—well, they'll just say, 'Why are you with him?' I know Bird hasn't said anything, but she must feel weird because he's not very warm to her.*"

"Warm!" Bird burst out laughing.

"*And he doesn't let her come here when we have company. 'She's not an artist,' he'll say. 'She's a has-been, coulda-been.' But he'll cool out, he'll get used to her. I keep telling him to give her a chance, he'll adore her, she's such a brain and all. He just looks at me and says something lame like, 'Only one of you has the smarts for art. You're the interesting one, she's just hanging on your coattails,' stuff like that.*"

Tears ran down Bird's face.

"Sometimes I wonder if he could find the two of us extraordinary. I don't think so, and I don't really care. I just want him to be nicer to her. There's no reason to be rude and shut her out. Where does he come from? What kind of women was he with? They must have been those little dishrag women you see coming in the art bars waiting for somebody to wipe the bar with them. He said he was 'sort of like married' before. What is that? Is that what this is?" Static.

Charles took the remote and turned off the tape. He looked at Bird's arms, touched them, ran his hands down her skin. "You got a little tan. I'd like to see the rest of it." He smiled. He was changing the subject.

"I hate to disappoint you, but it ain't tan all over. Tired of the tapes already?"

"It reminds me of being married. Speaking of which—" He made a more sober face, then gave a mock guilty look. "I was thinking—what do you think would happen if I called home and said I needed to be away for a month?"

"If you mean 'away' over *here*—divorce."

"So, before I do something stupid like that, what are we doing, Bird?"

She shrugged.

"Well, I'm going to call and say something. You really can't be here alone tonight if somebody's been breaking in. So, I hope you don't have any plans for a few days, 'cause you can tell them they're off." He got up and went to the phone.

"Them?"

"Well, you said that was your thing, 'them' rather than a 'him.'" He laughed and left the room so he could talk to his wife out of her hearing. He returned without saying what had happened and sat back down. Bird looked puzzled.

"You want to watch more," he asked, "or you want to get to the inevitable?"

"I want to call Bernard."

"I'm sorry, but I'm not into threesomes with guys."

"What if I am?"

He looked disappointed, maybe annoyed.

"I just want him to watch the tapes too. Okay? He'll go home in a couple of hours." She smiled. "I promised him."

Bernard and Charles greeted each other like old teammates. They were like that, could have gone to school together, or been in some club together, they just weren't. At the same time there was some rooster-crowing crap floating around that was thick enough for Bird to smell. Charles was cool. Bernard was cooler, but his cool was just reserve; Charles's was more like hostility. Sometimes Bird loved the energy surge when two men met like this in a room with a woman, maybe, or over a project, say, like building a dam or buying a car. Sometimes it bored her to death. First, they circled each other. Then they brayed or hissed or made one of those impolite animal signals. Maybe they disagreed, or one snapped. Then, if everyone was lucky, one man would decide to disengage.

Bird and Charles told Bernard someone had been in the apartment. He was not cool about that. He got ready to eye Charles like it was his fault, but then it was as if he remembered that he could have stayed in the apartment himself. Bird finally explained that Burton might have taken Alex's keys, including the one to the inside door. The two men decided they could rig the door so no one could get in and that one of them should stay the night. Charles volunteered. They all laughed.

[P.R.—ALIF, 1987, Entry #2]

Static. Night. Lights twinkling from across the street. Alex sitting on a stool in her workspace, facing the camera, surrounded by flattened shapes of dirt poured over a plastic sheet on the floor. She wears a T-shirt and jeans.

"September twenty-eighth. This is really an odd experiment. It goes against the notion of privacy to do it on a video. Can you really expect not to be watched? What else is a video for? Can you talk to a camera and not perform? I don't think so. No matter what, there is an audience."

Bernard shifted in his place on the couch, and sighed.

"It's weird, isn't it?" asked Bird, pausing the tape.

"Yep. It's eerie. I think it's very good to do this together, see what, if anything, strikes everybody."

"I'm thinking about this performance piece using The Thousand and One Nights. *The beginning of the book is very interesting. It's all about sex and race. The sexually aggressive woman gets it for 'getting it,' so to speak. Black man as forbidden object of sexual desire. Hey, nobody told me when I got these stories for bedtime reading.*

"Okay, well, first of all, this young king, Shah-Zeman, ruler of Samarkand, was going off to visit his brother and he packed up all the horses and camels or pack mules or whatever they used for all the tons of tribute, etcetera, and rode off into the 'deserts and wastes.' After all that, he suddenly remembered he'd forgotten something and rode back to the palace and ran up into his bedroom to get it. And what did he find but his wife in his bed, 'attended by a male Negro slave,' who'd also fallen asleep. I said damn!"

The trio of viewers laughed.

"Those male Negro slaves get around. Now here we are in Samarkand, which I had to look up. East Uzbekistan, okay?—which we know from the news is Russia—"

"Right," Bernard said.

"Who the hell ever thought the Arabian Nights *was in Russia? And I know this is an aside, but think about the border crossings here."*

"Uh-oh," said Bird. "We're about to be taken round the bend here." This was Alex at her best, Alex loony and excited over something that had nothing to do with the rent and reality.

"First of all, stupid me, I thought the Arabian Nights *was from Arabia. Now we're talking about Muslim Russia, which of course was not Muslim Russia then and ain't gonna be Muslim Russia much longer, but anyway, it's this whole Arab culture and they deal in Negro slaves. It's like the taboos we associate with slavery are the toys of times long before. And one version I read, Sir Richard Burton's—isn't that funny?—deals in all those minstrel images—bugging eyes, and big lips and all that—every time he describes one of these black males that all these women are sleeping with. And, you say, yeah? The minstrel face, put on by an Englishman, on a story from the Near East, by way of Russia—"* Alex made a funny face. *"Anyway—"*

Charles and Bernard and Bird all looked at each other and

cracked up. Bernard shook his head, saying only, "I can see we're in for a long autumn."

Alex is getting animated. "*On beholding this intimate and revealing slumber, this guilty sleep of his wife and a slave, King Shah-Zeman felt that, and I quote, 'the world became black before his eyes.' Well, there it is. And he pulled out his sword, probably it was a—what do you call those gruesome things with the wide curved blade—a scimitar, and 'slew them both.' Hmmh." In a West Indian voice all of a sudden, Alex says, "We call dem cutlass. We use 'em fe cut cane.*

"*But that's only the beginning. Why am I going through all this—well, it's good to talk it out, see what words and images are most compelling. I can see myself doing some visual pieces based on images in there, women put away in ornate chests and baskets, caves. They have women locked up in caskets, footlockers, things with dozens of locks, men carrying dozens of keys. Intricate rituals, women seeing and being seen. The nakedness or covering of the body.*

"*Anyway. The king gets depressed after that. He goes on to his brother's castle, villa, whatever, where he can't seem to pep up and enjoy. One day his brother King Shahriyar, who has given up on him, goes off hunting, and what's-his-name, Shah-Zeman, roams around and finds himself looking down on a courtyard." Alex gets up, leaves the camera's sight, still talking. "Pretty soon a door opens and 'there came forth' twenty slave women, and twenty male black slaves. Uh-oh." Alex appears with a paint-splattered sheet over her head and around her face.*

Bird and the men started laughing.

"*And among them is the king's wife, who was, of course, wondrous fair"— Alex acting fair and comely, bangles jangling on her wrists, feet bare—"the very picture of comeliness, walked like a gazelle, renowned in the land for her beauty, etcetera, etcetera." Alex, facing the camera, leaning against the glass windows at the back of the camera's view. "But then the women stripped off their clothes"— still leaning against the window, Alex rips off the sheet, laughing, and throws it to the ground—"and somehow Shah-Zeman realizes some of them are women of the court, that is to say concubines of the king, forbidden fruit." She shows the palm of her hand with a design drawn on it. "And the rest are 'white slaves.' I love it, this story has everything."*

Alex comes back towards the camera, disappears. "And then they all fell into pairs, and, as one book says, they 'sat down together.' " The camera moves and zooms in on the patch of dirt under the window. It is the impression of a small body laying spread-eagle on her back. The dirt outlines her outstretched arms, torso, and wide-apart legs. "Then the king's wife calls out, 'O Mes'ood!' But then in another version, she calls out, 'Here to me, my lord Saeed!' So, I don't know what his name was, but in both versions this big black guy jumps or climbs down from a tree." Alex reappears in front of the camera, sits. "Now, in the really gross one, he is called 'a slobbering blackamoor' (is that 'black amour'?), with rolling eyes showing the whites. He embraces her and she does likewise. And in the slobbering blackamoor version, he winds his legs round her, throws her down, and 'enjoys' her. And everyone else does the same. This is bad. And don't forget the guy is watching. King Shah-Zeman is on the balcony, looking down. Watching these guys laying upon the ladies of the court and doing the nasty, or 'futtering,' as they say, and he stayed and watched them doing this until nightfall. Well, until the call for prayer. What a day.'

"So, okay, let's get it over with. When the brother king comes back from hunting, Shah-Zeman has perked up, he's all cheerful and shit, because he's realized his brother's Negro-slave problem is worse than his own. He eats a big dinner and everything. He tells his brother what he saw, what a little hussy his wife the queen is, and King Shahriyar says he has to see it for himself. So they pretend to go away the next day, and then hide and watch and sure enough the same thing happens, and the black guy is still up in the tree there——I mean, does he live up there or what? But King Shahriyar is, of course, more than a little pissed and has them all killed. And, thenceforth, we learn, Shahriyar makes it a habit to have a virgin brought to him for marrying, takes her to bed, and has her killed by morning. And he does this for three years until people are packing up and running out of town with their daughters. There isn't a virgin left old enough to be sent off to his palace except for Scheherazade and her sister. But Scheherazade volunteers." Alex laughs. "This storytelling thing is very interesting to me." Static.

Bird stopped the machine. "What have you guys written down—anything?"

Charles answered first, as he got up to get beers. "Being listened to, being watched, don't forget the guy is watching."

Bernard took a brew. Bird passed.

"Yep," said Bernard. "I don't know if anything means anything but I'm just jotting things that stick out. The storyteller as a captive. Bird?"

"Yeah, I agree. It goes with this business of being watched. I have, 'being watched, sex, and race.' This is like a verbal Rorschach test or something. Also I have, 'nakedness and covering the body.' When she got to that nakedness thing, all I could see was her naked body in the street down there."

"Yeah. I know," Bernard said. "Charles, anything else?"

"Previous wives. Just connecting from there. Wife killer? A dead wife?"

"Yeah. Charles, in that other one we watched, you know the last one, she said something like Frank had sort of been married before."

Bernard thought that if Frank had a previous wife, it should have come up before. They agreed sloppy police work might have missed that. Bernard asked if Charles had anything else.

"Only one other thing, 'black man as forbidden object of sexual desire.' " He was serious, but as soon as they heard it, they all laughed.

"You know, we all hear our own concerns," said Bird. "I'm afraid you have spoken volumes, brother." They laughed some more. Charles recovered from his embarrassment and added, "Hey, we don't know. She was with a white man. In that circumstance, maybe the black man becomes a forbidden fruit, maybe it meant something to her that it hadn't before."

"Or to him. Yeah, 'cause we know she didn't regard y'all as forbidden anything before Burton came on the scene." The three laughed.

"Well, one thing is clear," Charles summed up, "we know why the police just sent the stuff back."

"If she meant to obscure something," said Bird, "she'd probably be happy to know she managed to do it while looking like she was being totally open." Charles followed Bird into the kitchen, claiming he would help make coffee. Standing behind her, he put his hand inside the right pocket of her jeans.

"You sure you didn't invite Bernard to spend the rest of the weekend?"

"He has other engagements. You s'posed to be the only black male object of desire around here?"

"Yes. I would think so. I'm probably going to have to get a

divorce for this weekend. And I haven't even been truly adulterous yet. But I do have hopes."

"That's your divorce. That is not my divorce."

"You don't know. It might be your divorce. I might be very serious."

Bird didn't look at him. "Bernard's going to help. He's going to see what we can't see. And he's going to help me get rid of the stuff next door. Ask him if he wants milk and sugar."

Bernard and Charles took a look around the other apartment, observing that the landlord had fixed the window glass and looking for anything that could be taken out before the probate people came, papers and things that wouldn't appear to have any value. Alex's mother had taken all the bills and promised to keep the services on till everything was out. Bernard offered to get one of his interns to help pack. "You know the probate court is going to ask where all the artwork went," he said.

"That's her mother's problem," said Bird. "They won't even talk to me, will they? I'm not a relative."

"Right. Probably not."

[P.R.—YA, 1989, Entry #6]

"I was thinking back to when I got hooked up with the Mexican art collector. You know when he called me I just went out to lunch with him because he was an art dealer. He came up to me at an opening and got my number and invited me to lunch and I went. I was annoyed at first that he wasn't, uh, buying my work, just wanted my number. Maybe he would if I went; I had nothing to lose." Alex is in her apartment, sun streaming through the windows over a table loaded with dirty dishes, newspapers, running her mouth.

Bird thought about how girlfriend needed to clean the place before doing her videos—the cinema verité effect left something to be desired.

"Well, but he was so nervous, I mean, sweating. I didn't get it. I mean, it wasn't hot. He just looked nervous."

Bird began to recall the story. "Well, we know that's Burton she's talking about. She's changed his profession."

"It was okay, but I spent the whole time trying to figure out what was going on because he wasn't eating the lunch and he was looking at me like he didn't care what I was talking about but he was interested. I kept on talking, and asking him questions. Then he asks me to come to Europe. Weird. To do what? 'I'll help you get hooked up.' I couldn't even react, and I sounded really dumb, I know, but I just blurted out that me and this man have a thing, you know, blah, blah, blah.

"It was kind of crazy actually because what was going on in my head was so different. I was trying to think, why not? What's wrong with this setup? I laugh now at my pretending to be caught up in some deep relationship. Sometimes now I do want to run off with somebody and have an adventure, but I'm not sure I can deal with starting over with new people. It has gotten so, if I didn't know them twenty years ago, fuck them. This was the last new fling I had in me. It's like Diego Rivera said, inspiration is for amateurs, and I would add, self-analysis is for youngsters. That's not what a love affair is for. One is not honest in a love affair anyway. One puts forward the myth of the self. A love affair is a vacation from the real self. The real self that becomes exposed day after day in a relationship gets exhausted. A love affair should be the lie of beauty.

"Of course it turns out that the maestro of the Yucatan is possessive and nuts. I've already said all these things to him. Probably shouldn't have. But then he must enjoy it. Personal drama keeps people like that going. He wants to know. I believe he'd hire detectives just to torture himself. I also believe he'd go out and fuck a couple of people just to mess with my head. He's like that." Alex is laughing, not a laugh of having fun, an awkward laugh. "He enjoys the drama.

"So back to my story. All he says is, he says, Just come. I'm saying to myself, shit. I mean, this ain't one of those dumbstruck young fawns we bump into sometimes. Then he says, 'Well, come with me on my trip this week. I'm going to see some ruins in the Yucatan,' and I'm like, 'Yum,' but go to the Yucatan with a guy I just ate lunch with? Even I am not that crazy. Thinking about it, I go, no, it's romantic. He's like in a movie. He's not doing woman killer, he's doing 'we just met and it's meaningful and let's go off like in the movie.' I told all this to Cynthia and she said it was weird."

"There she goes again," Bird said, pausing the VCR. "Calling me Cynthia. She never called me that." Even Bird's family didn't use "Cynthia" anymore. Rewind. Play.

"I told all this to Cynthia and she said it was weird. She sounded like she was almost alarmed. Well, I didn't think it was that weird, but of course it's me and

I'm seeing the guy as falling for me [starts laughing] which can't be that strange because, hey, this is me we're talking about. [Laughs.] Okay, okay. Hey, this is the lie of the love affair, the lie of beauty. Well, I was starting to get a little tiny bit annoyed with Cynthia."

"And I'm getting just a tiny bit annoyed with you." Bird paused the tape and sank back in the couch. "I just don't get why she's going through all this. She knew this story and he knew and I knew. Why would she need to put it on tape?"

"Let's just watch to the end, Bird," Bernard cajoled. "She's sort of trying to tell us something, and she's saying Burton wanted to know everything, maybe that's the deal here."

"What do you mean?"

"Let's just watch a bit more. There's not much left." Rewind. Play.

"Well, I was starting to get a little tiny bit annoyed with Cynthia. But this is the thing Cynthia says [very serious, imitating], 'It's too international.' [Breaks up laughing.] 'Too international'? Or 'too international'?" [Laughing.]

Bird started laughing too. She remembered it exactly.

"We both started giggling and then she tried to get serious and said it was too sudden. I agreed. You know, I got to thinking about her saying it was too international. We would never have thought that when we were twenty-five. Some people live like that. That's who we were going to be. Zipping off to Brazil for a holiday, romancing in Rome, hanging out in jazz clubs in Paris. I mean, I admit when I ran off with Baba I was going to renounce any material kind of life, but being an artist still seemed pretty close. Like guaranteed poverty, for one thing. Still, it was the attitude that seemed important. Well, perhaps that's the way it's gonna go for me, and maybe Cynthia is just an armchair adventuress."

"Thanks," said Bird.

It was almost as if the two men were no longer sitting with Bird and she was locked in a private conversation with Alex, who had on the mask of Alex the performer. She really didn't believe that Alex had been this dishonest with herself. That was at the core of her reaction to the tapes. She believed Alex would never have said some of these things to herself. She would only say them in front of an audience.

"I told Frank I couldn't deal. He said he just wanted to talk to me, he felt this

powerful connection to me from seeing me in a performance video, and all these things. I laughed. I asked if this was how he usually hooked up with women. He said he didn't 'hook up' with women, the woman he'd been with for the longest had died. I said I was sorry. I was. I felt bad. Then he started trying to criticize my work. What a switch. Out of the blue. Like seeing my work had burst his bubble or something. Said I was exercising too much control, not letting it get loose and raggedy like life. I was instantly in a complete state of rage—but I smiled. I wanted to wring his neck. Then I just got up to leave. He put money on the table and followed me out. Maybe I just couldn't resist the criticism. First man who didn't kiss my ass?" Static, pause. *Alex appears again in afterthought. "Did Cynthia like Sheikh? I can't remember."*

Bird shouted out a laugh. "Sister-woman, you don't remember?" Bird talking to the TV screen. The men looked at each other. Bird blushed and looked at them. "This is really none of your business she's telling you. God!"

"Anyway, thank God for small miracles. When I come out on University Place with this fool behind me, there is 'Sheikh-With' walking along. I was totally surprised to see him and he was really looking beautiful."

That's 'cause he's one of the prettiest men that ever breathed, Bird thought to herself. Alex wasn't into Sheikh but she did know what he looked like.

"I decided to run a 'showpiece' scenario on the art dealer. That ought to do it. I'd just get rid of him for good. I mean, Sheikh is one of the prettiest men anybody would ever want to see."

Bird snapped. She paused the tape. "Well, at least I know why she's telling this now. This is the whole thing right here," said Bird. The men looked puzzled. Bird knew the tapes were a confession of wrongdoing, meant to hurt. There was no reason to confess an old deception "for the record." Alex had made it up to him by moving in with him. No one knew what a showpiece was—only Bird and Alex used the phrase. No one knew it meant to front off in public with a man so handsome no one would doubt you were having an affair with him.

"I told Sheikh to play along with me just for fun. I grabbed him by the arm and introduced him to the art dealer, who glared at him with twenty eyes. He

managed to be cordial, I don't know how—he was still so flustered from me shutting down on him that he looked funny, like a demon was stepping on his shoulder.
I asked Sheikh how come he hadn't called me if he was dropping in from Paris. He
protested that he'd just gotten here.

"Well, he did believe that 'Sheikh-With' was more than a friend of mine
because you know Sheikh is very smooth with his shit and charming. He tells me
he thinks maybe I'm not as serious a woman as he thought. I just looked at him. I
told him I had to split and 'Sheikh-With' said he'd walk me, and I left. This later
turned out to be a bad thing 'cause that fool ended up meeting the other Sheik,
which made him crazy, and then he went off on 'Sheikh-With' in the Crescent. I
ended up taking him home 'cause I felt sorry for him. He never got it out of his
head that I was having an affair with somebody named Sheikh." Alex makes a
guilty face, raises her eyebrows, then smiles. Static.

"I know this is going to sound weird, guys," Bird said, "but it's
as if she decided to tell him that she'd pulled that number on
him. Leave it around for him to find. Lord knows he's the only
person who would have any reaction to that story. To me, it's
like a note that was meant to be found."

"And maybe she changed your name so he wouldn't be sure if
it was you that knew he'd been the butt of a joke," said Charles.

"Yeah," Bird said. "A joke he took so seriously he tossed a
drink at 'Sheikh-With' in the bar."

"Went there looking for him, maybe, when they talked about
meeting up there," said Charles. "She didn't show up and he just
couldn't help himself from starting up a conversation with
Sheikh. Then he thinks about her maybe preferring him."

"Oh, Mahmoud. Oh, Saeed," Bird cooed. She fast-forwarded
to make sure they had gotten to the end of the tape. "I think it's
almost worse that she's saying she took him home because she
felt sorry for him, don't you?"

Charles nodded. "And if this is a note left for him to find—"

"—why did she change his name?" Bird finished the question.
"I would have left his name in to get his attention."

"But she knew he would be paying close attention anyway,"
ventured Charles.

"Yup."

"Yup."

"And she covered for him, just in case anybody else found the tape," said Bernard. "Hell, if he wanted to assault a total stranger over a woman he'd just met, no telling what kind of scenes he might have made that she might have put on the tapes."

"Well, it sure seems to have done him some good in this case," said Charles. "If he threw her out a window, he's a lucky bastard. This would have been some funky evidence."

"Not really," said Bernard. "Just because a man has been violent doesn't mean in court what you think it might mean." They both rolled their eyes at him. "Sorry, but that's the way it is. Even if he had a record of assaulting a spouse."

"A record. Did he have a record? Did anybody look to see if he'd ever been hauled in for assault before?" asked Charles.

"Don't know," said Bernard. "I don't think so. He's a journalist, serious prestige white-collar job. They probably weren't looking for anything. Did I forget to add that he's a white guy? Like I said, it wouldn't necessarily help."

"Yeah, but she's practically pointing at serial killing in that other tape."

"Maybe he knew that already," said Bird. "Maybe it's the dead woman. It gives me the creeps just to think of it. Maybe it's that woman who died. If he knows it doesn't matter if he hit somebody, maybe that woman didn't die in an innocent way. Maybe that's what he's looking for. Let's hold this one aside."

"Even if she did, even if it just looked bad, that might make him want the tape," said Charles.

"That means we're assuming now that he's seen them all," said Bernard.

Bird felt things fall into place and spoke with authority. "He saw them all when she was making them. He took her keys when he left just 'cause he's that kind of scheming type. One day he remembered this one little bit of tape. It popped in his head and now he's looking for it."

"It makes him look more guilty and maybe he's not," said Bernard, holding out for them to remain rational.

"He's got a prestige newspaper job as you say—he has his name to protect," said Charles.

"If he's guilty," said Bird, "he's going to do something really stupid. Otherwise he'd leave well enough alone. But if he's guilty because he gets out of control, he's going to get out of control again."

"This sure raises the stakes," Charles said.

"Yeah, well, I'm sitting here with the tapes. I wish there was something I could do with them."

Charles suggested Bernard take the ones they'd seen and put them in his office.

"Sure. That's a good idea," Bernard agreed. "We'll get done with them as soon as we can, and I'll put them in a safe place."

"Oops, something just blipped past," said Bird, rewinding. "It's real short, whatever it is." She pushed the play button.

Frank Burton's face appeared in silhouette on the screen. He was sitting in a chair by the window of the apartment, having a glass of wine. At the sound of Alex's voice he looked at the camera, his blondish brown hair a little disheveled, his lean face a bit stern, his eyes wary. He did not say anything to the camera now scrutinizing him, slowly moving around him, taking in his long legs in dark corduroys, crossed at the knee, his somewhat battered leather hiking boots, black turtleneck, the hair sitting long on the neck at the back. Frank Burton in different angles, so aware of the camera he would not move. He did not follow the camera but waited impassively for Alex to face him again. She said something teasing, he blinked and looked away towards the window. Took a sip of wine. Alex's voice was cajoling him to smile, to look at her. She was being charming. She kept after him, come on, just one smile. Finally he turned, beamed, looked at her with eyes that found the camera irresistible. Static.

The group was silent for a moment.

"So what about the door lock?" Bernard asked.

"The super's going to get a new one, but there's no new one to be had till Monday morning," Bird said.

"Okay, so let's see about the door," Bernard said, "and I guess that means one of us will have to be here for two nights, not one."

"I've got that covered," said Charles. He paused. "I think." They all laughed.

"If you don't, let me know, Charles. I'll give you my number too."

Bird had an old door-chain they put on the door between the apartments and then they pushed in front of it Bird's antique oak sideboard which had a heavy mirror on the top.

"If somebody starts trying to come through all that," Bernard said, "call the police." Bird said okay.

After Bernard left, Charles went to call home. Bird lit a cigarette and sucked the smoke gingerly into her mouth.

"You haven't smoked all night, why now?" Charles asked, walking in.

"Bernard would act disapproving. I didn't want to hear it."

6

Saturday Night

Bird thought she would have a drink too. In fact, she got out
Dr. Rousse's list and looked for how many of the no-nos
she might try. She felt very contrary. She poured some
Myers's dark rum into a glass. Charles got another beer.

"Okay, I'm ready to experiment with some more of these
taboos," she announced, smiling. She sat next to him on the
couch. She took a sip of the rum and grimaced as it hit her
mouth. "This ought to do it. Now. Kiss me once on each cheek."
Charles complied, gently. "Now, let's try a little hug." He took
her in his arms and squeezed. She took another sip, swirled it
around her mouth. "Kiss me again." *I'm a young woman | and ain't
done runnin' roun'.* He ran his tongue across her teeth and then, very
slowly, explored the warm terrain within. Bird forgot she was
too old for Charles. She forgot she wasn't sure she wanted to

sleep with Charles. She was going to be good for Charles. She forgot she was embarrassed about gravity and her past getting hold of her body and whipping it out of its prime. In fact, Bird came into her prime right there on the couch.

> I'm as good as any woman in your town
> I ain't no high yeller, I'm a deep killer brown
> I ain't gon' marry, I ain't gon' settle down
> I'm a drink good moonshine and run these browns down . . .

"Shut up bitch, I'll shoot the shit out of you. Shut up, I'll shoot your ass."

"Fuck you."

"Shut your fucking mouth, bitch. Fuck you, you nasty black bitch."

"What the hell is that?" asked Charles.

"My neighbors," she answered flatly. He crossed to the window to look out. She went to see if Romeo really had a gun, or if he was just shooting off at the mouth. He'd never mentioned a gun before. They were darting in and out of the light and she couldn't really see. He kept heading up the street and turning back. This time she saw he had the hood of his sweatshirt on and his hands in his pockets. She stepped away from the window.

"This go on all the time?"

"Yup. And it will probably go on a while longer tonight. Let's go into the bedroom."

"Do you think he might shoot her?"

"Don't know. Don't know if he's got a gun. Or if he means he would go get one and shoot her. Or if he doesn't mean any of that."

"Shouldn't you call the police."

"There you go. It's very scary when they come."

Charles was flabbergasted, and indignant. He could not believe this woman he was spending the weekend with. He thought he was in danger of really getting caught up in something with her, which was confusing enough. "Scary? You don't think this is scary? He's threatening to kill her. Besides, they were perfectly fine when they came earlier."

"That was different."

"He's threatening to kill her."

"And he might, Charles. He very well might. We've learned that, haven't we?"

"What kind of attitude is that? You're damn right we've learned that. That's why we should call the cops. You people are nuts."

"You people?"

"You sixties types. Like living on the edge. Hate cops. It's so clichéd."

"I never said anything about hating cops. Where's all this coming from? You been reading magazine articles about former radicals or something?"

"I know where you're coming from."

"Shit you do. Where I'm coming from is something bad could happen. Something bad already did happen. I live with that. You need to start coming to grips with that. Hoping something won't happen is different from being able to prevent it. In the case of those two people out there in the street, nothing I've heard from them is as scary as what already happened right here."

"Why not just call the police, Bird? What have you got to lose? You say it's scary when the police come. Is that scarier than what you've already been through?"

"No." She didn't want to talk to him about calling the police. "This time of night, it's always these same two white guys—although that doesn't matter, it's hardly worth mentioning because the blacks that come, they're just as likely to be dogs—but usually it's these two white guys and they just fuck with him—"

"Him?"

"Romeo."

"Romeo? That his name, Romeo?" Charles had a bitter laugh.

"They fuck with him——"

"You worried about a nigger named Romeo who's beating his woman out in the street?"

"Charles, think about it! You're not thinking. If he lives, you think he might not surely kill her later? It's a horror show. That's why she doesn't call them half the time! When they come at him, calling him all kinds of black motherfuckers, they've got their guns out and all this 'I can kick a black motherfucker's ass' shit going on with them, chewing gum, guns drawn, getting in his face, 'Motherfucker we'll kick your ass, we'd *love* to kick your ass and then we'll take you and lock your ass up.' What they do is not exactly social work. They don't come here trying to stop domestic violence, babe." She wasn't even convincing herself but she couldn't stop. "The cops want Romeo to lose it; they push him, so they can just kill him. And he always gives them the same thing, very cool: 'Come on wid it.' " She did Romeo's stance and voice: "Come on wid it."

Charles was silent. He knew the moment.

"It'll go on till somebody yells. Maybe they'll go inside. His mother's in the apartment and she'll stop it if she can. So, if they really want to get into it, they go outside."

"And you live with it?"

She knew she couldn't explain that even though the Quarter was no longer a safe community—it was now perhaps a warped and distorted community—the people there did not rush to deal with outsiders. When she was a child down South she never knew anyone to call the police for anything, only the fire department. "Yeah. Hell, I lived with Alex and Frank. Naomi and Romeo will drop anything if a chance to get high comes up. That's all it's about. But Burton and Alex, they broke stuff and, you know, intellectuals can yell all night, on and on and on, ranting and giving fucking speeches." Bird was now headlong into excuses. "She would push him, I mean with her mouth, and then if he started coming at her, she would start screaming 'Get the fuck away from me' and throw soup bowls, whatever, in his path, at his feet." She paused. "You fight with your wife?"

"No."

"What do you-all do, sulk?"

"Yeah . . . yeah, I guess that's what we do. Sulk."

Bird and Charles sat in the bedroom listening to Naomi and Romeo fight. Charles had another beer and Bird smoked. Bird was hoping Mrs. Hayes would stop it. She wondered where she was. Finally, frustrated, Charles called 911. When he gave the address, the dispatcher asked if some officers hadn't been there earlier. He said yes but that had been about a different matter. No cops appeared for quite a while. Charles wondered aloud why they were taking so long. Bird simply replied that with noise in the street, the cops had to get a string of calls.

"When two or three more people have called, they'll come. They're not coming just for you, babe."

When they eventually showed up, there was a lot of fanfare to their arrival—flashing lights, screeching brakes, many car doors slamming shut. One, two, three—eight slams. Bird could tell how many cars from the numbers of door thuds. Weird science. Naomi and Romeo looked like they were merely having a discussion by the time the officers hit the sidewalk. Naomi stood far from Romeo and said he was pushing her around, "that's all, got a little outa hand." The cops' opening gambit was something about getting sick of coming to this building. Bird tuned out. Charles followed every word, every flex of every muscle, until the final series of eight car door slams. All Bird wanted to know was if they had taken Romeo with them. Charles was disappointed. He said no. From where she sat she could see the mirror covering the door to Alex's apartment. In her mind, she could see the door behind the mirror and the note in Alex's writing on the door that read, "Anytime."

Something hit Bird's chest like a brick. Her head jerked up and her eyes opened, but all she could see was a grainy haze fading from a dream to become the bedroom. She realized she hadn't been hit, it was the door, she'd heard a thump in her sleep. Or dreamt a thump. She'd had some kind of fright. Her chest hurt as if she'd had a seizure. Only a sliver of light from the street eased through her curtain. She jerked herself up in the bed. The clock said 1:28. Bird was sweating. Her hair was wet. She felt as if she couldn't move. Her arms and chest seemed locked into place. She kicked her legs, kicked back the sheet off her legs, and tried to sit up a little more. The light showed eerie white pools on her thighs. She could barely lift herself up. She instinctively reached over the side of the bed for her *boken* there on the floor. She got up and went to the window. She saw a figure darting around the street. Probably Romeo, she thought. Charles was sound asleep. She went back to the bed. She put her head back, eyes watching the mirror, felt the sweat on her scalp, behind her ears, on her neck.

If she could have broken down the fucking door between their apartments instead of just banging on it helplessly, crying and throwing things at it, screaming, "Alex, Burton, open the damn door!" Just screaming for them to stop. The bottom board on the door had a deep crack in it.

When they got drunk they were pretty loud, and eventually they got into an argument and got louder. Alex never backed down, Bird knew that. But that night it was about some letters.

A huge thud had hit one of the bookcases on the other side of the wall. The wall had shaken. Books seemed to spill to the floor. She couldn't tell what the screaming was about. As long as she could hear Alex— A body hit the door, the bookcase, she heard the lamp by the door go down. Bird started screaming. She called Alex's name. Burton bellowed, "I will break down the fucking door, bitch, get away from there. Stay out of it. That your bitch, huh? That your bitch in there?" Bird screaming, "Alex, Alex." Him screaming, "Shut up, bitch, get away. That your bitch in there, Alex?" She slid along the door to the floor. The noise stopped.

Alex had only taken shelter with Bird once. One time he came at her with something in his hand. She thought it was a knife. He had another lock put on their private door and hid his key. The two women then could never open the door without his permission, and rarely did. That time, Alex had gotten out her front door and banged on Bird's front door. Bird let her in. He kept yelling for Alex to come out or he would break it down. Bird said she was calling the police. They heard the other front door bang a few times and then the shunting of the elevator going down. The front door was steel, but Bird knew if he had wanted to he could have probably broken through the other one because it was pretty flimsy.

But that night she couldn't break it when somebody was falling, hitting the floor. Bird screamed for Alex to answer her.

"I found the letters, bitch. There's nothing you can say."

"They're old, Frank. They're old."

"And the diaries, I saw what you wrote in there."

"I don't keep diaries anymore."

"I found them, I saw where you had them hidden, and I've seen what's in them."

"That's old shit."

"Who didn't you fuck?"

"You fuck whoever you like, any time, any place. How dare you talk to me about somebody I might have had an affair with ten thousand years ago. How dare you go reading my shit!" Something flew across the room. Another thud.

"Here's your shit." Alex was sobbing, on the floor maybe. He was bending down yelling in her face, in her ear maybe. He liked to yell right up in her ear. Bird had seen him do it.

"Take your fucking love letters."

The noise stopped again.

If Bird had only called the cops sooner. They didn't want to come. They'd been there before. They'd never taken Burton downtown. He was a white guy who always told them he was a reporter and it would end up in the papers if they did. If she had only told them she was a reporter and it would end up in the papers if they didn't. She hadn't been thinking.

Bird's exhausted breathing woke Charles.

"What's going on?"

"Just woke up all of a sudden." Bird couldn't catch her breath, a wheezing pried its way from her throat. Her chest heaved with suddenness up and down.

"Are you okay? Are you having asthma or something? Your breathing sounds funny."

"Don't know." She didn't know what asthma was like.

He got up, went into the bathroom, and turned on the hot water in the tub. He took a towel down, drenched it in the hot water, and wrung it out. He put the plug in the tub. He returned and put the hot towel over her nose and mouth, told her to try to breathe in slowly. He lifted each arm slowly, sliding her T-shirt up her torso and off each arm, then lifting the towel and pulling the shirt over her head. Her whole body was sinking inward and then pushing out trying to get hold of enough air. He put the towel back on her mouth and folded one of her arms to hold it. He lifted her up and carried her, her head falling back, damp springy hair clinging to his arms and chest, into the still dark bathroom and bent down and laid her in the steaming tub.

"Just relax," he said, "breathe slowly, if you can."

Bird's face started to bead with sweat.

"Do you have these dreams all the time?"

She shook her head no.

"You sure? Just nod, you don't have to talk."

She shook her head no. "Not a dream."

"What do you mean?"

"Not a dream." She tried to breathe, laid her head back. "Something happens." Her words came slowly. "Not something I'm dreaming."

Charles didn't get it. "How long you been sleeping like this?"

"Like what?"

"Breaking out in sweats, short of breath?"

"It's not all the time. Things set it off."

"Including me?" he asked.

She looked at him and gave an exhausted smile. "I don't know. That might be unrequited lust."

"I don't think so, babe. I think I know lust when I see it.

Besides, your lust for me comes and goes so fast—no shelf-life whatsoever. It's okay. Don't talk." He got another towel and rolled it into a cylinder at the back of her neck. He pulled up the mass of her wild hair. "Put your head back. Why won't you let me take care of you?"

"Can't."

Charles sat on the corner of the tub and watched the water slowly cover Bird's body. She saw him staring at her body. A torso with an odd wasted color seeping out from the thighs, under the hair. A body visited by a changeling of some kind trying to take it over. She looked at him once, self-conscious at being helpless. She closed her eyes. He took the towel and drenched it again, wrung it out, and brought it to her lips.

When Charles was once again asleep, Bird crept out of the bed. She went into the living room and put on the TV with the sound very low. She took out another one of Alex's private reels and put it on. When Mr. Sloan upstairs got up for his 4:00 A.M. bath, she fell asleep there on the floor with the TV on, running from image to image, to static, to color bars.

III

IMAGE

I'm bound for Black Mountain
Me and my razor and my gun
I'm gon' shoot him if he stand still
And cut him if he runs.
—BESSIE SMITH

1
Sunday

Charles found Bird on the floor in the morning. At first sight of her he was alarmed. After realizing she was simply asleep there, the TV screen blank and bright blue, he was angry. He took it as a point of failure that after all of the night's love-making, and the drama, after he had bathed and dried her and carried her back to bed and had seen her to sleep, after collapsing himself from sheer exhaustion, she had gotten up and slept on the floor.

When Bird woke she could feel all the gods and demons of the household close to swarming. All the little beasts who ruled over slights and affronts were blowing in Charles's ears, and expelling toxic gases in his face. She could almost see them. And she didn't care because the really dangerous demons were taking their morning nourishment too. She could feel the red-eyed succubus sniffing the floor where she'd slept, ready to gnaw her flesh from the inside. The hate she was breathing in commingled with her desire for self-preservation. Her blood was up and practically flammable. She acted rather salty herself.

Charles went home after breakfast to do whatever he usually did on Sunday. Bird didn't ask. Charles left pretty pissed because she didn't say why she'd gotten up even when he asked. She said she couldn't sleep. He said she'd been asleep. She said that she later woke up and then couldn't go back to sleep. To Bird's mind, Charles was pissed mostly because he must have made a mess of things at home and then she had acted so weird.

He said he'd return, and he reminded her that if he was going to be delayed, he'd call Bernard and Bernard would come. Bird just said, "Yeah, okay, fine." Nothing too gracious. She wondered about Charles telling his wife he was seeing clients and if that story included going home Sunday, or did it permit him to stay as long as he chose. What could he add, the clients got sick? Car trouble? She didn't ask him any of that because she shouldn't have been messing with the boy's marriage in the first place, and he was pissed in the second place.

If Alex had been there for coffee Bird would have been the cruel coquette. She would have told Alex that Charles required nothing of a woman because he didn't have to be seduced. Alex would have said that was true of most folks.

Bird knew she couldn't think it through, what to do about Charles, because she had too much to do. If Alex were there for coffee Bird would have quoted that indomitable flower of the South, Scarlett O'Hara, who always found a way: "I can't think about that right now. I'll think about it tomorrow." She then would've had to ask Alex not to repeat to anyone that she was quoting Scarlett O'Hara.

The phone rang. She let it ring twice more and then the answering machine began its routine. The almost bashful voice on the other end was the now fully and properly ignored Prince of the Faithful. He was curious where she'd been. That was funny, she thought, she'd found no messages when they'd returned. Well, the light on the machine had not been blinking to register messages. The voice hesitated, trying to get around to the point that he'd heard from someone at her job that she'd been assaulted. She opened the closet door where she stored old artwork and materials and started dragging stuff out. He had to admit that he'd called her job. That was nice. That cheered her up. He sounded worried. He said he thought he would call one of her friends if he didn't hear from her soon. He tried to sound like he was in charge. "Bird, call me." When he finally hung up, Bird's head was still deep in the closet.

"Fiddle-dee-dee."

She crawled out and went to the answering machine and rewound the message tape to the beginning. Since the morning she went off with Charles, the Prince had left two messages, Alonso had left one, and one of the phonebook people had called back—four messages and no blinking light when she'd walked in. The light would always blink unless the messages had already been played. Someone had indeed listened to her messages. Bird lost her good mood. After taking it in her stride the day before that Burton might have been in her apartment, the machine was somehow more tangible proof, more frightening to her than the tapes being out of place. Those tapes were Alex's private life, this tape was hers. The enormity of her daring to try to catch Burton there or whatever it was she thought she was going to do really hit her. It was just plain dumb. There wasn't anyone else who could do it, though. No one else had something he wanted bad enough to blow his cover. No one else knew what would make him lose it, prevent him from thinking rationally. No one else knew how to press him to make a mistake. No one else knew how he was trying to restrain himself from acting to take total control. He probably wanted not only a tape, but to know what Bird had in her mind.

No one else was ever going to stop this night-stalking sleep-walking that passed for her life. No matter what Charles thought, some terrors do not abandon you simply because you get a moving van. Bird knew she was not having a real estate problem.

The messages did give her one idea, though. If she was going to go through with this idea she could just listen to Alex's tapes while she did the work she had to do. She would need every hour. If she listened to the tapes she would be able to hear if something was wrong, or if she should look. She didn't need to sit there. And she could still find what she was looking for on those tapes.

She knew what she was doing was crazy, but then, neither Charles nor Bernard had any better ideas. Besides, Ravana, the Demon King, had not taken any life in their homes, hadn't sent any Rakshasas to beat them up in an elevator, wasn't after anything in their apartments. They didn't really have the problem. She laughed at how she'd reverted to thinking of her stalker as Ravana. It gave her less terror than to call him a real name. Ravana, who always enters and leaves by the Gate of Illusion so that no one will see his twenty heads and forty eyes. Ravana would come through the door between two mirrored apartments. A Gate of Illusion indeed.

Bird pushed the oak sideboard from in front of the door to Alex's, unhooked the chain, and unlocked the door. She went into Alex's place and began searching among the packed labeled boxes till she found the one in which they'd packed Alex's VCR. She tore it open, took the machine out, and carried it into her apartment. She went back and got extra cables from Alex's box. She returned and took a look around the room, studied its tired, hopelessly used furniture, the baskets piled in a corner, and the many saints still standing on shelves and perches all over the room. She closed up the electronics boxes and placed some old mail on top of them, leaving them looking undisturbed, and went back into her own apartment. She sprawled on the floor connecting the cables of Alex's VCR to her own. With the two machines hooked up, she could make a dub of anything on the videotapes. She then found a blank tape to put in the second machine. She put on a tape and started listening, then went back to the "art closet" and continued pulling out pieces of her abandoned life. She left the door open between the apartments, and whenever she'd put an assemblage together or had an idea how to set up Alex's living room, she would dash in there and move furniture or turn one of the mounted sculptures to a new angle.

[P.R.—WAW, 1989, Entry #8]

Alex in the kitchen, unpacking bags of groceries.

"October thirtieth. I was in the grocery store today with a handbasket in this crowded aisle and I accidentally bumped a white woman with the basket. I apologized very politely, said I was sorry. She stopped and looked me up and down, and mind you, I had on my clothes, because I had been to another stupid gallery that never shows any women, and she said, 'That really hurt me!' I was about to say I was sorry again when she says to this other white woman in front of her, 'They really are animals, aren't they?' I lost it. I wasn't thinking. I said really loud, 'Fuck you.' And then this bitch, who had on the worst clothes and too much jewelry, all matching, you know, said to the woman, 'And listen to the mouth on that one, won't you?' At that point I didn't care anymore. I told her to get the fuck out of the store before I hit her. She reared up, and right away I knew she was one of those white people with the fantasy that we're all going to beat her within an inch of her life.

" 'What did you say you were going to do to me?' One of those people who freaks out at the idea of somebody touching them. I said, 'Don't fuck with me today, that's what I told you. Today I have no limits on what I might do, you hear me?' She ran out. I thought she was going to get the police. I stood there waiting like Harriet Tubman or Sojourner Truth—which one is it?—I stood there waiting to take the horsewhip or cops or whatever the hell it was going to be, and the black girls at the checkout had giggles in their eyes. What they must go through! They signaled me to come on to the cash register."

Bird had all of her old paintings out. She stared them down as she listened. It was strange to see them lined up there like old friends. Mostly her old friend herself—self-portraits. There were a few of other people. Two of Alex that Alex had never seen, done from photos. She cleared a space to work and put a tarp down on the floor. She got out her paints and inspected them, checked to see if the brushes were still usable, went for water. She pulled out all kinds of surface materials she'd been saving for God knows what: sheets of tin, pieces of canvas, bark, and wood. She pulled one of her wrist guards out of her knapsack and strapped it on her right hand. She wondered for a second if she could paint TV static. She began to paint.

"When I came to this country I really had no idea. I mean, I was coming here for what? I don't know. To go to school, be an artist. I thought I was South American. Whatever that means. I can't remember anymore. We call ourselves Americans down there too. How different could it be? I thought people would say, 'Oh, she probably doesn't speak English.' Well, I had no idea about anything, not even TV. I had hardly ever seen anything on a TV. I didn't even realize how I was learning English by being called nigger and whore. Then when the black kids started teaching me, I still didn't get it that they were teaching me race, having fun making me do white rhythms and then do black ones. I didn't realize the white girls at my school couldn't talk the same languages. I would switch up in front of them and they would ask me who I'd been hanging around with on the weekends. They recognized it when I sounded colored. After a while, they started to give me the treatment. They had their own code words, which it took me a while to get because they were only whispered when I came near. Well, one of them was very grown up today, broke through today—she broke through all the whispering and actually called me an animal to my face in a grocery store in New York City. I can hear her at home, proud, bold: 'I told her she was an animal.' Maybe exaggerating just a little tiny bit.

"Sometimes when I tell Frank stuff like this he asks me am I sure I didn't do something else to the woman, or something like that. I'm so 'volatile,' he says. He should get together with Carlota. Being a lot blonder than me, she didn't believe me either. When Frank starts to get it, he wants to know why does it only happen to me. I want to know is he checking my story with a list of ten black women to see if these things have happened to them lately?" Static.

Bird painted for several hours and thought about all these stories that Alex had laid down on the three years' worth of tapes. It was absurd to think of them as a collection of significant stories. They meant more as they accumulated than for any specific facts they might contain. The only thing they all had in common was the presence of some detail, or negligence, or mean thought—perhaps something untrue at that—that Burton would have found irritating. No one else. They had a common audience. Not every story had a charm, most were the mundane events of their lives. But all together, they had a peculiar effect on Bird, who integrated the changes in the stories and received the whole kit and kaboodle as a kind of document of a ripe time of life. It was a long performance work that was purposefully rough, that was meant to seem mundane, that used lies and revealed something really true.

She chose colors that matched Alex's images on the work videos. She flipped out the tape she was listening to, looked at the first tape of Alex making a work outside, studied the motion, falling into the earth, and the colors. She took it out, put in another tape, resumed listening, and stood studying what she'd been making. Everything needed to dry a bit.

The doorbell rang. She paused the machine and clicked off the TV screen. By now she heard a knock.

"It's me, Bird, Romeo." She yelled for him to wait for a second, and went to get her purse to save time. She put the purse behind the door and opened it with the police lock still in place. Having heard another voice from inside the apartment, Romeo peered in as if he was looking for somebody behind Bird, then remembered what was important.

"Hi, uh, you got a dollar you could spare?" He smiled his fake worried smile.

"Probably. Naomi okay?" She didn't look bored or exasperated as she usually did.

"Oh yeah."

"How's your mother?"

"Good. Good."

"Tell her I asked about her." She gave him two dollars, closed the door, flopped the police lock pole back into its slot, and locked the door.

Romeo hadn't had any sleep in a few days, she could tell. His eyes were yellow and his skin looked ravaged and cooked. He was one of the manic walkers who had lived through the first blast of crack down the canyon their street was built on. It left evicted furniture scattered on the sidewalk and filthy babies picked up by social workers in raids like the ones the police staged. Those who had survived it whispered hoarsely through holes carved out of bullet-proof doors when they could. Their flesh rotted while still young, their eyes were dingy, and their sweat smelled lethal, like carbon monoxide.

When somebody turned up dead for lack of cash, the walkers' wails could be heard on the sidewalks all night. They never called the police, but screamed out in pain that whoever it was didn't have to shoot him for it. They accepted the arrangement; few ran off. They usually got hauled away, sometimes for a short time, sometimes for long. Sometimes they left paintings of crosses and gravestones on the walls. Alex's sarcophagus was mourned along with the rest. They accepted Alex's seemingly undeserved and unpunished death as one of the roll call of ordinary deaths that went down without official markers. Romeo was third-generation unemployed, except for one uncle who had a job and two who made regular checks because they'd survived Vietnam. From all Bird could tell, Romeo came from a long line of survivors.

To many who lived on the street, the wanderers were nearly invisible. Bird remembered the afternoon that she'd looked up from cleaning by the window and saw a huge, shirtless black man in grungy pants emerging from a hatch in the roof across the street. Cops who were pulling up, jumping out of squad cars below, could not see him. A neighbor yelled that a man had climbed up the fire escape, into their window, and then run up to the roof. He bounded across the roofs, looking behind him and over to other roofs. Bird knew she was the only one who could see him. The police dragged another guy out of the building and threw him to the ground. The roof runner seemed too old, too hefty, to move so swiftly. To Bird, the moment was not real. She looked down at the cops and when she looked up again, he was gone. He was a two-hundred-year-old runaway.

Even though she could hear from the street that he had

robbed someone, even though Bird was scared of guys like him, especially after getting mugged once a few years before, she couldn't get it through her head that the man she saw through the window was real. Bird watched as if it were television. Romeo later said the two men had robbed a hairdresser's shop on the next street. To Bird, the present was a weird time. It felt to her as if there had only been slavery and then the past twenty years.

That's why Bird liked objects, evidence, proof, some sign of fact from the past. She liked objects with a specific time in their making. She longed for a Joe Louis clock she'd seen in a magazine. A clock folks would put on the mantel, back when people had a mantel, a clock with Joe Louis draped around the face, his boxing gloves all in bronze.

Bird turned the VCR up really loud so she could hear it in either space and began to pull objects to place in a kind of giant altar construction in Alex's living room. She took out each of the *retablos* she'd piled on one of the chairs and with hammer and nails began to hang them in a continuous arrangement, like one narrative, on the wall to the left of the shared door.

Bird's apartment full of market art was really a museum of shapes from antiquity, shapes that went back so far they couldn't be dated, and yet shapes that stayed around, that someone added something to or changed in a way that told her about time, that told her, we're still African, or Asian, but we like plastic. A Buddha who had reclined leaning on his right arm in India and Thailand and Bali since before the time of Christ, still contemplated in the same position, still carved of wood in the 1980s, but wearing gold paint and pasted sequins. A comb could be a wooden piece with tiny teeth and a white man riding a model-T on top. It was an ancient, useful shape but then the white man came to West Africa and someone just wanted to note that. And then a comb might be a cake cutter, or molded plastic with a fist and a peace symbol on the top, and then you knew that in the sixties people were trying to show where their sympathies lay, to do more than take a note. Black and proud from the back pocket, or the back of their heads. When all that was evident around her was slavery, then discos, Nixon, Rocky I–IV, Reagan I & II, Rambo I–III, and crack, these objects of continuity, of nondisposable usefulness and prayer, kept her sane.

The tape droned on. Alex described a script idea. *Something about the Three Ladies of Baghdad having tea in purdah with Father Divine.* Bird laughed. She knew Alex probably meant Daddy Grace. Father Divine wore suits, not Arab outfits. Alex had seen Daddy Grace dressed up like a sheik in pictures, liked the name. That's why Alex loved the States—the possibility of endless mix-up. Alex made the connections between generations by looking at the costumes and without knowing the history. But there were ties between folks she connected. Bird drew the outline of a popular religious image on a thick slab of board. She made a floating oval shape, puffs of cotton-ball clouds around the edge, and inside, a robed standing figure, feet perched on a crescent, crown on the head. Holding the bottom of the robes was a winged child, a peasant angel, arms raised out above his head. Rays emanated from all around this form, the traditional shape for a Virgin of Guadalupe. A shape that had been the same since colonial days. Some painters of souvenirs had added a Mexican flag or clouds of roses. Some added a note of thanks for a favor granted, a life saved. Bird massaged her wrists, which were beginning to ache. She got up and found the splint for her right hand and wrapped it up. Alex started talking again.

[P.R.—MIM, 1989, Entry #12]

"At the party me and the Prince were acting pretty intimate, well, acting in a way that no one had seen before."

Bird was startled. She ran over and played it back, thinking she was hearing things.

Static. Alex looking slightly dolled up and slightly beat, like she'd been up all night. "At the party me and the Prince were acting pretty intimate, well, acting in a way that no one had seen before."

"This—bitch. I do not believe this little biscuit." Bird was too shocked to burst into tears. She did want to cry.

"People were staring, almost inhaling the air between us. The tall handsome

man in the lemon silk shirt was at the party with his wife. He watched us as we talked to people, watched me as I slipped my hand around the Prince's waist, fingered his belt in the back."

Bird could feel her skin getting cold. She stood transfixed in front of her TV.

"When we moved to the floor to dance on a slow song, all the eyes moved with us. I put my arm around the Prince's neck and he put his lips near my ear, not saying a word, just breathing lightly. The tall man looked at us curiously, studied us while a friend talked in his ear. He nodded and sipped a drink and kept staring. I looked down at the Prince's shoulder, but when I looked up again, the man smiled."

Bird felt an enormous unhappiness. She remembered the heaviness of this kind of sadness from years ago. The double heartsickness of your best friend embracing the man you've acted a fool over long before she put her hands on him. She wanted to collapse but she could not move. She wiped her face with her hands as if to obscure the story by obscuring the view.

"Later Mr. Yellow Silk saw us on the patio whispering to each other—actually we were talking about somebody at the party—he watched the angles of our heads, the closeness. I guess he couldn't get over his surprise to see us like that in a public place, or any place, for that matter. He came out and blatantly interrupted us and flirted with me. The Prince acted like he didn't notice."

"Wait a minute, wait a fucking minute," Bird screamed. "Next, she dances with the man."

"He asked me to dance with him and I did. The man is so pretty. As we danced, we looked each other in the eye, smiling like old lovers, casually, as if it was no big deal, this lust between us, like the lust between me and the Prince. It's like a continuation of the same desire. It was all very low-key, but there's this heat. His wife found it annoying. When we finished dancing, I walked back to the Prince without looking at the tall man. I could hear his wife going, 'What was that all about. It's bad enough she's with him.'" Bird laughed. *"He played it off, saying that he looks at all women that way.*

"When the Prince and I got ready to leave, the tall stunning man offered to take us home—" Bird spoke in unison with the TV: *"—or wherever we were going."* Alex went on, *"We looked at each other and laughed and, after first saying no thanks, saying that we're going to the Prince's place, we said, what the hell, we'll take a ride."*

Bird laughed again. "Oh, shit." She wiped her face again.

"The man told his wife he was giving us a lift, he'd be back. She looked truly toasted. 'Don't think I'm going to wait around.' We squeezed in the two-seater car and started laughing, talking, and when we got there, the tall stunning man suggested that he come in for a drink. I got the giggles because it's kind of ridiculous, 'cause it's not like I see the Prince all the time. In fact—well, skip that. I'm wondering is he going to blow this for me, or is this something new I don't know about the Prince? I mean, the Prince is kind of private. See, well, these two are friends. I don't want to say any more than that about it. But the Prince just laughed. He gave me the what-the-hell look and said, 'Sure, come in, have a drink.' When we went in, the Prince got glasses and ice from the kitchen, and left me and the man sitting in the living room. From the kitchen door the Prince watched us chatting, and the man unfastened the straps of my shoes. I could feel my face turning red."

"You! I'm the one with the red face. I cannot believe you put this on a damn tape."

"The Prince entered laughing and said, 'I can see you want to fuck one of us. Are you planning to do both of us or just send me off to watch TV?'

"Mr. Lemon Silk kept looking at me, didn't turn his head, and said, 'I'm only interested in one of you, but I'm not selfish. I mean, we're friends, man. If we all fall in love, we can work something out, don't you think?'

" 'I don't know,' the Prince said, 'we've never fallen in love at the same party before.' They laughed. I laughed feebly like I thought it was funny too. I didn't think it was funny but I did think it was very exciting. Then the Prince said to me, 'What do you want to do?'

" 'I've never been in the middle of a sandwich before,' I said, 'I mean, whatever you and I can live with in the morning,' because I think this man is really sexy but I do love the Prince."

"You just blew it, girl. You wouldn't say you loved him. You were supposed to say something else. You would say something like you were experimenting."

"The Prince was pretty funny. He said, 'I don't think I'm going to want to have him over every time I see you. Besides, then we're all committing adultery.'

"His friend said, 'Well, it'll sure as hell still be adultery with me here.' The Prince thanked him for reminding us. Actually we kept talking for a while and

having drinks. When I finally got relaxed enough to curl up on the couch next to the Prince, I absentmindedly kissed him on the neck, and then he made his move. The tall man, that is. The Prince was just kind of waiting and sitting the night out, seeing what happens. The tall man kissed the back of my neck and slowly unbuttoned the back of my dress." Static.

Bird blushed. In her own apartment, by herself, she blushed.

"You weren't supposed to be telling that one, babe, that was my story," she said to the TV.

The tape was still rolling and all of a sudden it was another day. As always, Alex was talking. Bird was still so stunned by the story Alex had told that she wasn't really listening. Then she began to stare at her paintings again, and to hear the voice talking, and she would have sworn, had she heard it in the studio, that the voice was once again lying, yet it sounded like something Bird had been waiting to hear.

". . . then the art dealer tells me he didn't want to get married. I mean, I asked because I was into that at the time, but also I wanted to get to the bottom of this other crap about he was 'sort of' married before. So it turns out now he was married to somebody. How could a person not mention such a thing? And he said he didn't mention it because she later died. It was a sad time in his life. I kept asking him about it and he said the marriage wasn't happy, he'd caught her one time with another guy, or seeing another guy, or something like that, and he went pretty crazy behind that. Then he said something about her losing her hearing first and dying later. I don't get it, losing her hearing first, then dying? What does that sound like, a brain tumor? What did he do, hit her so hard she got a brain tumor? I am such a fool. All I can say is that something in the pit of my stomach turned and it gave me the creeps." Static.

Bird hurried over to the machine, ran the tape back to the beginning of the bit she'd just heard, set the other VCR on record, and played it again. "It ain't no smokin' gun, but it leaves a smell. I don't think he would want this tape going to a university archive. Hell, after what I've heard today, I don't think I want *any of it* going to an archive. That's what's eating him. I told him these tapes were going where anybody studying Alex could look at them."

The phone rang. She nearly yelled at Bernard over the phone, "I think I found a clip of tape that a man might want to retrieve or destroy."

"Really?"

"It's about his having been married and the woman dying. Well, to be honest, the way she was telling it, there was a little sliver of doubt left in my mind as to whether she was jumping to conclusions, especially after some other stuff I heard, but—"

"But it's perfect. I was just getting ready to call you. I have a clue of sorts, too. It took some doing to get this on a weekend, and it ain't exactly good news, but there were some visits from the cops for battery on a woman said to be his wife."

"Damn. It's good and it's horrible."

"Yep. I'm trying to find out what became of her, but I can't get anywhere with that till Monday."

"The tape says she died. Lost her hearing first and later died, and that's where Alex makes a leap, wondering if she had a brain tumor, wondering if the guy hit her—the guy said he'd gone crazy when he found out she cheated on him."

"Concussion, blow to one side of the head, possibly from head hitting a wall or something very hard, hearing loss in one ear."

"Or an elevator fucking floor. Oh my God." Bird felt sick. She didn't say anything for a minute. Bernard was on the other end asking was she okay. Finally, a cold feeling came over her and she said she was fine.

"Bernard, there's something else. I know this sounds real weird but I've decided that what all these tapes were about was keeping Frank at bay. She was using his curiosity, his jealousy, his insatiable desire to keep finding out more, to keep him from going too far. He could never be done with her, so to speak. You know how some couples torment each other with infidelities, keep each other's interest by torturing them? It's as if Alex didn't want to do those things, she just tormented him with stories instead."

"Yeah, I kind of get that. But why? Wasn't there something simpler and more efficient to do? Why didn't she just leave him, move?"

"It wasn't just a real estate problem. She loved him." Bird thought back on the phone sex Alex had been doing all those years with Dr. Swoon, but didn't mention it to Bernard. "And look at those tapes, she must have been *engaged* by the whole thing, know what I mean? She knew he wouldn't stop just because of a change of address."

"That's masochistic."

"Yeah. But what if, in her own little brain, she thought this was dealing with it rather than just being a victim? That makes sense to me. Besides it was her life, her place, where she did her work."

Bernard groaned.

"Yeah, okay. I can't make it make sense to you. That doesn't matter, though. I know she was just making those tapes to keep stringing him along with these tantalizing items that would make him crazy."

"How do you know?"

"I saw another tape."

"What's on it?"

"The particulars don't really matter. The point is, she must have really been desperate for material by Year Three because, let's just say, she was talking about things she didn't do at all."

"How do you know? You weren't there every minute."

"In this case, I was. Every minute."

"Is Charles still there?"

"Nope."

"Why not?"

"He *is* married."

"That's unfortunate in general, and this weekend in particular."

"Why is that unfortunate in general?" she asked.

"You seem to like the guy."

"Oh, who knows, Bernard? You know, I'm pretty crazy. This might be a whim."

"You haven't even had any whims lately."

"Watch your mouth, Bernard." She laughed. "And you?"

"I have my same old whims. Look, he's coming back as planned, right?"

"Yeah."

"I'll call later and check."

When Bird hung up she went into the bedroom and got her *boken*, and put it by the middle door. Then she went back to work. The buzzer rang. Alonso was on the intercom. She didn't know whether to be exasperated or relieved when, a few minutes later, he appeared. As she went to the front door, Bird swung shut the door to Alex's but it did not close.

"I was in the neighborhood."

"You were not."

"Okay. I wasn't. I thought we'd better talk."

"Why?"

"I talked to the lovely Charles." He took stock of her being splattered with paint, noticed her right wrist in its shinguard and then the mess on the floor. "What are you doing here? Don't tell me you're painting again?"

"Experimenting. When?"

"Great. I love it."

"When did you talk to Charles?"

"Yesterday. I called back. I'd forgotten to tell you I'd call some of the people in the phonebook for you."

"Oh."

"But before I could even get to that, Charles started rushing me and telling me he needed to use the phone, he wanted to call the police because someone had been in your apartment. Sound familiar?"

"Yes."

"So, it was a quick conversation." Essex took a long sigh, and then looked at her like a cross schoolmaster. "However, he said he thought you were acting kind of, shall we say, strange, and he was worried and could I come talk you down out of this tree you climbed up into. Are we still together?"

"Yep."

"So, he has done some weekend psychoanalysis on you and he thinks you have some secret scheme to set up Frank Burton in some way, or worse yet, to have a confrontation with him. And I know what a fierce little warrior bitch you can be, and how you like to flex your Amazon mouth muscles and get bad with folks, but you wouldn't do anything truly stupid, would you?"

"I'm not doing anything to Frank Burton. I'd like to smack the motherfucker, if that's what you want to know. Yeah. Bernard found out he beat up some other woman, and we've been looking at all these tapes here, and we know Alex was making a whole bunch of performance tapes to entertain his jealous fantasies or something, but that's about it. So it's scary, him coming in here."

"Very. But Diva, look, Charles thinks this is not about Alex at all, that you're on some kind of vendetta, that it's all about you. He's saying you should be doing everything to get away from this guy, but instead it's like you're trying to hunt him down. And this is the little psychoanalysis part, so get ready, he thinks you got some hatred for white guys 'cause there was the one you told him about that tried to rape you in college, and you have some irrational thing against two cops, and then Frank wrote that bad review of your work and you quit, and then he's here and our beloved Alex dies, and it's all too much. And from where we sit, they've all gotten away with all of this shit. And now you want Frank to pay."

"That it?" Bird was glaring at him, but cool.

"Like I said, it was quick. I may have even added something." He smiled. "What do you think?"

"Maybe." Alonso looked shocked. He'd expected a fight. "You want some coffee?"

"No, babe, I'm fine."

He was waiting, counting to ten, as she lost it. "I think Charles has a fucking nerve. A white man tried to rape me in college!" She went off, straight to raving. "That may be, and you could say being a Southern colored girl I had the *worst* time with that one. It was my life turned into some cliché movie walking back into a party full of people with my face bruised and my beautiful dress ripped to fucking shreds. I wasn't too anxious to go out with another one. No. I became very, very frightened of crazies, 'cause that guy was crazy, and of white guys. You already know all that, and you know it took me a *long* time to get past it. The white cops, I'm not going to even dignify that one.

"But those other things you mentioned, the review, and Alex—and the one thing the lovely Charles didn't mention"—she pointed to her black eyes and other bruises—"and this quiet little burglary, now they only involve one person, Francis Burton."

"You're right."

"I feel I'm in harm's way."

"You might be. You still have to find a way to let somebody else deal with it." Alonso walked over to Bird and hugged her.

Bird started to weep. "Who?"

"What is he after, do you know?"

"One of the tapes."

"Do you know which one?"

"I think so."

"So we'll move the tapes, we could even send a press release right to his desk at the paper announcing that the tapes are all at the university. Let him go there and try to get it. It won't be your problem."

"That's good."

"We can do it tomorrow. You have somebody to stay here tonight?"

"Yeah."

"Cool." Alonso looked at the open door. "We can get this stuff packed up in a day if need be." Before Bird could distract him, he reached to open the door, which was ajar.

"What is this? Bird!"

"Alonso, you gotta go home now."

"It's gorgeous. Bird?"

"It's an installation I'm making. Call it exorcising my demons."

"Bird?"

2

Sunday Night

Retablos *record the facts of physical distress in detail, without squea-*
mishness. [They] evince a kind of deadpan, reportorial directness; since
salvation has already been granted, there is no need for the rhetoric of
entreaty. The tale is told not to elicit pity but to settle accounts with God.
 —Hayden Herrera, *Frida: A Biography of Frida Kahlo*

lex's living room was hung with paintings. Without telling
Alonso what it really was all about, she got him to help
her get on Alex's ladder and adjust the track lighting in
the ceiling so that each painting shone. When she finally got him
to leave by promising he could come back the next day and see
the finished product, she went back to work. She was full of mis-
givings after Alonso's visit and hoped that Burton would just not
show up. Then perhaps they could do the simpler, more sensible

things: get the lock changed, pack the stuff, let Burton know it was gone. Yes, that might work. She was going to finish, though, because somewhere in her mind all of that was a pipe dream.

She still had to arrange all the market objects—gods and servants of gods, prayers to gods and memorials to human sacrifice. She culled the figures from both apartments and organized them on the floor. She pulled all the stands Alex had made for the sculptures and arranged them near the middle door, to be pushed back against it when everything was set. She then began to look for masks.

From her own apartment she took down Gede masks, hung with wires in her living room and hall, and demon-chasing masks from Bali, glaring and red, with bulging eyes, extended tongues, pointed ears, and golden brows. She piled them into a crate and slid them into Alex's apartment. She had African dance masks and Latin dance masks—masks with black, brown, and white faces, animal faces, strange horned faces, innocent child faces, and faces crowned with ribbons and bows. She needed one or two more to have twenty in all. While taking down the masks Alex had hung around her place, Bird pulled a Peruvian carnival mask from a nail over the hall doorway. Not only the nail came out, but a piece of wood she had thought was wall. It covered a little cubby left from the building's original design, a tiny closet of sorts.

Frank Burton put Alex's keys in his jeans pocket. He got out a satchel and put into it a roll of duct tape and a length of rope. Rummaging through the broom closet in his kitchen he found a hammer and two screwdrivers, one plain, one Phillips. He took off his expensive watch and left it on the kitchen table, and removed most of the cash from his wallet. He took fifty dollars, four or five singles, and some tokens and put them in his front pocket. He grabbed a dark jacket and put it on, taking a black knit article out of the jacket pocket and stashing it inside the bag. He left to catch a bus uptown.

Charles Marshall, who had not told his wife much of anything, found that this time his wife was not sulking. She was packing his belongings, if packing can be said to describe shoving clothes into Hefty garbage bags. His briefcases and office papers were piled neatly by the door. She went back and forth from one room or another to the bags in the living room, yelling out every spoiled idea that came to mind. Every regret and sacrifice she'd stored up during her marriage. She occasionally screamed out Bird's name, or Alex's, or something like "those weird artists you're so fascinated with," all of which helped him to conclude that, by whatever method, she had come close to figuring out what he'd been doing all weekend. This left him searching the files in his brain for a new rationale for his absence. Charles Marshall, who was already pretty pissed, found himself without a good account for himself, facing a woman who was spoiling for a fight. While he felt momentarily stymied, maybe even somewhat frightened, he was also a little bit excited. Right away he started screaming that he had spent two days confronting some dire circumstances she couldn't even imagine, peppering his tirade with outrage about how she was handling his clothes.

Frank Burton stood waiting on the corner near Bird's building. When Romeo rounded the corner, he spoke, and Romeo stopped. The two men smiled like warm acquaintances and walked to the corner, where Burton handed over the fifty bucks and Romeo nodded. Burton was in midsentence when Romeo suddenly looked off in the distance as though he'd seen something up the street, and ran, gesturing for Frank to stay put. Frank Burton waited.

Some of the paintings were still wet, would be wet for days yet to come. That idea alone was breathtaking to Bird, hanging wet paintings for someone to see. She would never have done it before. Bird swept the floor of Alex's apartment. Her last bit of setup was mostly for her own amusement. She brought the ladder into Alex's front hall and began to tape open sheets of newspaper haphazardly to the sprinkler pipes running along the ceiling. She could hear Alex's voice rambling on. The sound comforted her. She didn't hear her phone ringing. Once she had hung pages the length of the hall, she began to tape another set to the bottoms of those, resulting in oddly angled curtains of newsprint that would flap in the face of anyone entering. She put the ladder away and pushed her huge free-form living room installation all the way against the inner door. She stopped and studied the new world she had created in the room, a universe of its own, a crudely done art piece, a trap.

"Are you saying she will be reborn?" she was asking Viswamitra.

"She? What she?"

Bird retrieved her apartment keys from her pocket, left by Alex's front door. She shut it forcefully so that the locks engaged.

When Bird got into her own apartment, she saw the answering machine blinking. She played it back and someone had called and hung up. Then Bernard's voice came on, wondering if Charles had made it back over there yet. He said he thought since it was getting late, he'd call Charles's house and make sure he'd left. Bernard thought this would also provide Charles with additional cover should he need it.

Bird went into the kitchen and made coffee. She knew this was an odd idea, but she didn't know what else to do.

Bird sat and enjoyed the coffee she had missed so much since the elevator incident and remembered mundane things like her bills and other snippets of her life, as if it were an ordinary Sunday. There wasn't any reason in hell for Frank Burton to be stalking her and trying to hurt her, but that did not change the certainty in the pit of her stomach. And Bird didn't know if she would be able to get the police to show up quickly enough to prevent herself coming to harm. She wondered what the hell had happened to Charles. Maybe she just hadn't been nice enough to him. She didn't feel nice; she was in the middle of a war to keep her life. She knew she couldn't be nice. She didn't want to call.

Bird thought she'd better call Bernard and get him to come. She went into the bathroom first to put some packing in her mouth. She knew it was a feeble gesture, but the thought that terrified her most was of somebody bashing her face again. Her jaw and neck ached when the idea crossed her mind. She pulled her hair back and braided it quickly into a single plait. She knew why people kept using that expression "it made her skin crawl." Frank Burton made her jaws clinch and her skin crawl.

Bird had not heard either lock turn on Alex's door, but she did hear, quite suddenly, the rustle of paper and a man's gasp. She knew the lights were out in Alex's apartment except for the bluish glow from the TV. The newspaper would have made him jump. Bird could feel her own pulse quicken. She halfway expected the man to sneeze—if it was the right man, his allergy to newsprint ought to make him feel pretty claustrophobic. For a second, fear filled her head and she went blank, as if there were no plan and she could not react. She heard a man, most likely the man who was her quarry, moving with paper shuffling under his feet. She told herself to remember the night Alex died and how she *didn't* think then. She made herself recall the mistake she'd made. Stay calm, look where you're going, not at the distractions. She reached for a leather Jaguar mask that she had chosen for the purpose and strapped it on her head to protect her face. Her jaw felt snug inside its soft interior. She strapped a wrist guard to shore up her left wrist. The right one was spattered with paint. With her hands as wobbly as they'd gotten in the past two years, she wasn't sure she could manage her *boken* for more than one blow. For good luck she put on her leopard-print jacket.

Frank Burton smashed at the papers over his head, surprised and on edge. The sheets of newsprint actually frightened him, making blurred, blinding screens down the hall. A woman's voice—Alex's voice—was droning on in seemingly aimless conversation, as if coming through a window. He plunged forward through the hall, smashing the newsprint, sending some of it flying and crumpling loudly under his feet.

On her side of the inner door, Bird listened until the sound of the newspaper reached Alex's living room. She flicked the switch on a power strip at her feet where she'd run extension cords from Alex's apartment. The gallery lights came on, gleaming eerily with yellow bulbs. Bird Kincaid, former artist, imagined the reds in the room bursting out at the eye, the blues becoming ominous instead of gay, the browns of her skin getting richer, the beiges glowing, the white eyes popping out. She remembered how she'd seen the shapes on her skin this time like a warrior's scarification marks. Like designs one had chosen and painted on. She could see the browns and beiges of her skin covering the walls of Alex's apartment.

Frank Burton dropped his bag of tools. The paintings were lined up across the walls of Alex's living room. Bird's paintings. The top row were heads, some dating back to when she'd met Alex in the seventies. Below them were long, narrow, vertical nudes. Bird's whole body in strange blotches of color and colorlessness, as if islands in her limbs were disappearing from the painting. Sometimes around the mouth and eyes, a white outlining that seemed an image borrowed from antiques—cartoons and hateful renderings of blacks.

Beneath them, carefully placed on mountings and lit, were a hundred little figurines from the Yucatan, hands upraised, mouths blackened, necks and chests loaded with necklaces, bodies wrapped in skirts of clay. Some showed teeth in their open mouths, some curled tongues, some loose pieces of jade Alex had placed in them to replace jade lost centuries ago. A stone in the mouth where the tongue had been, to show that the spirit is immortal. Some had scalloped skin, like an armor of rose petals, to indicate that they had been flayed. Frank Burton would know they were figures of sacrifice, some with outstretched arms who had fallen, mouth open, screaming to their hungry ruler's gratification. Maybe screaming as they fell into the well of Chichén Itzá, or into the body of Ah Puch, the Fleshless One, god of death. Some lost their heads, some fell, and some lost their hearts.

He turned towards the voice of his lover Alex Decatur, talking on and making a tape for him to watch. The TV was submerged inside a shapeless altar of sorts, a huge morass of Alex Decatur's real sentiments. It was like the real Alex, not the disciplined mind in her work, not the abstract shells she made in organic shapes, but a collection of passions, sympathies, crucifixes, flowers dead and alive, santos and unlit votive candles. There were animals, some of recognizable shape, some not; skeletons; boxes of saints made out of flattened soda cans. And he saw masks of awful leering faces, masks glaring with bulging eyes from everywhere in the altar. The display was overwhelming. Only Bird knew this was an all-purpose kind of altar, a prayer thrown up to many gods and many saints reborn in the Americas—in short, everybody to whom Bird knew to throw up a praise song or prayer. Bird had studied the altar and seen it as she thought Frank Burton would take it in, all that he would notice, and all that he wouldn't.

Burton couldn't see the African jaguar smiling behind the jaguar borrowed from Chiapas. The Mayan snake which is also the sky, next to Da, the snake of Dahomey, who turns the creator's intentions into deeds, who became the Haitian sky serpent, next to Muchalinda, the serpent king who protected Gautama Buddha, who was probably born of a Hindu cosmic serpent like the snake on whom Lakshmi rested. There was the sinful Serpent, which, for him, would be enough. Burton would never know Bird had made a point of placing there twenty masks for twenty heads, forty arms, as many legs, all the limbs of Ravana, the Demon King, severed from his death-seeking body.

The altar was both ecstatic and grisly, strewn with mannequin arms, legs, feet, wooden limbs from broken sculpture. To Burton, they could only be the tributes to saved body parts one sees in a Mexican church. Saved by a miracle granted after

229

prayer. Even a set of plastic teeth Bird had added in gratitude for still having her own. Frank Burton collapsed to his knees inside the horseshoe shape Bird had made in the room. For a minute he looked away from the altar and then he turned to examine it again.

The wall around the door was covered with wet paintings—Bird's *retablos.* And Alex's mirror was still there, which forced Frank Burton to look at his own face, distressed, boyish, angry. Some of the paintings hung there had been made so hastily they were dripping, disfiguring the saints painted on them. Saints—Madonnas, all in the same shape, with ribbons of writing across the bottom. Madonna forms, some even had Alex's face. Bird thought Burton would never describe them as saints with the face of Alex Decatur. He could never regard Alex as a saint. Bird had learned from the tapes, and of course from their famous fights, that it must have been rather important to Burton that Alex be a fallen woman. He seemed very attached to the idea that a woman once fallen could never again be raised up in a loved one's eyes.

All the dripping *retablos* around the door showed the Virgin of Guadalupe: one with a photographed face, two with little hand-renderings of Alex's features. Even Bird had laughed to herself at how the pictures looked on first glance like Alex as an art school saint. There was a tawdry taste to the whole assemblage that seemed just right to her in the end.

The creator knew that it was on the second glance that her work took on its eerie power. The small *retablos* depicted a series of violent moments using a woman's body—the scenes of his last fight with Alex. The pictures represented events no one had seen but Frank Burton: Alex crouching, trying to reach up and open the lock of her front door; Alex facing forward, thrown against the police lock, its pole surfacing above her neck as if it had gone through her; Alex's body slammed against the inside door, legs splayed, face flinching from an attack; Alex falling. The writing on each contained a narrative, a cryptic line that offered thanks that the victim had escaped after being thrown against a door, and on and on. The story progressed as the eye moved from one to the other.

Bird was sweating profusely inside the Jaguar mask as she listened on the other side of the door. All she could hear was the voice of her friend Alex saying, *"Frank says he was sort of like married before."* The loop would repeat a few times like a mantra and then Alex would start to tell the story of King Shahriyar and his brother, King Shah-Zeman, of Samarkand, and their imprudent wives. Suddenly the lock by her ear slipped from its place and she heard the screws fall. Burton's voice was loud.

"You should come out, little girl, and take a bow." Bird gasped and jerked her head back. "It's your best work. Better than anything you've ever done in your whole miserable failure of a career as an artist. I always thought you had no guts. But you're starting to show some nerve. Now, let's see how much you've really got." Bird reached down and plugged in the remaining extension cord lying by the power strip. She lifted the bottom of the mask and spoke.

"I hope you don't think I'm interested in your critical opinion," Bird said, letting him know she was right there. She wanted him to keep coming for the door.

"I don't know what you think you're going to prove here," he bellowed. "I thought you'd decided to let it go. That's really what you ought to do. You need to leave it alone. You think I killed her, but I'm nothing more than the suspect in a murder that didn't happen."

"I know you killed her."

"You weren't there. You don't know. Look, we don't need to go through all this cat-and-mouse, all I want is a tape. I gather from your presentation here that you know which one I'd like. You give it to me, and I'll leave you to your playpen here. You won't hear from me anymore."

"Why didn't you just take it before? Why come for it now?"

"It was that idiot at the radio station. He made me think of it. And then you were gracious enough to say her things were going to a university." Bird had moved away. She was only half listening. She pushed the oak sidebar back in front of the door, turned off the lights, and grabbed her *boken*. She crept down her hall for the front door. The phone rang and kept ringing.

Bernard was calling, and when Bird's machine clicked on, he became alarmed. When he called Charles he found him still at home. Charles apologized and said he could not come. Bernard tried the police, who were really skeptical and wouldn't listen to him because he admitted that it was not his address and he was not there, or across the street. They wouldn't buy that he knew there was trouble. They said they had been there twice in the past twenty-four hours, once already to that apartment. What was going on? Finally the dispatcher got nasty. Bernard got his coat.

Burton yanked the lock off the middle door. He shoved and banged, pushing the door into the furniture behind it. He took out the hammer and began to smash at the door's plywood panels. Bird put her key in Alex's front door as quietly as she could. She could hear Burton banging his way into her apartment. She turned the knob and opened Alex's door, crept in, and left a wedge of fallen newspaper on the threshold. He was banging and still talking.

"I don't know how much trouble you can cause with that tape but I don't need it. Even if you can't get an indictment, it will end up in the papers, and my life is over, finished. I'm a self-made person, I don't have anywhere to fall back to."

Bird spread her feet in the proper stance, held her *boken* with both hands down by her hip and pointed backward, so he wouldn't see it until it was too late. She stepped around the sheets of newsprint on the floor. Frank felt her presence, turned, and looked in horror as she struck for his head. He dodged, and then instantly screamed, first in fear, then in pain, as her blow glanced off its target but landed forcefully on his neck and collarbone. Bird knew from experience that the *boken* was made out of the hardest wood and weighed like an iron coming down on a body. When she then saw herself in Alex's mirror, she nearly jumped. The huge animal face she wore was grotesque above her shoulders.

Frank grunted and swung wildly for the sword. "Bitch, I wasn't going to hurt you," he said. "You want to be stupid about this. You're going to force me to hurt you." She stepped back and raised the sword again, breathing hard.

"Like Alex forced you?" She remembered that wild raging look.

"She was very, very good at it. The best."

"She did nothing to deserve to die." Bird kept her stance, watching him warily like a cat measuring every breath of an interloper.

"She killed herself. She was a liar and she's even made her death a lie. She lied about a lot of things. And she killed herself. I didn't kill her." He was bobbing and moving to see if she was jumpy. She stayed calm, cold.

"I heard it. I heard you beat her, taunt her."

"She lied to me. She lied about me. She thought she was going to make it all work for her. She tried to terrorize me. She demanded a response. Always." He was looking around for a weapon.

"She made you do it. And I wanted you to stalk me? To attack me in the elevator?" He picked up a wooden limb from the altar. She knocked it from his hands.

"You were in the way. I was just coming in your place to get the tape. I had to get you out of my way. And I needed time."

Bird had the sudden realization that he had not only attacked her in the elevator, but had lain in wait, waited till after the cops left, waited till she went to the hospital, and then got into her apartment. It gave her the creeps. She'd never noticed. How could she?

Frank saw her thoughts connect and laughed. "Your little notes were very helpful," he said. He grabbed his crotch. "I thought about masturbating while watching the tapes and reading your own little personal notes about your dear little Alex."

Bird exhaled hard as she lunged at him. He ducked. The sword landed in his back and hit part of the altar, scattering flowers, limbs. She inhaled, breathed out slowly, counting her breath, beginning to sweat.

"You don't like that idea." Frank laughed.

He reached down and grabbed his hammer and threw it low. The head of the hammer landed on Bird's knee and shin. She yowled in pain and with one hand still holding the sword, grabbed her leg with the other hand. He grabbed the tip of the sword with both hands.

Using both her hands again, she shoved the sword forward, grunting as she extended all her strength. The blade slid upward along his side, forcing his arms out and his elbows up into the air. He kept holding on, although another shove would break one of his arms. With her good leg she kicked him in the balls, as suddenly and roughly as she could, shouting out from her own pain. He roared and crumbled to the floor, letting go. She yanked the sword back fully into her power, stumbled backwards on her bad leg, nearly falling, and steadied herself. She breathed in and as she exhaled, smashed down on his collarbone in the same place she had hit before. She heard it crack. A chilling scream came up from inside him.

In this strange dance there were only the thumps of their bodies as they fell and stood again, their loud, exhausted breathing, and the drone of Alex's endless monologue.

Frank stood up and lunged at her and she put the sword in his sternum, right on the bone in the center of his chest, and shoved him back, smashing him into the door, his elbow bursting into one of its panels. He groaned, and groped to get to his feet. He was breathing hard and bleeding from little cuts made all over by shards of the pottery gods and glaring broken masks.

Bird could barely stand on her right leg; the hammer seemed to have broken it somewhere in the shin. She backed away and took a position on the floor. She folded her legs underneath her as if about to make a prayer but had to lean all her weight on her left leg. She straightened her posture, pulled her head up, and held the sword upward across her chest with her two gladiator wrists.

He came at the sword with both hands. Hauling up all the strength she had in her lower body, Bird dragged herself up on her left knee, raised her arms and sword up into his body, shifted her whole weight with her hip, and threw him around and down. She jumped and sat on top of him, holding the sword down across his throat with her left hand, turning his right hand back in on itself with her right hand.

"I will break it. It's not like this is any artist's hand."

"She fell. We had a fight and she fell."

"You're a liar. She didn't fall."

Alex's most shocking tape clip leapt loudly into the silence. *"So it turns out now he was married to somebody. How could a person not mention such a thing? And he said he didn't mention it because she later died. It was a sad time in his life."*

"That tape is a lie. She made it sound like something that never happened."

"Is that why you wanted it, 'cause it's a lie?"

"I kept asking him about it and he said the marriage wasn't happy, he'd caught her one time with another guy, or seeing another guy, or something like that, and he went pretty crazy behind that."

Bird felt anger swelling every cell in her body. Pain grabbed her legs, moving up, like one crushing hand after another, up from her shins into her hips. She pressed her weight down as much as she could, stretched out her broken right leg. *"Then he said something about her losing her hearing first—"* She could keep herself steady on her knees. But Frank took the chance. He lifted his hips as high as he could, shifted, and knocked Bird over on her right leg. She screamed. She keeled over and he knocked the sword from her hands. He pulled her head back by the hair and yanked her arms behind her, just like he had in the elevator, and began to punch at her body. Once he climbed on top of her, he put one large hand easily around her neck and began to choke her. He banged her head and choked her and ripped the Jaguar mask back from her face.

"I believe this ought to take your magic powers away." Frank smiled. He punched her in the face. She grunted, unable to make any big noise with his weight on her stomach. He punched her again. She spit out a piece of the gauze in her mouth and bit the nearest piece of flesh. He jumped, letting go of her hands. She picked up the bloody gauze and stabbed it with her full force into one of his eyes with her thumb. She spit out another piece of bloody gauze and stabbed it into his other eye. He reeled back, momentarily resembling one of the painted masks now on the floor. When the gauze fell, his own blood mixed with hers running down his cheeks. He punched her two or three times and grabbed her throat with both hands.

"Hey!" someone yelled. Romeo appeared, standing a few feet away, a long gun held straight out in both hands aimed at the two of them.

"You said you were coming to get a videotape. You having a fucking voodoo ceremony?"

"Thank God," Frank said. "I gave up on you."

"Oh, yeah, I'm here alright. And all the noise you making, everybody else going to be here soon."

"We'll just get the tape and go. She's going to be nice enough to tell us where the original is, and we'll take this one out of her VCR and, presto, we're outta here," Frank said.

He started to get up off of Bird, crawling around till he was behind her head, still holding her hands. From the way he struggled, Bird thought maybe he couldn't see.

"Let her hands go and don't move another inch, mother-fucker," Romeo said. Frank did not let go.

"But, man, we have a deal."

"But nothing. Fuck you. Don't move another inch." Bird thanked every benign deity on the planet, took a deep breath, and hoisted her weight up and over her head, kicking Frank's head with her good leg. Frank fell over onto the floor. Bird rolled back and sat up, exhausted, and stared at Romeo.

"Damn, Bird. You should be on TV! That was good. Martial arts, huh?"

"Black woman's yoga."

"Yeah, that's cool." He nodded his head in appreciation.

"I need to teach Naomi some." Bird struggled to her feet. Her leg was definitely broken.

"Ha-ha. You look like shit." He looked at Frank. "He looks worse." The TV flickered and droned on. Romeo was in a good mood. Bird figured he'd taken whatever money Frank gave him and got high before grabbing the gun and coming up to see what was up.

"My leg is broken. But I think his collarbone is smashed."

Frank was curled up and groaning. "Let me lie here," Frank asked.

"Sure," Romeo said. "She would kick my ass."

"Who?" Bird asked.

"Naomi," he said.

"Yeah, maybe she should. You know last night I heard you and I was wondering if you really had a gun." Bird grabbed her sword, and using it as a cane, hobbled across the room to get some rope. She tied Burton's hands.

"I knew where I could get one. I was just talking."

"Yeah?" She was looking at his clean new gun.

"I borrowed it."

"Yeah? I would have called the cops but I thought they might take you away. Frankly, I hoped you'd be keeping an eye out."

"So you gonna call 'em next time, huh?"

"I think I might move, is what I think I might do." Bird laughed. "But you need to cut that shit out."

"Yeah. What you want to do with this piece of shit?" Bird thought it would be pretty easy to let Romeo kill him. Romeo was so high he probably would.

"I want him to tell me something."

Romeo came over and held the gun to his head.

"I told you already. She killed herself."

"Romeo, that what your friend saw from the roof?"

Romeo looked surprised. Romeo didn't know what she was

237

talking about, but he went along. "Uh, no. No, he didn't see her jump out the fuckin' window." He went for the icing. "He saw the whole fucking thing."

Frank Burton was stunned. He resigned himself to something. He nodded in the direction of Bird's paintings of Alex's death.

"I can't see them anymore, but it's all there except the one panel. The one that would be next to the last." He started to cry. "I can't see anything."

Bird looked at her paintings and she heard the tape on the TV grinding away as it rewound itself for the umpteenth time. In her head she heard the delighted voice of Alex's swami: *"He stopped his breathing. He closed his eyes and watched all light die before him. He saw every experience of his life as a mortal and thought, it's like something I once created."* Maybe it didn't come back to her just right, and she still didn't understand its true meaning, but she heard it, which was interesting to Bird.

"Tell me," Bird said.

The front door to Alex's apartment broke in with a loud blast. They all ducked towards the far wall and the floor.

"Don't anybody move. Get down on the floor, put your hands above your head. Now. On the fuckin' floor. Your hands above your head." Half a dozen cops burst in, a SWAT team in black T-shirts and pants, armed with black shields, black metal nightsticks, black helmets, and black guns. They were not the usual guys. They were very scary. In the rear, Bird saw two guys with a mounted machine gun. Behind them were more cops. No door slams this time. The cops headed straight for Romeo, took his gun, and grabbed him in a choke hold. Two other guys came down from the fire escape, yelling through the windows. Bird was on the floor. All she could hear was Romeo going, "Wait a fuckin' minute. What is this, some kind of commando operation?" Bird heard handcuffs snapping shut and a rough thud as they threw Romeo to the floor.

"We can't really tell you what was in our information."

"It wasn't him" was all she said.

"Shut up, lady, we'll ask questions in a minute. We know this guy, he's a troublemaker. He's standing here holding a weapon on this man's head." She could see Frank, frightened out of his mind, but managing to give a little smile. His little hopeful smile gave her courage.

"It wasn't him. It's the other guy, arrest him." The cops could not get it together.

"What the hell is going on here?" Back by the door, she could make out Rae from across the hall and Mr. Sloan from upstairs, inching their way closer. She heard Bernard's voice: "Excuse me, I'm her lawyer," explaining that he'd called them, politely working his way in.

It took some talking to get them to cuff Frank and charge him with harassment, stalking, and assault. Bird had to explain that he'd tried to hire Romeo to help and that Romeo had borrowed a gun to protect her. Romeo, in turn, had to explain that he didn't know how long it might take the cops to get there. He had to explain that he'd forgotten the name of the guy who loaned him the gun. He said again and again that he'd seen Burton come in the building a number of times. Bird had to volunteer that Romeo would be only too happy to come downtown and testify, although she knew in her heart he might not ever be seen down there. Bernard volunteered that he had called several times and that he was the one who had finally phoned and said there were explosives and a cache of guns in the place.

"That explains it," Romeo said.

Bird had to ask them to send up a doctor. Frank became too overwrought to contribute anything except that he was in pain and couldn't see. They wanted to know how that had happened and they were not quite ready to believe that she had done it with her thumbnails. Bird added that she thought maybe his collarbone was broken. After hearing that, they wanted to know why she was wearing an animal mask on the top of her head and roller-skating guards on her wrists, and most of all, why she was clutching a wooden sword. By this time, blood was released by every word and flowed from her mouth.

"Ninja voodoo, sir," Bird said.

"This is not funny stuff," the officer said.

"Do I look like I was here to be funny?" Bird's gods of effrontery, stupidity, and indignities spat. "You can write down in your little notebook that it's an elaborate form of self-defense." She could hear Bernard clearing his throat for her to cool it, not to lose it now that she'd maintained it so long. Bird said she'd be happy to cooperate but she needed to get some gauze or something to put in her mouth because it was hard to talk.

As she was poised to leave, Bird turned and said, "One more thing, officers." She pointed at the cubby above the hallway door. "Up there." Taking Bernard's arm, she hobbled to the hall and showed them the ladder. The burly guys at the door carefully lifted the machine gun off its tripod and carried it to the elevator. One of the remaining officers climbed up and pulled the wood panel out of the wall. Alex's video camera was rolling along, its red light blinking.

She told them that Burton was on the tape trying to break into her apartment, and admitting to her that he had been in there before and that he had beat her up in the elevator. Romeo pointed out that they were on the tape too, with their choke hold on him and all.

Bird summoned up all of Arthur Kincaid's savvy and said, "And I saw it too, but we don't have to worry about that necessarily, as long as we have our day in court with Mr. Burton." She could hear her father on the phone already, "Get the best man in town, I'll pay for it."

3
Saturday

Bird couldn't clean on crutches, so Essex and Reenie came over and made a wonderful reconstruction of her altar, tossing out the shards and limbs and saving the whole pieces to divide among all their friends. Bird showed them where to hang one of her self-portraits in her own living room and left the others where they were for the party. Bird sat, occasionally giving instructions, and stared at the series of *retablos* she had made, sometimes just staring at the space between the last and the next to the last.

What Bird had heard Frank Burton say:

"I had to go through her things. I knew she was a liar. You told me that yourself. But I had to have proof. She was running

241

out of lies too. She was telling everybody else's lies, I imagine. Maybe yours. Maybe if you'd known, you would have been as mad as I was. She was making fun of me. I found those letters and then I had the proof. No more stories. No more keeping me hanging on with her wily stories. No more. That night you should have called the police. You should have. Because it was a terrible accident. You would have been able to sleep better. I've seen you tossing and sweating. I came right up near you in your bedroom and I said to myself, she's a liar too. She's trying to make it out to be my fault. You're pretty, I would have fucked you if you weren't such a contentious bitch. You're like some kind of maniac. You should look in the mirror sometime. See, Alex, she had fire and she pretended to be arrogant, but she wasn't. She knew she was a fraud, deep down inside she knew she was a fraud. And I saw it. I didn't fall for her shit like the rest of you romantics, and that's why she wanted me. That's why she wanted me. She kept wanting to leave me but then she'd realize she wanted me. I kept her honest. She wasn't nearly what she made herself out to be. She didn't do half the things she claimed to have done. Those adventures she was trying to make so tantalizing in the tapes, they weren't hers. They were bullshit. At first she made me believe it, and I sullied myself, stained our relationship. I went with many other women to punish her. And it was all for nothing. I told her. I wanted to absolve her. You don't understand that. I told her she could stay with me and I would absolve her. I told her it was like the ancient Mayans who also practiced autosacrifice, you know. So it wasn't simply that they pulled you out and killed you, but you could choose to participate, make a voluntary submission. One could attach a device to cut the body and hand it to the supreme ruler, the chief, and he could pull the string, allowing you to make an autosacrifice. A voluntary submission to the rite of death, but not suicide, which you really do for yourself. That's a selfish act. Sacrificing oneself is different. She would have to come clean and accept some kind of absolution because even just to kill herself was to forget the rest of us. Those who loved her. I talked to her. I told her what she had done. And I told her to tell me, tell me what she had done. I asked her, didn't she realize if she would do this to me, it meant everything she did was dishonest? Her work was dishonest. She admitted the letters were old. She admitted that she didn't have any other men. I told her she should ask for my forgiveness. Then she tried to get away. She tried to come to you. And I knew she was still a liar. She handed me the string. The window was the string. The window was only to scare her into absolution. To ask my forgiveness. She didn't like looking down from any height. The window was just to scare her. Don't you see that?"

Bird couldn't decide if she would paint the last piece. She thought maybe she would move on. Paint something else. The super had hung a new door and new lock, "only temporary," he said. Reenie brought fresh flowers and asked why Bird had never shown anyone her paintings.

"Wasn't comfortable in my own skin," she said. She thought about her mother's horror when the light patches of skin had first showed up. She remembered all the long-sleeved shirts and makeup on nights when she wore slinky dresses to dances. She thought about maybe showing the paintings to her mother sometime.

Angie the Terrible had come to visit once Bird's injuries had been declared worthy of at least an overnight in the hospital. She still had to be told by several people she thought sensible that in fact Bird had put someone else in the hospital. And Arthur Kincaid had to warn her not to ask Bird even once what she had done to make Frank Burton want to stalk her. Bird thought better of showing her mother the paintings when she remembered how she'd reacted to Bird's hair. Bird had put herself, cast and all, in a cab to the hairdresser's and came home with her brown hair the color of Miles Davis's favorite trumpet, a rosy copper. Angie, stretched out having coffee on the new couch she'd had delivered, sat up and made a horrified face when Bird pulled off her hat. She spewed something that sounded like "Eeww!"

Bird opened all the windows in Alex's living room and her own. It was a warmish autumn day and Bird also thought it might keep folks from complaining about her cigarette smoke. Not that she *really* cared, she just didn't want to hear it. They opened the super's new door, cooked in Bird's kitchen, and drank in Alex's living room. They made rice and beans, a crab dish for Bird, *platanos* for Alex, pound cake for everyone. Sheik-Without showed up, on tour by magic, to stir the pot of *thiebou dienn*. Sheikh-With called from Paris talking croonsong.

Essex came dressed as a little bit of several women he always admired, but mostly Miss Ross. Bird kissed him and said, "You tired cliché, you," and reminded him that had Randall been there, he would have burst with exultant laughter. Essex saluted Randall with a bit of Lyndon Johnson: "I never trust a man unless I've got his pecker in my pocket." Even Carlota laughed. She was probably from the same school, Bird and Essex thought. Carlota got drunk and admitted that what her daughter had needed was a good party. Bird wrapped up a fat balsa baby angel from Bali and put it in Carlota's purse.

They made a libation and toast for every one of their friends now dead, not just Alex and Randall and Paul. They poured for Eric, and Hayes, Luis, Henry, and Lew. They told tales on all of them, laughed, and performed wicked imitations of moments famous among the friends.

When the Baguette showed up with his wife, Bird decided she'd have to stop calling him that. His wife admired Bird's paintings and even tried to buy one. She gave them a pair of Hindu statues, a musician poised on one foot playing the flute and a shapely maiden admiring herself in a mirror. Every Catholic took a cross, and every woman left draped in a piece of Alex's handmade cloths. Alonso Jackson Essex draped one over his shoulders, under his Miss Ross wig. Everyone cracked up—

especially Charles's wife and Carlota—over the unearthed bracelets made from napkin rings and butter knives, the sequined platform mules, and the purple crocheted skirts, hats, and maxi-vests. They packed up everything in Alex's place and closed and locked it for the last time.

"When they put me in a nursing home," Reenie said, "I can make seventies accessories in the arts and crafts class." Bird decided to keep the sequined mules for when they put her in a home. Bird gave to Bernard a tin red flaming heart pierced with an arrow.

Frank Burton's arraignment in court was covered by all the papers and ruined his life more or less as he had imagined. What he had not imagined was being blind for a few months. His lawyer had him appear with bandages wrapped around his eyes and head. When his lawyer asked him to explain in court how he'd damaged his eyes, the story sounded strange and worth printing in the papers, too.

He gave a rather sensational account of a public radio engineer named Cynthia Kincaid coming up on him from behind, dressed in a leopard outfit, and assaulting him Ninja-style with some kind of karate weapon. After the arraignment, a photographer caught Bird standing on crutches outside her office. She was wearing a new leopard-print jacket Bernard had bought that sparkled, very dark sunglasses, and black wrist guards with night-riding Day-Glo patches, a gift from an athletic shop. Her picture even pushed the mayoral candidates off the front page of the tabloids. No one could tell she had a mouth newly packed with gauze because her makeup was pretty good. She was smoking a cigarette in the autumn sun. Her dentist had a fit.

After reading the stories in the paper, her old martial arts teacher called to say, "The man was stupid calling it karate.

"Tell them it's aikido you studied. Okay? I'm telling everybody, 'That's my student,' even though you haven't been to class in so long. But you know, once a student, always a student. You need to come back to class, get back on the mat. You're not even a black belt yet." He was in a great mood. He queried her very seriously about every detail, and made comments as she described her moves, sometimes "good," sometimes "oh!" He joked that the fact that the man was alive meant she was a little rusty. But it was a joke, the kind of line tough guys say in karate movies. She knew there was no good or bad, only glad you are okay.

Having gone as far as she did, having stopped anyone trying to harm her, Bird knew she would have to try to save him, whether she wanted to or not. She wasn't planning to kill him, probably would not have killed him, but somehow she needed the choice to be hers. She needed to decide to let him live in his hell, and she needed to decide to live in hers as well. She knew no other way to get rid of that killer she was carrying around in her. She had to smash that world of night wanderers and let it go with Alex. Frank was only one of the demons. She didn't know if they were keeping her from prayer exactly like the old sage said, but they had been keeping her from something. *"My friend,"* the new silence was saying, *"we have not seen you for a moment in heaven. Return to yourself."*

What Bird saw in the missing painting:

That Frank would, in anger, come after Alex. That he might back her into a corner or against a wall, that Alex might scratch him, and fight back. That he would threaten to do worse, that he had no idea how far he would go. That he had no idea if he could stop. That he might not ever say he would kill her, or he might say he would. That he might say she was like all the rest, that her deceit was even greater than the deceit he expected. That he might not know what he was going to do next but that he was really frightening her. That she might think that he would kill her, if not this time, one time. That she would scream, No, please don't. No, Frank, put me down. No. That he might pick her up because she was so little, so tiny and light. That he might pick her up because he could. That she might have spent every second in terror. That she knew he was going to kill her even if he didn't think he would. That she had no idea all creation would go with her and have to be made again. That she might be kicking wildly, trying to hurt him, stop him. That she might be totally uncontrollable. That he might not have a good grip on her. That the wind could be sucking at the window.

Epilogue

God made paradise, and redeemed man. To each man He left a living through his work. Some are fitted to do damage, others are good Christians, others, card in hand, gamble to support themselves. And I can be grateful that I am a maker of saints.
>   —Florencio Caban Hernandez, Puerto Rican *santero,*
>   *The Folk Art of Latin America*

A s the middle of October came, Bird stayed up pretty late and watched the aftermath of the San Francisco earthquake. Romeo was on a furlough from his regular haunts. Bird thought the cops had taken him for something, but when it turned out they hadn't, she knew that street law had won. Naomi was at her post, in a hurry for something to come. Neither woman saw his figure darting on the roofs overhead across the street.

The world was still offering up disasters to get lost in, but Bird did not stay up all night watching them. Almost any night she went to turn out the lights she would look through the doorway to her workspace, and her eyes would fall on the figure she'd always kept by her paints. The small clay sculpture squatted down on her haunches serenely giving birth to another fully developed being. The brushes next to it were freshly cleaned. She remembered hearing somewhere that a saint who is not seen is not worshipped. She was working on that. When Mr. Sloan upstairs got up for his 4:00 A.M. bath, she was already sound asleep, the Jaguar mask above her head.

FOR THE BEST IN PAPERBACKS, LOOK FOR THE

In every corner of the world, on every subject under the sun, Penguin represents quality and variety—the very best in publishing today.

For complete information about books available from Penguin—including Puffins, Penguin Classics, and Arkana—and how to order them, write to us at the appropriate address below. Please note that for copyright reasons the selection of books varies from country to country.

In the United Kingdom: Please write to *Dept. JC, Penguin Books Ltd, FREEPOST, West Drayton, Middlesex UB7 0BR.*

If you have any difficulty in obtaining a title, please send your order with the correct money, plus ten percent for postage and packaging, to *P.O. Box No. 11, West Drayton, Middlesex UB7 0BR*

In the United States: Please write to *Consumer Sales, Penguin USA, P.O. Box 999, Dept. 17109, Bergenfield, New Jersey 07621-0120.* VISA and MasterCard holders call 1-800-253-6476 to order all Penguin titles

In Canada: Please write to *Penguin Books Canada Ltd, 10 Alcorn Avenue, Suite 300, Toronto, Ontario M4V 3B2*

In Australia: Please write to *Penguin Books Australia Ltd, P.O. Box 257, Ringwood, Victoria 3134*

In New Zealand: Please write to *Penguin Books (NZ) Ltd, Private Bag 102902, North Shore Mail Centre, Auckland 10*

In India: Please write to *Penguin Books India Pvt Ltd, 706 Eros Apartments, 56 Nehru Place, New Delhi 110 019*

In the Netherlands: Please write to *Penguin Books Netherlands bv, Postbus 3507, NL-1001 AH Amsterdam*

In Germany: Please write to *Penguin Books Deutschland GmbH, Metzlerstrasse 26, 60594 Frankfurt am Main*

In Spain: Please write to *Penguin Books S. A., Bravo Murillo 19, 1° B, 28015 Madrid*

In Italy: Please write to *Penguin Italia s.r.l., Via Felice Casati 20, I-20124 Milano*

In France: Please write to *Penguin France S. A., 17 rue Lejeune, F-31000 Toulouse*

In Japan: Please write to *Penguin Books Japan, Ishikiribashi Building, 2-5-4, Suido, Bunkyo-ku, Tokyo 112*

In Greece: Please write to *Penguin Hellas Ltd, Dimocritou 3, GR-106 71 Athens*

In South Africa: Please write to *Longman Penguin Southern Africa (Pty) Ltd, Private Bag X08, Bertsham 2013*